A Shadow in the Past

Melanie Robertson-King

King Park Press

Published by King Park Press

Cover design by Melanie Robertson-King

Green-eyed brunette: Shutterstock, Inc.
(Signed model release on file with Shutterstock, Inc.)

A Shadow in the Past is a work of fiction. Names, characters, places and
incidents are the product of the author's imagination or are used fictitiously.
Any resemblance to actual events, locales or persons, living or dead, is purely
coincidental.

ISBN: 978-1-9994257-1-5

DEDICATION

For Anne (1953-2012). You were taken from us too soon but you will always be in our hearts.

ACKNOWLEDGMENTS

Thanks to everyone who put up with my daft questions during the research of this novel. Without your help, the book would not have come to fruition.

Chris Longmuir, you've been an angel. I've bent your ear more than once asking for help, and sometimes it's been the same questions repeatedly. You've always taken the time to answer them graciously, and offer support.

If I've missed any member of my team by name, I apologize.

Special thanks to my husband, Don, who continues to support and encourage me, and provides a shoulder to cry on when things don't go well. He redesigned my website making it mobile-friendly and taken charge on the domestic front giving me time to write..

PROLOGUE

Nine-year-old Sarah Shand struggled to keep up with her grandmother on their way to the stone circle. "Wait for me," she called.

Caught up, she slid her small hand into her grandmother's, and they carried on to the crest of the hill. The tops of the stones soon peeked over the horizon. The upright ones, taller than Sarah's grandma, stood in a semi-circle with broken pieces piled against them. Off to the edge, one of the huge rocks lay on its side. "I like it when you come to our house. You make it fun. Mummy never comes up here."

"Thank you."

"Who built the stone circle?"

"I'm not sure, but in olden times."

"When you were a little girl like me?"

The woman smiled. "Much longer than that. Many thousands of years ago."

"Why?"

"I don't know. Maybe to use as a calendar or a clock to tell the time? Mark the changes in the seasons."

The explanation satisfied Sarah's curiosity for the time being. Still, she loved to listen to the woman talk about the 'olden days,' "Tell another story?"

"Let me think. How would you like to hear about how my parents met?"

"Yes, please. I love your stories."

"All right then." The woman made herself comfortable on the fallen boulder. She gathered Sarah on her knee and began. "It was in the early part of the Second World War. The army billeted my father at Weetshill."

"What's that mean?"

"Lodging. Much like the people who stay at your farmhouse."

The ruined building stood high on the distant hillside. "He stayed there? But it's falling down."

"Yes, but back then the place was beautiful. Anyway, the village council held a social down at the community centre, and all the soldiers went. My mum and a group of her girlfriends went, too."

"Like at Robbie Burns night?"

"Yes. It was at that dance they became enamoured with each other. He was tall and slim and handsome, Mother told me. He had the bluest eyes and the nicest smile and treated her like a queen. She said it happened when they were dancing the Gay Gordons."

"What?"

"They fell in love. She said they looked into one another's eyes, and she knew it was the real thing," the woman reflected.

"Don't be sad." Sarah traced her fingertip over the lines around her grandmother's eyes. "Tell me more?"

"I think you're too young to hear."

"Oh come on, please?"

"Well, most of the young men never expected to come back from the war alive, so they wanted to … before they left."

"What?"

"This was to be a romantic story of how my parents found each other, nothing more. Let's just leave it at that."

Sarah folded her arms and pouted. Why didn't her grandma tell her more? She would have understood. She was nine for pity's sake. "What about the mansion then? What happened?"

"Well sometime in the 1950s, I believe. The taxes became too much for the owners, and they pulled off the roof."

"Why?"

"Because once a building becomes a ruin, the government no longer levies taxes against it."

"So sad," Sarah said as she stared at the house. "Someday, I'm going to live there."

"'Tis a beautiful dream, my sweet girl, but how will you raise the money? First, you'd have to buy the place and then make the restorations. You would need to win the lotto, and then, I don't think the biggest jackpot would be enough."

Regardless of what she was told, someday Sarah would live in Weetshill. How or when remained a mystery, but she would. She imagined the building's appearance newly built. Then a flash of movement distracted her. Two children with brown, curly hair appeared and ran toward them. The boy wore a blue suit; the girl a long, green frock with a white pinafore.

"Gran," she said haltingly.

"Yes."

"Who are those kids?"

"What kiddies?"

"The ones dressed like the people in my old story books. The stories I'm too big for now," she said, pointing near a cluster of rose bushes.

The lad stopped and pointed toward Sarah.

"Gran look. Don't you see them?"

Her grandmother smiled and pulled her into her arms, hugging her. The children were gone when she looked back.

1

Ten years later...

Sarah lay on her bed, a pillow bunched up under her chest. In her hands, she gripped a photo of Blair and herself taken in front of the Mercat Cross in Aberdeen the previous summer. A mascara-stained tear dripped off her face and splattered on the picture. They were so happy then. What went wrong? Bad enough he cheated on her, but why with Niamh? Her best friend? Well, not anymore.

From the moment she turned off her alarm clock that morning, she had a premonition something dreadful was going to happen. She shrugged her misgiving off until she encountered the two snogging in the woods. The discovery devastated her.

Her mother tapped and called through the closed door. "Supper's ready."

Attempts to regain some semblance of composure were unsuccessful. With conviction, she responded. "I'm not hungry."

"Stop this moping. Down in five minutes, no longer."

Sarah dragged herself off the bed and surveyed her reflection in the dressing table mirror. Her eyes were red and watery, and eyeliner and mascara stained her cheeks. She couldn't go to supper looking like that.

She tried to wipe her face clean with a tissue but smeared the darkened streaks instead. Her cleansing cloths were in the bathroom. Sarah listened at her door to ensure nobody was there, then crept across the hallway.

With no time to remove and reapply her makeup, she washed and applied toner. In the mirrored cabinet above the sink, a bright, orange plastic container with a Boots prescription label sat on the lower shelf, glowing like a beacon. She took it out for a closer inspection.

The door opened, and Murphy, Sarah's ginger and white tabby, poked his head around the door. The cat purred and rubbed against her legs. Sarah put the medication in its original position and shut the cabinet door, then picked up the moggy and cuddled him until he squirmed to be let down.

The tantalizing spicy scent of her father's Tikka Masala chicken wafting out of the kitchen tickled her tastebuds as she came downstairs. The aroma made her mouth water, despite not wanting anything. Her dad sat at the table, his face buried in the farming section of *The Press and Journal*.

"Where's Rachel?" Not that she cared where her sister was.

"Down at your granny's," her mother called out from the galley kitchen. "Sit down. I'm dishing up now. Naan bread is in the basket. Should still be warm."

A few minutes later, her mum placed a bowl of steaming hot curry over Basmati rice in front of her. Sarah's primary school photo mocked her from the sideboard. She wished that disgusting photograph from P5 or P6 would be put away. Overweight with a face full of freckles, a mouthful of crooked teeth and short-cropped fringe. Weight lost, some courtesy of orthodontic work, she was nothing like the image in the picture.

Sarah reached for the bread then stopped.

Next to the hated photo was one of her younger sister at the same age. Slim, with a clear complexion and perfectly aligned teeth, her sibling was gorgeous by comparison.

"Jimmy put the newspaper away," her mother said as she set her husband's evening meal before him.

He grunted but did as he was asked.

The back door slammed. Rachel flounced in and collapsed into her chair.

Mrs. Shand came back with Rachel's curry and turned to Sarah. "I need you to move your things into your sister's room after supper." She tore off a chunk of bread and dipped it in her Tikka Masala sauce. "We've got guests arriving around half-eight, and they need the family room and yours as well."

"A boy asked me out for Saturday night," Rachel interrupted.

"Who would that be?" asked their mother.

"Only Alexej Svoboda, the hottest guy in The Gordon Schools. His eyes are the dreamiest blue," she swooned, "and the blackest hair. He reminds me of Daniel Radcliffe."

"Just where is this lad taking you?" Mr. Shand asked.

"He's picking me up here, and we're going to a film in Aberdeen."

"We don't know anything about the boy. How he drives. You're only fifteen years old, dammit."

"But Da-ad."

"Oh Jimmy, don't be such a curmudgeon."

"You never let me go out with a bloke who had a car back when I was Rachel's age," said Sarah.

"Times are different since then," Mrs. Shand said.

"It was only four years ago," Sarah retorted and glared at her sibling. Rachel stuck her tongue out.

Redirecting the talk back to before her sister had turned things around to be 'all about her,' she asked, "How long are they stopping?"

"Who?"

"The people who are coming and turfing me out of my room!"

"I believe a week. Don't fret. In a few days, when the en-suite becomes available, I'll move the couple down. Then just their three kiddies will be up there."

"Great." Sarah rolled her eyes. Things went from bad to worse. She didn't need to be stuck sharing a bedroom for one night, hearing Rachel gloat about being asked on a date. This was one of the times she wished her mum didn't take over her grandmother's Bed and Breakfast business when they swapped houses. Her appetite disappeared, and she picked at her food.

"You must eat, Sarah."

"I'm just not hungry." Her sister banging on about her hot date made her more depressed, and her eyes burned.

"What's the matter?"

Before she had a chance to answer, her father spoke up. "You're not still moping about over Blair? I made my feelings about that lad clear from the beginning. I never liked him. You're better off without him."

"Sarah and Blair broke up?" Rachel's eyes widened.

Tears ran down Sarah's cheeks, and she began to sob. She started to stand, and her dad yelled for her to sit back down, but instead, she darted out of the room.

The cat was curled up in the centre of her bed. She fell to her knees and rubbed her face in Murphy's fluffy fur.

Now her family home was the last place she wanted to be, regardless of how much she loved it. The further away she was from rural Aberdeenshire, the better. She shrugged into her beige cardigan and glanced around the room once more before closing the door silently behind her. After a brief stop in the bathroom to retrieve the sleeping tablets, Sarah would teach Blair a lesson he'd never forget. Pocketing the bottle, she crept down the stairs and out the front door.

2

The derelict mansion's granite façade reflected in the dwindling twilight under a purple, cloud-streaked sky. Tonight, the ruined building appeared as if someone had switched on the lights. Flashes of light sparkled on the non-existent glass in the huge window openings. Granny Duncan's stories of how her parents had met during the Second World War always made her smile. Sarah's great-grandfather Cochrane lived at Weetshill when he was in the army. She put on her mother's old dresses and pretended to be the Lady of the estate, married to the handsome Laird when she was a little girl. Back then she was a silly, naive child. Marriage was no longer in her future.

She had yelled at Blair when she busted them. Asked how he could cheat on her but he shoved his hands in his front jeans pockets and stared at the ground, silent. Then she vented her anger on Niamh, who implored, "Wasn't like that, Sarah. We were all friends. I didn't want it. I didn't encourage him. It-it just happened."

Three months didn't just happen.

Blair was Sarah's first serious boyfriend. They started dating the same year she turned sixteen. Every event since January was hashed over. More and more, he insisted they take their relationship to the next level.

"Come on, Sarah. We've been together three years. I'm tired of taking cold showers. I'm beginning to think you don't love me."

"Of course I do, you daft thing," she had told him over and over. "I'm just not ready. I don't want that kind of relationship until I'm married."

"You silly mare. Everybody who's been with their partner as long as us are doing it."

"I'm not everyone."

He retaliated and called her old-fashioned.

Maybe Niamh agreed to do what Sarah wouldn't.

Pill bottle extracted, she removed the cap and shook out the contents. Six, no seven pills lie in her palm. Hand clapped to her mouth; she swallowed the narcotics.

After a few minutes, her vision blurred, and her surroundings swirled around her. She tried to stand, but her legs buckled. Sarah collapsed, groped for a boulder, crawled on all fours, then pulled herself up, and sat. Once the dizziness subsided, she stood. Thinking she was returning to the farmhouse, she wandered away from the stone circle and staggered over the hill.

The volume of the traffic noise increased as she approached the Kendonald single carriageway. A motorbike's high-pitched whine faded into the distance, and the rumble of a lorry's diesel engine became louder then dwindled.

Sure she was on her way home; she followed the road noise. A bat swooped past her head, almost hitting her as she cut across the meadow. Disoriented, she regretted swallowing the pills. No matter how bad things were, she did not want to die. Her death would devastate her parents, and that was unfair to them. At the edge of the grass verge, she stepped out without looking.

Sarah spun around at the sound of the approaching engine. Headlights sparkled and danced in the closing darkness, blinding her. The next few seconds unfolded in slow motion. A horn blared, brakes screeched, and smoke surged out from beneath the tires.

Hypnotized by the dazzling light, Sarah couldn't move. The impact of the car's bumper shot a searing pain through her legs. Her bones snapped like twigs as she flew into the windshield and over the car. With a sickening thud, her head smashed against the tarmac.

Vomit and blood rose in her throat. She tried to roll over to keep from choking, but her body refused to obey. All the strength drained from her, and her world faded away into nothing.

"Oh my God! Oh my God!" The hysterical woman repeated.

"Don't die on me, please don't die. I called 9-9-9. Help will be here soon."

The soft touch of a hand caressed her forehead. A wide-eyed girl of about her age bent over her. Behind the girl, a mangled car rested against a tree. Sarah opened her mouth to speak but couldn't. She shivered.

"You must be freezing. Here, let me cover you." The young girl removed her coat and laid it over her. "Please just stay with me," she prayed, looking over her shoulder. Everything went dark as the approaching sirens wailed.

3

Sarah's eyes flickered open, and the frantic girl and her wrecked car had vanished. Instead of the paved surface of the Kendonald Road, Sarah sprawled out on her back on a narrow gravel lane.

Her chest ached with every breath like her father's herd of cows had trampled over it. Were her ribs broken? She gasped for air and tried to prop herself up on her elbows, but collapsed as stones gouged her arms.

With her last ounce of strength, Sarah hauled herself to an upright position. Something wet and sticky ran down the back of her neck, and her head throbbed. Dirt and blood coated her clothing, and her trainers were gone. Sharp gravel bit into her stocking feet as she staggered, trying not to fall, surprised she could stand. She was sure the impact with the car had broken her legs and maybe her back.

She wiped her palms on her shirt and cried out. They were bloodied and filthy. Her knees stung like someone scraped sandpaper over them.

Barely able to make out a faint glow shining far away, she stumbled toward it. Was it the yard light near the barn? Ears ringing, she clapped her hands over them in an attempt to block out the irritating noise, but to no avail.

Sarah blinked and stared at one of the ghostly trees lining the roadway. The trunk expanded and contracted before her eyes as if breathing. A gust of wind rasped through the branches, and a sudden cry of a long-eared owl made her jump. Chilled and shivering, Sarah folded her arms and rubbed, but the pain shot all the way to her fingertips, forcing her to stop.

At the narrow bridge, she stopped and rested. A shrill whistle pierced the silence, drowning out the ringing in her ears. It vibrated beneath her as she tried to catch her breath, and black smoke clogged the air. Sarah wheeled around and gasped. In the distance, the speck of a headlight emerged, growing larger and brighter as the locomotive advanced before finally thundering under the bridge. The train dropped out of sight into the darkness. The railway was further from her house. A flat dirt trail lead to the hamlet, unless ... unless she crossed the Kendonald Road.

Soon the smells of fresh cut hay, manure, and livestock replaced the lingering aroma of the train's oily coal smoke. If the barn was this close, she was almost home. The sound of horses snorting and the scrape of hooves pawing at stall floors drifted through the night air. Other than Murphy, the only animals on their farm were beef cattle, sheep, and a few barn cats.

Stumbling away from the stables, Sarah faced a sprawling three-storey building. Weetshill? No. The place was roofless. Trees grew inside its crumbling walls. The slates on this structure shone in the moonlight like they were installed yesterday, and glass sparkled in enormous casements that should have been gaping dark holes.

After her fingers made contact with the heavy oak door, she jerked her hand back as though the surface was on fire. Like the rest of the building, the door was real and in nearly new condition. A thick cord hung from a bell by the door, but before she reached the knotted end, her head began to spin, and she lost consciousness.

"Did you hear that, Granda?" Robert put down his newspaper and strained to listen.

"Not a thing."

He tried to go back to his paper but couldn't concentrate. He walked to the front door, disengaged the lock, and pulled the creaking door open. "Is anyone out here?" he called into the darkness as he stepped outside to better survey the area.

Robert stubbed his toe against something on the step and cast his eyes downward. A pile of rags laid on the stoop, but a bloodied leg protruded from the jumble. Squatting next to the crumpled heap, he reached out and stroked the matted hair. The dishevelled figure flinched at his touch and moaned.

"Archibald, Mrs. MacEwen. I need your assistance."

His grandfather, holding his cane over his arm, shuffled into the entryway. "Whatever are you bellowing about?"

"I found this laddie outside on the ground. He's been seriously hurt."

The housekeeper popped up behind the old man. "Och dearie me," she said as she crouched down. "Bring him in the book room, and put him on the settee."

Robert hoisted the injured boy and carted him indoors. Blood and dirt covered his suit after he positioned the lad on the sofa.

"Poor laddie met wi' a horrible fate. I dinnae ken what. Just it be awful," she jabbered covering the body with a woollen throw.

The shape under the blanket groaned, and a hand worked its way out from beneath the cover. A muffled voice spoke, "Wh-here am I?"

"You'll be fine. Can you tell me what manner of misfortune has befallen you?"

"No clue."

"What is your name?"

"Sarah Shand."

"You're not a laddie at all," said the old man, the shock evident in his response.

"Of course not. I'm a girl." The tone and volume of her voice shot a white, hot searing sensation through her head.

"Granda, please. You're not helping." Robert pulled over the ottoman. A pair of emerald green eyes framed with long, thick dark eyelashes stared at him. In spite of all the dirt and blood covering her skin, it was smooth and feminine. He sat and took one of her scuffed and scraped hands in his. "Do you understand what's happened to you?"

"I need to call my parents. Tell them I'm all right."

Robert raised his arm and waved to his servant. "We need Doctor Burnett. Can someone summon him?"

"Straight away, Sir."

"Wh-who are you? How did I get here?" She rubbed her eyes as she spoke.

"I don't know who or what brought you. I heard a noise and found you on the doorstep. You might not have survived the night on that cold granite slab."

Streaks of bloody muck coated the young man's brown wool suit. Sarah shivered. The blood came from her body when he toted her into the house. "Where am I?"

"Weetshill."

A knock on the door preceded a balding, rotund man sporting mutton-chop sideburns. A character out of Dickens in his white shirt, black tie, and gray trousers topped with a black jacket and green waistcoat. "Sir, you called?"

"We've summoned Doctor Burnett. Show him in the moment he arrives, Archibald," Robert advised.

Sarah's eyes darted about the room. "Did you say Weetshill? That can't be. That place is a ruin. Please, I need my mobile so I can ring my mother, tell her I'm all right."

"Whatever are you talking about? A what?"

A shock of dark curly hair fell on his forehead as he leaned down to scrutinize her. Sarah stared into his golden-brown eyes, attempting to make sense of his question. Everyone had a cellular phone of some brand or another. Her iPhone was new, and if she lost it, her parents would be well miffed with her. "Can I use your landline so I can call home?"

"What is this thing you speak of?"

Sarah grimaced as she struggled to sit up. Every part of her body hurt, including her hair. The morning after an end of term celebration in Glasgow was the last time she was in this much agony. "Who are you?" She repeated her question.

"Robert Andrew Robertson, grandson of the Laird of Weetshill." He extended his hand toward her.

Did he say Laird of Weetshill? "What an odd name."

"Not at all, Miss Shand. I was named after my maternal grandfather."

"Sorry. Not taking the mick. Caught me off guard, is all." She couldn't remember telling him her name, but how else would he know? Staring into his eyes, she wiped her dirty, sweaty palms on her shirt and held her hand out in return.

"Where do you live?"

"With my parents at Gordonsfield." Her stomach quivered.

"Where is that?"

"Near Kendonald."

"I'm not aware of such a place. Perhaps it is in another shire?" Robert asked.

"Not far from here. The road from the village to Leslie."

He furrowed his brow. "Gleanstane, the Christies' lands, are in the locale you're speaking of," he said, stroking his chin.

Sarah had heard of it before, but when? Her father said a stately home once occupied the farmland at the bottom of the far side of the mound where the stone circle stood. What happened? Barns, a cottage, and nearer the ancient monument, two standing stones, but no house.

"Nothing makes sense. I know where I live. Gordonsfield Farm by Kendonald." Sarah flinched and shrunk back as Robert reached for her.

"Don't be afraid. I'm only going to brush your hair out of your face." He tucked a lock behind her ear. "Pardon me, but what manner of trappings are you wearing? It is not appropriate attire for a lady."

She lifted the blanket. Her clothes were filthy. Her rugby shirt torn like she had taken part in a match and lost. "I don't understand. Why am I so dirty?"

"You can't recall? Were you in an accident?"

"I-I don't think so. I don't remember. My head hurts, but I don't know why." Sarah palmed the back of her head with her left hand and winced. "I don't suppose you have any Paracetamol."

"What is that? Your legs appear to be wounded as well," Robert said. "We best get you cleaned up, and your injuries seen to, and into some fitting lady's attire. I'll summon Mrs. MacEwen, our housekeeper. She'll look after you."

"I don't want clothes from you." Sarah snatched a newspaper from the coffee table. The masthead read *The Aberdeen's Journal*. Difficult to focus, it took her a few minutes, but   finally, she found the publication date on the front page. The month and day were right, but the year was 1886. Sarah's stomach lurched, and a wave of blackness consumed her.

Someone slapped the back of her hand, waking her and she opened her eyes. A gray-haired, heavy-set woman sat on the ottoman Robert occupied earlier.

"Och, Sir, wherever can that doctor be?" she bemoaned.

The woman, clad in a long full skirt, striped blouse, and half apron, patted Sarah's hand in a comforting gesture. Too bad it didn't work.

Rumours of the mansion's conversion to flats circulated throughout the district, but a renovation of this scope was impossible to complete in this short a time. Were these people actors cast to portray a simpler time for prospective buyers? Their accent was stronger and more formal than the northeast brogue she was accustomed to, especially that of Robert and the elder Mr. Robertson. The servants' speech was more like the seniors she saw at functions in the community centre.

"Och, you poor wee hen," the old woman clucked. "Let's take you up the stairs and saw to properly."

"Who are you?"

"I be Mrs. MacEwen." She helped Sarah stand and shepherded her to the kitchen. "Where are your shoes?"

"Beats me." White socks bunched at her ankles were filthy and bloodstained. Blood trails covered her pant legs, and scrapes and cuts were visible through the gaping holes ripped in her jeans.

The stone fireplace was massive, dwarfing the enormous cookstove on the opposite wall. The scent of onions lingered in the hot, steamy air. Two heavy benches sat under the long table. Various linens hung from a

Victorian clothes-horse suspended from the ceiling.

The woman took a kettle of steaming water off the wood burning cook stove and deposited it on the wooden table. Wiping her hands on her pinny, she turned. "Crivvens," she babbled. "Where did I put my Lambert's Listerine?"

Wasn't that a mouthwash and a rather strong one at that? And this woman was going to use it to clean her wounds? Sarah opened her mouth to object but stopped. Too many far more critical things raced through her mind. How did she get here? Who were these people, and how would she find her way home?

"You'll be needin' washin' up for starters. I'm not sure where you been or what doin', but you's terrible feechy." The housekeeper took off her wire-framed eyewear and swiped them with her apron. She had tired gray eyes. Sarah guessed her to be in her sixties. The woman put her glasses back on and retrieved the kettle, "Come wi' me, Miss Shand."

Pain seared through Sarah's legs with every step as she went up the narrow servants' staircase. About halfway up, she stopped. "I can't," she squeaked. "Hurts too much."

The senior staff member hesitated. "Och, I ken it does. I'll gie you a hand." She encircled the injured girl with her free arm and supported her up the remaining steps.

Sarah sighed with relief when she made it to the upper floor. "I wish I could remember what happened to me." She reached up with her left hand to swipe a lock of hair away from her face.

The older woman narrowed her eyes at her. "You doesnae ken? Och, dearie me. Ne'er mind, we'll take care o' you."

Mrs. MacEwen ushered her into a bedroom with a fireplace, gorgeous mahogany furniture, and plush burgundy drapes. The four-poster bed's mattress was so high off the floor; a person needed a ladder to climb onto it.

Hot water poured into the basin on the washstand, she added cold from the pitcher. "Take those dirty, tattered things off, and clean yoursel' up. I'll fetch you a nightgown," she said as she left the room.

Sarah sighed, relieved she was alone. Nothing made sense. People running around in period costume in a mansion she was sure remained derelict. The sooner she found her way back home, the better.

The servant came back with a clean, white nightgown over her arm.

"I need to use the toilet. Can you show me where it is?"

A puzzled expression crossed Mrs. MacEwen's face, but she led her to a small room at the end of the passage. "In here," she said as she turned up the lamp.

Sarah gasped. It was nothing more than an outhouse. She had used those antiquated things at Girl Guide camp, but they were outdoors. This one was inside the house. Once over her initial shock, she took advantage of the primitive facilities, went back to her assigned room, and changed into the nightgown provided for her.

"Much better," the housekeeper said after Sarah put on the bedclothes. "Now for your hair." She plucked a blade of grass from the back of Sarah's head before picking up the tortoiseshell brush and running it through her long, thick, brown hair.

"Ouch! That hurts." She reached behind her head and found a sizeable lump.

"I's sorry, Miss Shand. Young Mr. Robertson did say you has a sair heid. I dinnae mean to hurt you. Lets me take a gander." The woman parted Sarah's hair with her fingers and inspected the wound. "Isnae wonder you flinched when I touched you. That be a braw bump you's got."

"I'll do my hair if you don't mind." Sarah took the hairbrush in her left hand. The woman crossed herself in the mirror.

"I-I'll fetch the doc up when he gets here," she stammered, shuffling with difficulty out of the room.

The ornate grooming tool was returned to the dressing table. What had made the servant so uncomfortable?

"Doctor Burnett is here," the butler announced as he knocked on the door.

Robert and the elder Robertson man came into the room, accompanied by a tall man with salt and pepper hair and bushy eyebrows. The doctor's hands were enormous, with long, thin fingers. One hand encircled Sarah's wrist with room to spare as he monitored her racing pulse. His extremity was large enough to wrap around both her arms and still leave room. Bent down, it was apparent his nostrils and ears needed a proper trimming. "What have we here," he commented as he began his examination.

He examined the bump on her head and shone a crude, candle-powered torch into her eyes. After completing the initial exam, he rummaged in his satchel and retrieved a stethoscope and shoved the earpieces in his ears. This one had a bell-shaped horn instead of a disc on the end of the piece of medical equipment.

"I can't find a thing wrong with her but for the external injuries and bump on her head," he said as he removed the instrument from around his neck. "Mrs. MacEwen, if you would be so kind as to bring me a basin of lukewarm water." The doctor rooted through his bag and pulled out a small vial and clean strips of cotton.

The housekeeper came back, and he emptied the contents into the water swirling the fabric in the liquid. He wrang the fluid out of the calico and dabbed the dampened cloth over her injuries.

"That stuff stings. What is it?"

"Carbolic acid and water."

"You're rubbing acid on my skin?"

"A nonirritating solution to cleanse the abrasions and lacerations and help prevent infection."

"And who knows what else," Sarah said under her breath.

After he cleaned and bandaged Sarah's wounds, Dr. Burnett addressed the curious onlookers. "Everyone, please leave the room so I may speak to my patient in confidence. Would someone bring the young lassie a single malt?"

"Would you like one, too, Doctor?" the butler asked.

"Thank you. It would be sublime."

"Come, Granda. Doctor Burnett wants us to go," said Robert, his voice barely above a whisper.

"I'm not leaving her. I don't trust a young woman who runs around at night wearing laddie's clothing. 'Tis not right."

"I think you're making something of nothing. Come, please."

"You can't believe her." The old man drove his cane against the floor punctuating his statement.

"She's not apt to cause trouble in the condition she's in," Robert said as he guided his elder out of the room.

The manservant returned with two glasses of whisky.

The doctor gave one to her. "Drink this," he said. "Now lassie, why don't you tell me who you are and what happened."

Although Sarah didn't commonly consume liquor, she accepted his offer. Her mother always made her tea when she was hurt or unwell. Now, she wished she was at home and being cared for by her mum. She fiddled with her glass as she spoke. "My name is Sarah Shand. No clue how I got here - just I'm cut up and scraped, and there's a huge bump on the back of my head. It hurts like mad, and no one will give me any Paracetamol." She wanted to say the crazy people who surrounded her pretending the year was 1886, but stopped herself.

"I never heard of such a thing, but I carry medicine for a headache. Would you like some?"

"No. This seems to be helping." Deception, yes, because she didn't bring the glass to her lips. She refused to believe she was back in the nineteenth century, but she didn't want anything from the doctor's bag.

Who knew what sorts of poisons and potions his black case held?

"Continue with what you were telling me."

"I live at Gordonsfield, or at least I think I do. My father has beef cattle and sheep."

"Where is that?"

"Only a couple of roads from here, near Kendonald."

"Tell me more about you. When you were born for instance?"

"Seventeenth January."

"What is today's date?"

"Ninth August." She set her glass on the bedside table. "Um, Doctor, I don't know what year it is."

"Why, it is 1886 my dear lass."

Hands clapped over her ears, Sarah rocked back and forth, biting her tongue to keep from screaming.

"What is wrong lassie?" He patted her knee as he spoke.

She recoiled at his touch and drew her legs up to her chest.

"Please tell me what you do recall," the doctor said.

"I went to the stone circle by my house at Gordonsfield, and that's the last thing I remember until I ended up here."

The physician scratched his head. "I'm going to speak to the family," he said and left the room.

Sarah waited a few moments, before tiptoeing to the door to eavesdrop.

"Well, Doctor?" said Mr. Robertson.

"Is she dangerous?" asked Mrs. MacEwen.

"I shouldn't think so, but she is bewildered. She couldn't tell me what year we are in, and she thinks the collection of rocks at Gleanstane, or Gordonsfield as she called it, is on her father's land. I'll leave some tinctures of laudanum with you to calm her if she gets agitated."

"How much do we gie her?" the housekeeper asked.

"I'll write instructions on the dosage. In the meantime, I suggest you try not to agitate the girl. Once I get back to my surgery, I'm going to refer to my medical books. This loss of memory and confusion, well, it is not something I encountered before, and I'm not so sure I can treat the ailment. I want to consult some of my colleagues in Aberdeen. Perhaps one of them has come across a similar situation and can offer me advice."

"Thank you for coming with such promptness," said Robert.

The conversation ended, and Sarah backed away from the door. She sighed and walked to the window where she pulled the plush burgundy curtain aside. The heavy fabric was the same as the winter drapes her mother hung every autumn.

The weird people and surroundings frightened her more than the gaps in her memory. Unless they were lying to her, Gordonsfield didn't exist. So where was she? Clearly, she was not at Weetshill, was she? She needed to escape and determine for herself.

"Doctor Burnett is away," Robert said when he came back into Sarah's room with the old man and the servant. "Did someone attack you? Perhaps we should summon the police?"

Now that Sarah was cleaned up, she was quite attractive. Her long dark hair fell in soft waves around her face, and she stared up at him with wide, fear-filled emerald eyes.

"I don't remember."

Robert changed the subject, to try and put the lost and confused young woman at ease. "Only last month, Granda and I went to the Edinburgh Exhibition. The things we saw. What impressed me the most were the electric lights. The grounds and pavilions illuminated with them. Over three thousand the literature said. One day, Weetshill will have them, too."

Sarah's eyes widened.

"Whatever is wrong?" The blank expression on her face puzzled him.

"Nothing. This exhibition was when?"

"Prince Albert Victor, himself, opened the exposition in May and it continues until October."

"Who is he?"

"Why the Queen's grandson, of course."

"Don't you mean William or Harry?"

"No, who are they? Word is; Queen Victoria will visit before the event closes."

Sarah's bottom lip quivered, and she began to cry.

"What has you so vexed?"

She shook her head in response.

"Why don't you take her to Gleanstane?" the old man suggested. "She did say that was the last thing she remembered. Seeing the place might help the young lassie."

"Would you like to go there?"

"P-please. I must see for myself." Her eyes filled with tears.

"We'll go in the morning. You need your slumber tonight. Things will appear better then, I assure you."

"Why do we have to wait?" Sarah's voice quivered.

"At this time of night, you won't see anything. Even the light of the moon won't be enough. Along the way, we might find someone who knows your family. Drink up, and we'll call it a night."

"I really do need to know. You understand, don't you?"

"Yes." He turned to his employee and said, "Well, Mrs. MacEwen, it appears we have a guest for the night."

"Sir. It does."

4

Mrs. MacEwen shooed the men out of the chamber and shuttered the window. "When the mornin' sun comes in these windies, it's very braw."

Sarah sat in the armchair in front of the fireplace. "This is a beautiful room," she said. "A woman's at one time?"

"Aye, Mrs. Robertson's."

"Robert's wife?"

"His mother. Young Mr. Robertson hasnae yet married," the housekeeper said as she turned down the covers.

The last thing Sarah wanted was to stay overnight in this house, but she had no other options. Maybe she would wake up and find it had all been a dream. Sarah struggled to climb up on the mattress, but no matter how hard she tried, she was unsuccessful. Then she spotted the steps next to the bed and used them.

The housekeeper tucked her in. "I got you another blanket here if you needs it, Miss Shand. This auld place can be frosty at night."

"Please, you don't need to be so formal. Sarah is fine."

"I cannae do that. It wouldnae be proper for a servant to address you as such. Now, you willnae waken too soon. You need your rest. I'll turn down the lamps, so they doesnae bother you."

"I'm exhausted, so I'll probably be asleep in no time. Goodnight."

"Now settle in for a good night's sleep. I'll see you in the morn." She closed the door quietly behind her.

Had Sarah suffered a concussion, wasn't sleeping the worst thing?

Handsome and seemingly concerned, she found Robert arrogant. The old man didn't believe a word she said, and rightfully so. She landed in on them out of nowhere in the middle of the night. Were they real or just characters in a dream, or worse yet, a nightmare? Why was she unable to remember what happened between the stone circle and when she woke up here?

Satisfied the head maid went back downstairs, Sarah leapt out of bed. She pulled back one of the thick red curtains and scanned the horizon. The yard light at Gordonsfield should be visible if this were Weetshill. Not a speck of luminance in that location.

The full moon, partly obscured by clouds, bathed the landscape with an eerie bluish glow. Something in the direction of the main thoroughfare captured her attention. A blink was followed by a double take. Beyond the grounds, on what would be the Kendonald Road, the recognizable blue lights of an emergency vehicle flashed. The squad car, ambulance or fire truck was stationary, so was at the scene of an accident. She was both relieved and scared. If the light was real, she didn't go back in time, and the people around her were crazy. She jumped away from the sash, and the let the curtain fall into place.

Expecting to discover information on the inhabitants of the house and anything else to prove she was still in the twenty-first century, Sarah snooped. Inside the wardrobe hung beautiful clothing. The gowns appeared to be handmade, and she couldn't find any tags affixed to them. No zippers either, only buttons or laces. She walked to the dressing table and picked up the tortoiseshell hairbrush, turning it over slowly and admiring the grain and silver trim.

Sarah rummaged through the drawers but found nothing except women's underthings and jewellery. A jewel-encrusted box caught her eye. The orange stones were amber, accented by teardrop shaped pearls. She opened the container. Inside were tortoiseshell and ivory combs, and an eye-shaped brooch with an identical red-yellow gem. Disappointed, she returned the items to their rightful place and returned to the window, but the emergency lights were gone.

"Jimmy, Sarah's not in her room. She's not moved her things into Rachel's yet, either."

"Is she in her there? Maybe the loo?" He put his newspaper down.

"I searched all over upstairs, but there is one other thing. My prescription sleeping tablets are missing from the bathroom."

"Damn it to hell, Moira! Why didn't you mention it in the first place? You know what a mood she's been in since... since... Goddammit, if anything's happened to her, I'll swing for that lad – the torment he's put our girl through." He stomped out of the room.

Moira's husband had a temper and stood by his word. Had Sarah done something daft because of Blair, the boy wouldn't survive to rue the day. She tagged along behind Jimmy to the back door where he struggled to shove his feet into his shoes. "What are you doing?"

"I'm going out looking for her. You ring the police. Where's my bloody torch when I want it?"

"The same place as always. On the shelf in your office."

Mr. Shand thundered out of the room. By the time he came back, his wife had her jacket on and was tying her shoes.

"Where do you think you're going? I told you to call 9-9-9. That meant for you to stay here for when they arrive."

"I'm going with you, Jimmy. I can't let you do anything you'll live to regret."

"Not necessary. I'm only going up to the stone circle to find out if that's where the crazy fool girl went." He scrubbed his hands down his face. "You're aware she likes that place when she's not able to face the world. Tonight is one of those times."

The beam was of little use because he continually waved the torch around as he walked. Moira held his forearm tighter to keep up with him. There was no trace of their daughter.

"Sarah, where are you? Quit playing silly beggars and answer me," her father shouted in the darkness.

"We're worried sick," her mum called, anticipating a calmer voice would elicit a response. Not that she felt composed.

Mr. Shand sat down on one of the boulders. His arm went limp, and the torch's beam shone on the ground. The sleeping tablet container glinted in the shaft of illumination with the cap beside it.

"Oh Lord, Sarah, what have you done," she grieved, choking back a sob.

"How many pills were left in the bottle?"

"I don't remember exactly. Not many." She collapsed against her husband.

A blue light flashed on the main route through the village. "Jimmy. You don't suppose ...," her voice trailed off.

"Let's pray she's all right. Come on. We'll go back to the house and get the car. It'll be faster," he said as he sprang to his feet and started for the farmhouse.

Mrs. Shand ran as fast as she could, but her husband's strides were longer. He already had the engine fired when she flopped into the front passenger seat. Gravel sprayed from the tires when he hit the accelerator.

Moira clutched the handle grip above the door as the Vauxhall Astra roared out of the yard.

The emergency lights still flashed as they rounded a bend on the Kendonald Road. An officer stood blocking their way, holding up his hand. "Sorry, the road's closed. You'll have to turn around."

"We're not going anywhere. Our daughter is missing, and she might be here," Jimmy said, shutting off the motor and undoing his seatbelt.

Moira got out in time to overhear a distraught young woman talking to another policeman behind a rescue truck. "Sh-she ran out in front of me. I tried to stop, but I couldn't. I dialled 9-9-9 right after I found her. I looked back when I heard the ambulance, but when I turned around again, she was gone."

Startled by a noise outside the room, Sarah turned down the lamps and scrambled into the warm bed. Her heart raced as she hid beneath the blankets. Fleeing from this crazy place was her number one priority, but finding her way home wearing nothing but a nightgown would be difficult. Still she had to try. Sarah climbed back out and tiptoed into the passageway, looking both directions in the darkened corridor. At the central staircase, a voice scared her.

"What are you doin' out here, Miss Shand?" the housekeeper asked.

"I-I can't stay here. I need to go home. My parents will be worried."

"You cannae go prowling about the countryside in the wee hours of the night in just your night clothes. Come, back to bed."

"No. I have to go," Sarah insisted.

"Young Mr. Robertson will take you tomorrow. Your folk will understand."

"You don't know my father."

Mrs. MacEwen put a motherly arm around Sarah's shoulder and walked her back into the bedroom. "Things will look better in the mornin'. They always do."

"I'm not so sure," Sarah said as she crawled under the covers.

"Maybe you should take some o' the med'cine Doctor Burnett left for you."

"No, I don't want that."

"You'll no get a good night's rest wi'out it." The housekeeper dispensed some on a spoon. "Here, take this."

Not knowing what else to do, Sarah opened her mouth. The bitter tasting medicine made her tongue go numb. Was she dead and been consigned to purgatory or worse for killing herself? She didn't want to be drugged and lost, like a shadow in the past, but too late. She'd taken the laudanum.

"That's a bonnie girl." The servant pulled the blankets up around her, bid her goodnight again, and left the room.

The narcotic put Sarah to sleep immediately but gave her vivid nightmares. She was with Blair and Niamh when she found them in the woods. "How could you cheat on me?" she cried. "And you, I thought you were my friend."

"It wasn't like that," she begged. "We were all friends. I didn't want it to take place. I didn't encourage him. It-it just happened."

"Like this just happened?" Sarah held a gun in her hand. Her body jerked as two shots rang out in quick succession.

5

Sarah woke with a start. She was in the room at Weetshill. Still in the four-poster bed; its crisp white sheets and patchwork quilt drenched with sweat, as was her nightgown. Her heart pounded, and she gasped for air, fearful if she didn't it would burst through her chest. She was relieved she didn't shoot her cheating friends but disappointed to find herself in the strange house. The events that happened to her since she left the stone circle had to be a dream. She hoped to wake up back in her room at Gordonsfield.

The fire no longer blazed. Only embers remained on the grate, and the paraffin lamps were turned up to their full illumination. Sarah jumped at a movement in the corner. "Wh-who's there?" she called.

"You're awake, Miss Shand." The voice was female, but not the housekeeper's.

"Yes, I am. Who are you?"

"I'm Janet. Janet Cochrane."

The maid wore a long, black crepe dress with white collar, cuffs and apron. An object resembling a doily perched atop her head. In minutes the heavy draperies were opened and the lamps extinguished.

"Mrs. Mac … was right about the sun," Sarah said, unable to remember the woman's full surname as she slid off the mattress. The hardwood floor was freezing, so she jumped to one of the area rugs.

"Aye." Janet pulled up the sash.

Sarah stared out the window, hoping she could catch sight of her home, but dense fog obscured everything. She could barely make out dark silhouettes of trees, and the aroma of wood smoke lingered in the crisp air.

By the time she turned around, the bed had been made and a gown laid out along with a corset, clean chemise, and petticoats.

"Mrs. MacEwen tells me I'm to take care of you."

"I don't need looking after."

"Beggin' your pardon, but if I doesnae, herself will be fair vexed with me."

"Oh, all right then. We wouldn't want that."

"Let's get you washed, dressed, and hair done for the mornin' meal," Janet said pouring hot water into the ceramic basin, sending billows of steam into the air. "Let me help you."

"I'll do it myself. I'm sure there are other things you need to do," Sarah said. She stabbed her finger at the corset. "I refuse to wear one of those medieval torture devices."

"You're lucky you dinnae has to," said Janet, staring at Sarah's extended arm.

"What?"

"You're left-handed?"

"Yes, why? Do you have a problem with that?"

"W-well, they say the devil possesses left-handed folk."

"And you believe in the silly superstition?"

"I ain't never seen someone who is so I cannae say."

Sarah shook her head. Superstitious nonsense. "I'm most definitely not possessed by him or anyone. My dad is a leftie, too, so it must be hereditary." The pale blue frock with black piping and white lace trim was beautiful. Clothed in the garment, she sat at the dressing table. Long hair brushed, she tied her tresses into a low ponytail with a ribbon hanging on the mirror frame. Closing the bedroom door behind her, Sarah strolled to the staircase and went downstairs.

In the vast anteroom, the salty aroma of frying bacon combined with the yeasty bouquet of fresh-baked bread made her ravenous. She opened a pair of double doors to her right. The enormous room housed a grand piano at the near end. A violin case lay on top. On the opposite side of the panelled area, she discovered the empty dining room as the housekeeper came around the corner.

"Nae here, Miss Shand. You has to go to the breakfast room. Come along. I'll show you."

This room was bright and airy. Stacks of plates, cups, saucers, cutlery, and napkins were laid out on the massive sideboard. Both the Robertson men sat at the table and stood at her entrance.

"Good morning. Sleep well?" Robert said guiding Sarah to the chair directly across the round table from his place.

Robert's grandfather nodded, acknowledging her presence. "Hmph, you're still here," he grunted.

"You look most appealing," he spoke up. "It's been a long time since I saw someone wear that frock. Mum wore this one many times."

"You don't mind me wearing your mum's things do you?" she said, smoothing the skirt.

"No. I'm happy someone is using her things rather than them being packed away in the wardrobe. I told Mrs. MacEwen last night to make them available to you."

"Oh Lord, I hope she didn't die in it," Sarah muttered.

The old man laughed and said to Robert, "That sounds like something your dear old Gran would have said, God, rest her soul."

Sarah's face flushed, and she put her head down. "I was looking for this room, and I went by another one with a piano and violin in it. Who's the musician?" She tried to divert their attention.

"Granda plays the fiddle, and my mother played the piano."

"That she did. So did your Grandmother," the old man said.

She turned to him. "Would you play for me sometime?"

His face lit up. "Delighted."

"As promised last night, the carriage will be ready after we finish our meal. We'll take you where you want to go."

Sarah smiled and plucked a rasher of bacon from her dish with her left hand. Robert's brow furrowed. Was it because she had used her fingers? She dropped the slice of cured meat and turned back to the elder Mr. Robertson. "I have to go home first, but later?"

"Of course."

Robert accompanied Sarah to the front door. A cloak lay on the settle for her along with an overcoat for him. He placed the garment over her shoulders.

Archibald disengaged the locks. The dense fog had dissipated, and fluffy white clouds drifted in the sky. A chestnut horse harnessed to the open-top carriage pawed at the gravel and snorted.

Unbelievable. The lush, green lawns surrounding the house were well manicured, unlike the overgrown, weedy mess Sarah was accustomed to from her vantage point at the stone circle. Flower gardens of assorted shapes and sizes reminded her of castles she'd visited with her parents. The house resembled Weetshill, but she had seen it only a few days before, in its ruined condition. Such extensive renovations would be impossible in this short a time. A shiver ran down her spine, and she turned away from the building.

The lack of engine and tyre noise was eerie. At this time of day, travel was brisk. School buses delivering children to the local primary, milk tankers, and other heavy goods lorries travelling between Huntly and Duninsch, joined the regular commuter traffic on the Kendonald Road. Robert's voice snapped her out of her reverie.

"Thank you for attending to this so promptly. Miss Shand, permit me to introduce our ghillie, Angus Cameron. I asked him to accompany us on our journey since he knows this locality so well."

The man tipped his moth-eaten deerstalker hat. "G'day, Miss Shand. 'Tis lovely to meet you."

Sarah nodded. The gamekeeper was about six feet tall; his face and hands weathered by the wind on the hills. Parts of his tweed coat were threadbare and the collar and cuffs frayed.

A huge man stood behind the ghillie. At least four inches taller, he was broad-shouldered and muscular like the men she had seen compete in the Ironman competitions on television. A leather thong at the nape of his neck kept his shiny, jet-black hair in place. He leered at her with icy blue eyes.

"Ah, I didn't realize you came along. Excellent, you can drive. Miss Shand, this is Hamish MacMillan, our groom."

He extended his hand and bowed slightly in greeting.

Sarah collected the multiple layers of skirt and planted her foot on the small step before taking the groom's hand to climb into the brougham.

"Miss Shand," Robert exclaimed.

"What?"

He indicated her exposed calf and knee. "You're behaving in an indecent manner. You, Hamish, avert your eyes."

"You never saw a woman's leg before?" Sarah climbed aboard and settled into the forward facing seat. "Bet you never tried climbing into a carriage wearing a long skirt."

The groom winked at her.

"Show's over perv." Once the words were out of her mouth, she wished she could take them back. The man stopped smiling but continued undressing her with his eyes.

"Perhaps you should stay here, Hamish. Angus can drive. You go back to the stables. I'm sure chores are requiring your attention." Robert boarded and sat next to her. "We'll go by way of Kendonald to Gleanstane, sorry Gordonsfield, as our visitor refers to the place. We might find someone between here and there who knows of her family."

Sarah anticipated her homecoming as they travelled further away from the residence. After they turned right to a dirt track, the surroundings were unrecognizable. "Where are we?"

"On the Kendonald Road."

Swaying and lurching along the bumpy path, she watched the passing scenery with growing dread. While familiar, something was wrong. The tarmac surface of the carriageway she knew no longer existed. This lane was gravel and chock-full of deep ruts. In place of the distillery, grazing sheep and cows occupied a green pasture. The small railway station with its broken windows and missing slate roof tiles was resplendent. She spent the night in a house full of crazy people, but now the whole world had gone insane. The further they drove, the faster Sarah's heart hammered. Her breathing quickened, and the backs of her eyes pricked.

"Are you all right?"

Fearful of saying the wrong thing or bursting into tears, she only nodded.

The ghillie turned on the trail to the location described as the setting of her home. Sarah gasped. Few trees. No houses. Nothing but vacant fields. "No. No. No. You didn't bring me to the right place. Mine looks nothing like this. Where did you take me? Let me out. I want out."

"Help Miss Shand, would you, Angus?"

She ran to the middle of the empty field and turned to face them. "Please take me to Gordonsfield."

The men caught up with her and Robert whispered, "But no place of that name exists in this area." He wiped a tear from her cheek.

"Yes, there is, but we aren't there. The driveway would be right here if this were our farm. Even though my sister and I are too big, the swing set would be over in the corner near the clothesline. The barn should be over there." Sarah turned and extended her arm in the direction of the missing structure.

"There was but one house on this land, and the place burned about ten years past." The gamekeeper nodded to a roofless shell in the adjacent farmland. "Isnae Shands here. Ne'er been. This be part of Horatio Christie's holdings."

"You took me to the wrong place. I know you did. Parts look like it, but this isn't it."

Angus's expression became thoughtful. "Sir, Miss Shand. The burnt out house o'er yonder belonged to auld Gordon Eadie, one of the Christie tenant farmers. The small plot the cottage sat on was sometimes called Gordon's field."

That name, Gordon Eadie, was familiar to Sarah, but where or who had mentioned it was unknown.

Robert put his hands on Sarah's upper arms. "Calm down. Things will work out."

"Like hell, they will!"

Shaking Robert off, she started for the hill. The waist-high grass made running difficult, and her long skirt, petticoat, and boots added to her woes. At the top, she stopped and screamed. In the same place for thousands of years, stood the ancient monument.

Chilled to the bone, a bead of cold sweat ran down Sarah's back.

Weetshill sat on a distant ridge, gleaming in the midday sun. In the direction from which she came, was the empty field where her house should be. She gave a strangled cry. Her knees weakened, her stomach lurched, and she blacked out.

Sarah turned a sickly greenish-gray, and Robert lunged forward and gathered her up before she hit the ground. "I think it is best we return to Weetshill now. I believe Miss Shand has had enough for one day." He transported her to the carriage and positioned her on the seat, covering her with his coat. "Take us home, the quickest possible route. We can't do anything more for her here. Mrs. MacEwen will get her seen to on our homecoming."

"As you wish, Sir."

Robert caught himself thinking about the glimpse of Sarah's legs he had seen when she lifted her skirts. A decent lady would never do that, but she was so innocent in other ways. Even her accent was unusual, and the words and expressions used were foreign to him. Her claims to her history were impossible, but she was adamant. Torn between wanting to be rid of her and the desire to protect her and tell her everything would be all right he sat in silence.

"I dinnae ken if I should be the one to say, but there is something else, Sir."

"What would that be?"

"She could be frae the lunatic asylum o'er by Ladysbridge Station or e'en Aberdeen."

"Oh, I do pray that isn't the case."

She hauled herself up, shooting daggers at him with her eyes. "I'm not an escapee from the loony bin, and I don't appreciate being called one."

6

Sarah glared at the men all the way back to Weetshill. Wrapped in Robert's coat, she shivered. Painful to believe, she had travelled back in time to 1886. She would have to beware of everything she said and did from now on, or the mental hospital was right where she would end up. If that happened, she would never figure out how to get home.

The carriage crunched to a stop. Angus and Robert supported her between them as they walked to the front door.

"Och, dearie me, what happened?" Mrs. MacEwen asked as they came inside. "Quick, bring her in here." She opened the library door.

"My head hurts."

"Doctor Burnett left some med'cine for you. Would you like it?"

"What's all the fuss?"

"Miss Shand is not feeling well, Granda."

"I'll be right back," the old man said. He reappeared a few minutes later, violin case in hand. "I haven't played this in years."

She smiled and hoped the violin wouldn't yowl like a cat having its tail rocked on.

Bow rosined, he drew the hair across the strings, creating the exact screeching noise she dreaded. The sound was worse than chalk on a blackboard. Sarah cringed.

The old man grinned. He'd done that on purpose. The strains of *O Gin I Were Where Gadie Rins* filled the room. The tune was on one of her father's Old Blind Dogs CDs.

Powerless to contain herself, she tapped her toes and clapped her hands against her thighs in time with the beat. She caught herself bouncing in the chair and immediately stopped.

"Why don't you ask the lassie to dance, then laddie?"

Robert stood and held out his hand in invitation. "Can you do the Gay Gordons, Miss Shand?"

"Y-yes, but I'm dreadful. I'm always turning the wrong way." Of all the Scottish folk dances to mention, it had to be the one her great-grandparents danced to when they fell in love.

"You'll do fine. I'll lead you."

Once she was on her feet, he led her around the room. "You're doing sublime, Miss Shand, when did you learn the steps?"

"I can't remember for sure. I think at one of the Burns suppers at the community centre when I was a young girl. My grandpa played the fiddle in a local ceilidh band."

Despite dancing and the music lightening the mood, the scene brought back memories of watching and listening to her grandfather. She wished she could be in the small lounge at their cottage now.

Sarah stopped and walked to the window.

"Are you all right, lassie?" The old man gawped at her as he put down his bow.

"I-I'm fine. Your music reminded me of Grandpa Shand."

"Shall I continue?"

"Please."

Robert joined her. "What an amazing effect on my granda. It must be down to you. He's not played in years."

She nodded; her mind elsewhere.

Taking her in his arms again, he signalled to his elder who resumed his performance. "Can you dance the polka?"

"No."

"I'll teach you." He demonstrated. "Just remember, one and two and one and two, and you'll be just fine."

Sarah was less expert in this than she was the Gay Gordons, yet he didn't appear to mind, even when she trod on his feet.

"You're doing marvellous," he said as her foot mashed down squarely on his.

"I-I'm sorry."

His golden brown eyes sparkled when he smiled at her, and the dimple in his left cheek grew deeper. "I'm not fussed about my feet. As it goes, I only use the bottoms."

Sarah laughed. Soon she became used to the dance and managed a complete turn around the room without stepping on Robert or kicking him.

The music stopped, and they flopped on the sofa in fits of laughter.

"Thank you. Most entertaining." He squeezed her hand as he spoke.

"I had fun, too," she said as she applauded the elder Mr. Robertson's efforts before a feeling of sadness overwhelmed her.

"Are you all right? A moment ago you seemed happy. Now, you seem on the verge of weeping."

Sarah walked to the fireside.

"I didn't make you too sad, lassie, playing for you?"

"Not at all. It was nice to think of my grandpa."

"Did he pass on?" Robert followed and put his hands gently on her upper arms.

After considerable thought, she formulated a response. "No. I miss him."

Mr. Robertson returned the violin and bow to the case and snapped it shut. "You see laddie? Some young folks appreciate their elders. Would you like to view some more of the house, Miss Shand?"

"Y-yes, please." Sarah went with him.

In the foyer, she stopped and admired a huge painting. The man could have been Robert, but the eyes were dark brown, not golden brown like his. Shiny black hair styled in a chignon, the woman's piercing blue eyes bored through Sarah. Her costume was velvet, the colour of cocoa, trimmed with ivory lace. The long full skirt swept the floor in front of her chair. At the neck of her gown, the woman sported a brooch. Its black, oval gemstone had narrow stripes of whites and browns running across the top half. Surrounding the rock was a silver filigree frame.

"You like the portrait," the old man said. "That was my Elizabeth and me to commemorate our nuptials."

"She was beautiful."

"Much like you in some ways, now I'm getting better acquainted with you. I must apologize for my previous behaviour. Not genteel on my part."

"I don't blame you for not trusting me with the way I landed in here out of nowhere."

"Would you like to see more paintings?"

"I'd love to, but only if it's no bother."

"None, whatsoever. Come, I'll put my fiddle back in the ballroom, and we'll be off."

Even though the old man carried a cane, he only used the walking stick when he bashed it on the floor or got up from a chair. The rest of the time, he hung the thing over his arm.

The remaining portraits were of Robertson ancestors dating back to the 1700s. "Old Louis, here, well the family lore conveyed down through the generations says he was quite the rogue. Invested a great deal of time in the exclusive gentlemen's clubs in Aberdeen."

"In the what?"

"Oh, until he met the right lassie, he spent much of the family's fortune on prostitutes. The talk was, he was particularly fond of one old gal and requested her services every time he visited."

Sarah had seen the hookers in the red-light district of the city down by the harbour. They were aged beyond their years and tough, although some were probably no older than she was. "So what was so special about this one?"

"That part of the story never was imparted. Louis's bereft widow, my great-grannie, was too much a lady ever to say."

An image of an overweight, toothless and harried woman wearing only a corset and drawers popped into Sarah's head. Unable to help herself, she laughed.

The old man turned to her and smiled. "Come. There are more." He showed the way to the first floor.

The portraits here were more current than those already viewed. "Who are these people?"

"This is my son, John Alexander – he preferred Alex, and his wife, Elspet. She was a delightful lassie. Good for him."

The resemblance between all three Robertson men at the same approximate age was uncanny. All had that wild curly brown hair, the kind eyes, and mischievous smile.

Sarah smiled and moved on to the next one. The couple again, but this time with a small boy and an infant.

"Is that Robert?"

"No, Johnny, my oldest grandson. He died not long after that," the old man said, his voice choked with emotion. "And the baby is Robert."

"I'm sorry. What happened to Robert's brother?" Was her question nosey and insensitive?

"He had the diphtheria. We kept Rabbie in the nursery in the far wing, so he didn't take sick, too. Bad time, horrible."

She didn't push for more information.

"He was a delightful boy, my Johnny."

"I'm sure." She reached out and touched his arm.

The subjects of the next picture were a boy and girl with dark curly hair. Sarah gasped. These were the same children she had seen on the hill at Gordonsfield many times. "Who are these two kiddies?"

"Robert and his sister, Margaret."

"Um, did they ever play over at the stone circle?"

"Yes, the silly pair. The two used to climb on the stones and come home filthy with their vestments torn. Drove their mother to distraction. Why do you ask?"

"Oh, no reason." After a brief pause, she continued, "Where is Robert's sister now?"

"She bides in Edinburgh and isn't able to come around much," he said, his eyes moist with sadness.

A loud crash from below startled them, and they hurried to the head of the stairs. Lying on the floor in the great hall was the picture of Mr. Robertson and his wife. The housekeeper shrieked and crossed herself when she burst into the room. "Archibald, Dougal, come quick. I need you. The painting of the Laird and his missus come off the wall," she called. "We gots to put it back up right away."

"I'm off to lie down for a while," the old man said. "I'm not feeling so well." He took out a handkerchief and blew his nose.

"I hope it's not down to me."

"No, my dear lassie. Just my age. I'm not a young buck anymore, and sometimes I tend to forget that."

Sarah turned back to stare at the picture of the children. Any doubt in her mind they were the same ones she saw at the stone circle was expunged. All the times she had seen them, she thought they were ghosts, but now she was dumbfounded. Maybe whatever magic allowed them to materialize had somehow transported her into the past. The thought made her head ache.

The library's massive bookcases strained under the weight of numerous leather-bound tomes. Sarah wandered around until a spine with bright gold lettering captured her interest. She stared at the book, likely the first edition.

"Do you like to read,?"

The voice startled her. "Y-yes, I love to."

Robert seated her and summoned the butler, who carried over a tray with a full crystal decanter and two matching glasses. "Who are your favourite authors?"

Seized by panic, Sarah couldn't think of an author from that time. She loved novels written by Diana Gabaldon and Barbara Erskine and far darker works by Stephen King. She pointed to the hardcover with the gold script on the spine. Taking a deep breath, she said, "I like this one."

She took it off the shelf and opened it to the flyleaf - *Middlemarch* by George Elliot. She hoped he wouldn't want to discuss it since she'd never read it.

Peering over her shoulder, he said, "A fine work. Did you enjoy it?"

She swallowed. "Um, yes. More than once and would love to again. Such a great story."

"Your wish might come true. Who else do you like to read?"

"Ah, no way. I told you. Your turn now."

"Well, I do take delight in Dickens. *The Pickwick Papers* I would say is the one I like best."

"Can't say I know that title, but read *A Tale of Two Cities*. Talk about depressing, but I loved *The Christmas Carol*." She had seen the black and white film with Alastair Sim many times. If he wanted to discuss the book, she hoped it remained true to the movie.

"I'm also fond of Jules Verne and Robert Louis Stevenson. Maybe someday the adventures in Verne's stories will be possible. Imagine travelling around the world in eighty days. The books here in the library are at your disposal during your stay here at Weetshill."

Eighty days? With modern jets, passengers could traverse the distance in a week. Less than.

"*Middlemarch* was actually written by Mary Anne Evans. She wrote under a man's name to gain credibility. I'm not sure why I'm aware of that," she added.

"The dickens you say." Robert glanced at the mantle clock then pulled out his pocket watch and confirmed the time.

"Why do you do that?"

"What?"

"Take your watch out to double-check the time."

"Timekeeping instruments are such intricate things, aren't they? The idea of time itself fascinates me. I read a story called *The Clock That Went Backward* by Edward Page Mitchell about a timepiece when wound backwards, allowed people to go back in time."

If he only knew.

"Beggin' your pardon, Sir. 'Tis time to gets ready for dinner. Miss Shand, if you come wi' me, I'll find you something to wear," Mrs. MacEwen announced.

"What's wrong with what I'm wearing?"

"'Tisnae one for this meal. Now come."

Sarah went with the servant. On the bed was a beautiful velour burgundy gown with short, puffy sleeves. After changing, she admired herself in the cheval mirror. She never owned anything this gorgeous in all her life and likely never would. "It's tight here through the bust. My boobs are going to burst out."

"You be fine. Dinnae fash. Let us gets off to young Mr. Robertson."

"You are a vision of loveliness," said Robert when she appeared at the head of the staircase.

Her cheeks grew hot, and she imagined her face was the same shade as her clothing. "Th-thank you."

The low-cut neckline made her self-conscious since the garment was so tight. The one she wore earlier had been snug, but at least didn't leave her feeling about to pop out if she moved the wrong way. With her left hand, she tugged on the bodice trying to keep everything tucked in and gingerly descended the stairs, adjusting herself as she went. How did women manage to function under the weight of such heavy fabric? The gown had to weigh fifteen pounds. The housekeeper scurried ahead of her and took her place with the rest of the household staff.

Robert moved to the newel post and took Sarah's hand. They walked to the head of the line.

"This is our cook, Morag," he said indicating a plump woman with frizzy hair and an ample bosom.

Sarah suppressed a giggle. She envisioned this woman as the old ancestor's favourite from the gentlemen's club. If her size was any indication, the woman was an excellent chef. "Judging by the aroma, dinner is going to be to die for."

"I'll has you ken, me cooking isnae poison!"

"I didn't mean anything bad. I meant it would be delicious. I can't wait to find out."

"I needs to go back to it, or it willnae be fit to eat."

Excused from the receiving line, the cook took the kitchen maid with her.

"This is our laundress, Maggie."

The woman, wearing work clothes, curtseyed slightly.

"These are our maids, Anna, Catriona, and Lesley," he said.

The young women dressed in identical black crepe gowns, white collars, cuffs, aprons, including the same doily-like things on their heads worn by Janet.

"Pleased to meet you, Miss Shand."

"I'll never remember everyone's names," she said. "Does everyone have to call me that?"

"They're respectful."

"The term is so old-fashioned. I'd just as soon everyone called me by my given name."

"I can't abide that. Calling you by your forename is not courteous."

"Dinner is ready," the butler announced.

A fire crackled in the giant stone fireplace. The table, covered with white jacquard linen, was massive and able to accommodate at least twenty people. Robert seated Sarah in one of the high-backed, wooden chairs before taking his place directly across from her. His grandfather already sat at the head, and the staff took up their positions in the room.

Beads of nervous sweat formed in Sarah's underarms. This room was far more formal than any dining room she had ever been in before. Terrified of making a mistake, she envisioned using the wrong piece of cutlery. Or dropping something on the perfect white tablecloth.

Napkin on her thighs, Sarah rubbed the handle of one of the forks next to her plate with her left hand. Her eyes darted around the room. She felt as if she were on display.

Mrs. MacEwen carried a platter holding an enormous roast and placed it in front of the elder Mr. Robertson. After giving the blessing, he stood to carve. Aromatic juices dripped from the meat when the fork pierced the surface.

"What is it?"

"Venison. I daresay cook has been fussing o'er it all day."

Never having eaten game in her life, she was hesitant about starting now, but the mouth-watering aroma coming from the haunch won out.

A maid stood beside her holding out a bowl of boiled potatoes. Sarah took the spoon in her dominant hand but transferred the cutlery to her right. She managed to pick up one, but her wrist gave out, and the vegetable fell, breaking in pieces on the linen table covering. "S-sorry."

The maidservant scooped a generous helping from the dish onto Sarah's plate before making her way to the others. Another domestic carried bowls of carrots and turnips. She inhaled and served herself a small amount.

Sarah reached for the silver salt cellar, and the bodice of her dress slipped. She grabbed at it to keep from exposing herself, and dropped the small bowl, spilling its contents all over the tablecloth.

"Och, Miss Shand, seein' how you's spilt salt you must throw some o'er your shoulder to stop death frae happenin'."

"What? No one in my family ever said anything about doing that."

Watching how the men held their forks and knives, Sarah imitated them. She felt like a baby learning how to feed herself. Her knife fell with a clatter on the China plate. The piece of venison she'd cut off skittered to the white tablecloth.

Because of the problems with the cutting utensil, Sarah gave up and used a different piece to stab a potato. Then, what she feared most of all happened. She had it almost to her mouth when it fell off the flatware and down inside the neckline.

Embarrassed, if she could shrink and become invisible, she would. The chunk of root vegetable was hot, mushy, and disgusting. However; this elegant space wasn't the right place to put her hand down her front and pull it out. Her cheeks burned with a blush the same colour as the burgundy fabric.

"Are you all right, Miss Shand?" asked Robert.

She shook her head and dropped her fork on her plate.

Sarah tried to push her chair back, but one leg caught in the rug, knocking her against the tabletop. Her goblet tipped over, and a dark, red stain spread over the white jacquard covering. Her napkin fluttered to the floor as she dashed out, slamming the door behind her. At the base of the staircase, she stopped and broke down in tears.

Mrs. MacEwen sat down beside her. "Come now, lassie. 'Tisnae that bad."

"But the wine. I ruined the tablecloth."

"You let Maggie be worrit about it."

"I don't belong here. I want to go home and be with my family." She fell into the housekeeper's arms.

"I cannae help you wi' that, Miss Shand, but I will make your stay pleasant whilst you be wi' us. Let's get you settled. A good night will do you the world. Come along." The woman helped Sarah to her feet, put her arm around her, and they climbed to the first floor.

7

"Don't just sit there, laddie, go after her."

"Why? I don't even know what her problem was."

"The clothing and surroundings made her uncomfortable."

"I should ask you, why the sudden change of heart, Granda? You were the one who was suspicious and didn't trust her when she first arrived."

"I made an error in judgement. Miss Shand is a charming lassie," he said cutting his venison. The old man took a sip of his wine and popped a hunk of meat into his mouth. He scowled at Robert as he chewed. "We had a delightful time when I took the fiddle back to the ballroom. She was interested in the family portraits. In some ways, she reminds me of your Gran."

"How could that be?" Robert's fork slipped out of his hand.

"She's much like my Lizzie when I first made her acquaintance, most likely about the same age. Headstrong, impetuous, full of life." A faraway expression developed in his eyes when he talked about his late wife.

"Yes, she is. Why the sudden talk of Gran? You hardly speak of her."

"I miss her enormously even now after all these years. She died giving your father life."

"I never knew. I'm sorry. That explains why I never knew my grandmother. I frequently wondered why every so often you seemed to be miles away. I wish my marriage will be as happy as yours."

"So do I, laddie."

Robert went to find their houseguest. "Miss Shand, wait."

Sarah and the housekeeper made the last turn on the staircase and disappeared. He ran after her, taking the steps two at a time. "I must apologize." He puffed trying to catch his breath when he caught up with her.

"I'll be fine, Mrs. MacEwen. You go on now," she said.

Once the woman had vanished through the door to the servant's stairs, Robert spoke. "I must say something to you. You were extremely uncomfortable at the table. Should you need to use your left hand, which is what you're accustomed to, then by all means. You shouldn't feel forced to do otherwise."

"What makes you think I'm left-handed?"

"Besides the fact you couldn't hold on to your cutlery and dropped almost everything you handled? Well, after I brought you inside when you first arrived, you favoured that one. You touched the back of your head with it many times. This morning at breakfast, you ate your bacon with your fingers, something I never saw a young lassie do, but that's the one you used."

"So you don't think the devil possesses me?"

"Of course not. What would give you such an idea?"

"Just something Janet said." Sarah paused before she proceeded. "I should be the one apologizing. I mean, I'm the one who spilled stuff all over the tablecloth. The gravy and wine stains will never come out. The harder I tried to do right, the worse things got. And I was afraid ..."

"Of what?"

"Falling out of my dress. My boobs must be bigger than your mothers were. Oh drat, I shouldn't have said that. Why can't I keep my mouth shut?"

Robert laughed.

"What's so funny?"

"You. You talk in ways I never imagined. Most refreshing."

The next morning Sarah made her way down the massive central staircase. She perched on the bottom step, one hand holding her skirts up and the other on the substantial newel post.

The housekeeper fussed with a fern and stopped as she came in. "Good mornin', Miss Shand. How are you this mornin'?"

"All right, I guess. I was hoping to wake up in my bed at Gordonsfield, but it didn't happen."

"Things'll look brighter after you gets some breakfast down you. Go on. The Mr. Robertsons are already down."

"I'm not sure I want to go in. After all, last night didn't go at all well."

"Dinnae be worried. Now off you go," Mrs. MacEwen said as she walked her to the door.

Sarah wavered and turned around. "Er, maybe fiddling to keep my boobs from falling out wasn't the right thing to do at the supper table. Why can I show off that part of my body but not my legs?" She reached up with her left hand and fiddled with the top button.

The housekeeper's face turned crimson. "A woman doesnae show her legs to any man but her husband," she said and scurried away.

"Good morning, Archie," Sarah said as she breezed into the room.

Mr. Robertson smiled but remained silent.

Unable to look the men in the eye, she focussed her gaze on the area off the breakfast room. "I'm sorry about making such a pig's ear of things last night. I ruined the tablecloth."

"Don't be daft. Accidents happen."

His comment eased her mind somewhat. "Can we take our drinks over there when we finish eating? It's so bright and sunny." Sarah nodded to the conservatory.

"A fine idea," Robert's grandfather said.

Robert winked at her, making her blush.

She quickly bowed her head and finished her breakfast, relieved she could use her left hand. No repeats of the mealtime disasters from the previous night occurred.

After their meal, the elderly man helped Sarah to her feet. "My grandson is a lovely fellow." He showed her to a chair near the window.

The housekeeper followed with hot refreshments and oatcakes.

"Miss Shand, I would like to become better acquainted with you. We've discussed our love of the written word. What else do you like to do?"

What was there to tell? Already, she said she lived on a farmstead that didn't exist – yet. A few things slipped that shouldn't have when the doctor visited. By now, he was likely having the commitment papers drawn up, and she'd be locked up by lunchtime. "I-I started my post-secondary schooling in Glasgow. I'm due to start University at the end of this month," she hesitated, rubbing her thumbnail against her index finger.

"You, a lassie, attended such a place? Not many women can do that."

"Yes, you look surprised."

"I can't say I ever met any lassies who studied at that level." Robert twisted to his grandfather. "Did you hear that Granda? Miss Shand went to University."

The old man nodded and smiled.

"Not there yet. I've done two years getting my Higher National Degree at Glasgow College of Food Technology, and the Caledonian University accepted me for this fall's intake. Another two years and I'll receive my Bachelor's in Hospitality Management."

Robert returned his attention to her. "What is the nature of that subject?"

"Hotel and restaurant management."

The men looked at her quizzically.

"I would run the establishment, be in charge of the employees, and that kind of stuff." She blinked hard to keep the teardrops from escaping. She had been doing just that at the B&B, except with no payment.

"Our Mrs. MacEwen already performs those duties without a degree."

They were distracted by a knock on the breakfast room door. A gray-haired man clothed similarly to Angus walked in and tipped his hat. The ends of his middle two fingers on his right hand were missing.

"Did you forget the hunting party is comin' in today, Sir? If you like, I can take wee James to the railway depot wi' me."

"No, Callum. We're running a smidgeon late this morning." Robert pulled his silver, half-hunter from his waistcoat pocket and checked the time. "I'll be with you in a moment. I'm sorry, I must go." After a short pause, he said, "Where are my manners? Miss Shand, this is our coachman Callum Stewart."

"Pleased to meet you, Miss. We really must be goin', Sir."

"Yes, you're right."

After Robert left, Sarah walked to one of the enormous conservatory windows. The holly bush in the garden was alive with birds. She turned her back to the window. The old man sat quietly with his tea. Suddenly, a vision of him bound in a white cloth to his waist materialized. It remained only for a second or two then vanished. Feeling dizzy, she groped for a chair and flopped down.

"Whatever is wrong? You look as though you saw a ghost."

"I think that bump on my head is making me hallucinate." She rubbed her eyes.

The old man dragged a chair over and sat next to her. "Why don't you tell me?"

"I could swear I just saw you, wrapped up to here," she said holding her hand about waist high, "in a sheet."

His eyes brimmed with sadness. "First the portrait and now this."

Overwhelmed, Sarah dashed out of the room. She sighed with relief when the door closed behind her. The last thing she wanted was to suffer a meltdown in front of the man.

She came across the ghillie down by the burn.

"You look like you's seen a ghostie, Miss Shand. Whatever is wrong?"

"N-nothing," she said and sprinted toward the gate.

About midway, she spotted the groom, Hamish. He was naked from the waist up, and his back glistened with sweat. He rested one hand on the handle of a shovel and wiped his forehead with the other. Sarah wanted to slip by unnoticed.

He snatched up his shirt and mopped his face. "Off for a stroll?"

She ignored him, but his leering and undressing her with his eyes made her uncomfortable.

With no chance to react, he lunged at her and grasped her arm.

"Would you like some company? Such a fine looking lassie shouldnae be out and about on her own."

"Get stuffed," Sarah snapped. She tried to yank herself clear, but he tightened his grip.

"A wildcat been about killin' lambs. Big as a panther. You should be protected."

"So? It won't be out during the day."

"You dinnae ken that. The beasts hunt when prey is there."

"Besides, cats that big aren't around here. You're only trying to scare me, but it won't work. The only wildcats in this area aren't much bigger than my ... Murphy." She wished she could pick up her ginger and white tabby and bury her face in his fluffy fur. "Let go of me," she insisted to no avail. "I'm not going to tell you again."

"What are you going to do to make me?"

"This." Sarah spun around and kicked him in the shin as hard as she could.

Hamish grunted and loosened his grip enough for her to break loose, and she darted away. She didn't stop until she was beyond the iron gates.

The crunch of footsteps on gravel weren't audible, so she hoped the groom had given up on chasing her. A sharp stitch in her ribs caught her by surprise, and she paused and clutched her side to ease her discomfort.

While Sarah rested and caught her breath, a woman's voice breathed her name. She chased the sound, but it stopped.

At the bridge over the railway line, the voice spoke again but louder. "Where are you?" The familiar ethereal voice said.

"I'm coming, Mum," she answered and ran off in the direction of the farmland where Gordonsfield should be. Maybe everything would be back to normal when she arrived.

At the Kendonald road, she turned towards the village, searching for the path to her parents' home.

Her mum's voice called to her again.

"I'm on my way."

"I can hear you, Sarah but I can't see you?" Mrs. Shand's voice was louder now than when she first shouted for her daughter.

"I'm right here. Are you?" Sarah stopped in her tracks. It came from right beside her, but her mother remained invisible. She called out again awaiting a reply, but none came. The air in front of her shimmered, and the woman came into view. She tried to touch her face, but Sarah's hand passed through the translucent image. Tears spilled down her cheeks, and sweat trickled down her sides from her armpits, chilling her.

"Sarah. Come back to us. We love you. Don't leave us. Sarah," her mother's voice cried out.

She extended her arm again, but the figure vanished. "I can hear you, but I can't see you. Mum, help me, please. I need you!" The vision of her body lying on the Kendonald Road flashed into her mind, and the memory of the accident surged back. Now, she stood in the exact spot where the catastrophe happened. Sarah hurried toward the ancient monument, hoping her home would reveal itself, but it was only the empty pasture.

In the novel *Cross Stitch*, the heroine was sucked through a crevice in a rock in a stone circle and catapulted through time. Did something similar occur with her? With trepidation, she brushed her fingertips on one of the boulders. Nothing happened. There was no magic in the piece of granite. She fell to the ground crying.

After a few minutes, the faint sound of a woman singing drifted towards her. The melody was *Skye Boat Song*, but the words were in a foreign language, perhaps Gaelic. She lifted her head as the music grew louder.

A woman appeared at the apex and walked toward her. Dressed in a long-sleeved, royal blue gown partially concealed by a full-length black velvet cloak, she was stockier and slightly shorter. She carried herself with her back and shoulders straight akin to practising walking with a book on her head. Her dirty blond hair was styled in a French twist with lots of curls at the front and sides. She held a fan, obscuring the lower portion of her face.

"Who are you?" the woman questioned, "and what are you doing on Gleanstane lands?"

"Lived here all my life." There was no sign of Gordonsfield, but she refused to let herself believe her home did not exist. The only familiar things on the tract were the stone circle and the burnt out shell of a house in the meadow behind her non-existent cottage. This was the place where she was raised. She swallowed hard and said, "I'm a friend of the Robertsons from Weetshill. Who are you?"

"I am Letitia Christie. You couldn't possibly have occupied this land your entire life. You are on my father's property." The woman clicked her fan closed and glared.

Sarah opened her mouth to retaliate, but nothing came out.

"I'm going for Father. He'll set you right as to the ownership of Gleanstane." She turned and stormed away.

"It's Gordonsfield," Sarah hissed.

"Father, where are you? I need to speak with you," she called out as she walked through the front door and tossed her cloak at their ageing butler, Carlyle.

"He's busy in the drawing room, Miss Letitia. He gave me orders not to disturb him," he said, shuffling toward the door to impede her entry.

She shoved the servant aside and burst into the room, slamming the door.

"I'll do my best to raise the rest of the money by week's end," Horatio said. He pulled out his handkerchief with one of his massive hands and mopped his sweaty brow, scowling at his daughter. The well-dressed man on the opposite side of the desk glowered at her.

"I left word with Carlyle that I was not to be disturbed. Did he not tell you?"

His tone brought tears to Letitia's eyes. "But Father, I need to tell you about the woman I encountered near the stone circle."

"Could this not wait until our meal this evening? Couldn't it wait until then?" His eyes narrowed.

"No, Father. I think she is insane. She insists her family owned Gleanstane and said she's always lived here."

Mr. Christie apologized to the man at his desk and dismissed him. He put his pen down and moved to sit on the sofa.

She remained by the door, glaring at the visitor when he exited.

Once they were alone, her father patted the adjacent cushion. "You are distraught. Why are you so vexed, my dear lass? Why?"

Letitia sat down beside him. "Father, it was most distressing. She sounded so convincing," she blubbered. "It isn't true, is it?"

"I still own this house, the lands and chattels. Don't worry your pretty head. I say, don't worry your pretty head." He bundled her in his arms and held her.

"What were you and that man talking about when I came in, Father?"

"Nothing to concern yourself about," he said, pulling her head to his shoulder.

Sometime later, a man's voice in the distance called Sarah's name. Smoothing her skirts, she stood and turned in the direction of the sound. "Dad? Is that you?"

"No, it's Robert. Where are you? We're worried to death over your disappearance."

"I'm here at the stone circle."

"I thought you might be. Stay put; I'm on my way." A few minutes later he reached the summit. "Are you all right? Were you crying?" He pulled a handkerchief from his inside breast pocket and offered it to her. "Granda sent me to track you down."

"I thought I heard my mother calling me. I followed her voice, and it led me here. She sounded scared, terrified. I had to find out what was wrong. I even thought I saw her once but couldn't touch her. My hand went ... went right through her." Sarah wanted him to take her in his arms and tell her everything would be okay. "I wanted my house and family to be here, but they're not." She wiped her eyes and blew her nose on the neat square of white cotton, then clenched the hankie in her hand.

"Come back home with me. You can stay as long as you need." He took her hand and escorted her down the knoll and back to the side road to Weetshill.

At the murmur of voices, Sarah turned toward the sound. She stopped in her tracks and gasped. Niamh and Blair stood on the far side of the field. "It can't be." She broke away from Robert and ran toward them.

"What can't?" Robert chased after her.

"My two-timing ex-boyfriend and the girl I thought was my best friend."

"I don't see anyone."

"They're right there." She continued. Their voices were odd and muffled. Still, she was able to make out most of their conversation.

"What we did to Sarah was wrong," Niamh sniffled. "Why weren't we honest with her from the beginning?"

"She'll get over it," Blair said, moving to kiss her but she pushed him away.

"You don't have a clue, do you?" Niamh wailed. "She's missing. Her mother called me, looking for her. She's not been seen since the day she caught us. It's all our fault."

A tear ran down Sarah's face, and Robert brushed it away with his thumb.

"No one is there. Just your imagination."

"They're real. I know they are. Please believe me. I'm petrified. Am I losing my mind?"

8

"No. You're fine." Robert desperately wanted to give credence to his words, but Sarah was beginning to frighten him. No one with his or her wits about them saw or heard people who didn't exist.

Near the tree-line along the Kendonald Road, he stopped. The air shimmered, and a young couple materialized out of nowhere. The girl had long red, curly tresses and leaned against a large oak tree. The man stood in front of her, his hands on her shoulders. Both wore the same bizarre type of apparel Sarah had on when she arrived unannounced at Weetshill.

"See? There they are."

Robert didn't answer. He squinted, shook his head, and blinked, but the mysterious people remained.

"You saw them, too. I can tell."

He tried to rationalize the vision, but couldn't. "Miss Shand, was one of these people you just saw a redhead with long, kinky hair?"

"Y-yes. So you did clap eyes on the couple."

Doubting his sanity, Robert turned around, but the pair were gone. Rather than dwell on the apparition any longer, he redirected their discussion. "You and Blair were close at one time?"

She nodded. The painful memory of their break-up remained fresh in her mind.

"He hurt you terribly. I can tell. What happened?"

"Don't want to talk about it."

"You might feel better."

After Robert's reaction to her bare leg, Sarah couldn't imagine telling him she suspected Blair cheated on her because she refused to have sex with him. She explained the only other reason that came to mind. "Well, when he and I started going out, I was quite a bit heavier than I am now. I didn't like myself much back then, so I dieted and exercised and lost weight, but he still thought I was too big. Niamh is thinner than me, but her bone structure is a lot different, also. If I were as slim as her, I'd look like a skeleton with skin over it."

"Why would he want you to be so skinny? It doesn't seem logical. Curvaceous women are beautiful."

"Then explain why they stuff themselves into corsets?"

"I don't understand myself. The ladies appear uncomfortable trussed up in that fashion. I am sorry for you. Blair should never have forced you to lose weight. He was a fool. To me, you're handsome just as you are." He put his arm around Sarah's shoulder and pulled her close. "We should be getting back," Robert said. "The hunting party will be there for dinner."

"Who are they?"

"Old friends from Aberdeen. They come every year."

"So how do you propose to explain my presence?"

"Hmm, you're a friend of the family from Edinburgh?"

On their arrival, Archibald ushered them inside. Mrs. MacEwen came from the direction of the dining room. "You's back. You had us worried. Come along now. Dinner be ready," she said.

"I need to change my clothes first, don't I?"

"Isnae time. E'eryone's waitin'."

The elder Mr. Robertson and four other well-dressed men stood when they went into the room.

Robert made the introductions. "Here on my grandfather's left is Mr. Kenneth McIntosh. His late father used to be Granda's solicitor, and now he attends to the family's legal requirements. Next is Mr. Benjamin McCrae, Proctor of the University of Aberdeen. On his right is Mr. William McKeever, Lord Provost of Aberdeen. Beside him, Mr. Ian Ross, Professor of Archaeology at the same institution as Mr. McCrae, and is recently back from an expedition in Africa. They come up every year for the grouse. Gentlemen, this is Miss Sarah Shand, an acquaintance from Edinburgh."

"That we do," the men echoed.

Robert seated her beside Mr. Ross and took his place across from her.

"Will you be joining us on the hills tomorrow, Miss Shand?" Benjamin's beady eyes gleamed.

"No. I'm not much into hunting," she said as she unfolded her napkin and smoothed the linen square on her lap.

"Where did you folks disappear to?" asked Ian Ross.

Before she could answer Robert spoke up, "I found her at the stone circle over at Gleanstane."

"Why did you mention that? Now we'll be forced to listen to the man carry on about old, dead things," bemoaned William.

"Fascinating place is that. Thousands of years old." The professor's eyes lit up as he talked. "Charles Elphinstone-Dalrymple took part in an excavation at the location in 1857 after an urn was allegedly found on the site in 1821."

Sarah's curiosity piqued, she quizzed, "Did they find anything in this second dig?"

"A cremation pit complete with bone and charcoal. Exciting find. Still not the primary reason for the circle's construction. We may never understand for certain, but the hypothesis is these ancient monuments were much like today's calendars, telling the seasons and the lunar cycle. I attended a presentation some time ago given by William Henry Black. Most interesting. He theorized geometrical lines which radiated mystical energy intersected at sacred places like stone circles."

"You mean ley lines," said Sarah.

"I'm not familiar with the term."

Although the wood fire crackled on the grate, she shivered. "An archaeologist and his students studied the theory of ley lines where I live. He said one runs from Fortinghall in Perthshire through the stone circle at Gor- Gleanstane and beyond." He said they were superstition, but what if there was more? What if they had caused her time leap? "Do you think one follows or intersects with the Kendonald road?"

"In the presentation I attended, they claimed the construction of many followed those lineations, but my esteemed lassie, wherever did you hear this terminology? I'm abreast of the current archaeological theories, but never heard of such things."

"I-I'm not sure where."

"A good day hunting, gentlemen?" The old man changed the subject. "Talk is; this is the best year for the grouse in a long time."

A sigh escaped her lips, and she smiled at the old man, grateful he had turned the conversation away from her. Extra care had to be taken. A wrong thing said, and it could be bye, bye Sarah, and they'd pack her off to the asylum.

"Fine day, John," William said, smiling.

Mrs. MacEwen sat a generous soup tureen on the sideboard and ladled the contents into bowls. "Venison stew tonight. I'll bring the bread through right away." She departed and soon came back with a plate of thickly sliced home-baked whole wheat, still warm from the oven, and an earthenware bowl of home-churned butter.

The men turned their attention to the meal. Sarah's thoughts raced. Until a few days ago, the idea of time travel happening in real life was ludicrous. Still here she was, eating dinner with a group of Victorian gentlemen in the year 1886. Until now, her greatest fear was being trapped here and never getting home. What if she bounced about in time forever like the character in *The Time Traveler's Wife* and never put down roots anywhere? The doorbell rang, snapping Sarah out of her grave thoughts.

"Who would be visiting at such an hour?" Mr. Robertson mused and tossed his napkin to the table. "Don't people have any manners? Dropping in on folks at mealtime is downright vulgar. No calling cards arrived today, so I'm certainly not expecting anyone."

"Excuse me, Sirs, visitors to see you – Mr. and Miss Christie. I said you sat down to eat, but they insisted," said the butler.

"You stay, Granda. I'll go." Robert left to greet the company.

He found his unexpected guests waiting just inside the front door of the mansion. "Mr. Christie, Miss Letitia. What brings you out at this time of day? As Archibald told you, we've only just started our meal. Why don't you join us?"

"'Tis very kind of you, my good man. Very kind. I only came to tell you of a strange woman who my dear girl found on the Gleanstane lands near my beloved Philomena's rose garden. She insisted her family owned the property. I thought you and your grandfather should be aware."

Horatio meant Sarah, but Robert was lost for words. Say the wrong thing, and trouble would follow. Instead, he swallowed hard and said, "Thank you. It's good of you to think of us."

Letitia fluttered her eyelashes at him and smiled. She looked at her father. "Please, may we stay?"

In the doorway, Robert stood with the visitors. She was the woman from the stone circle accompanied by an enormous man with a long face, drooping jowls, and puffy bags under his eyes.

"We'll have two more for our meal, Archibald. If you would be so kind as to arrange for the extra places to be laid." He turned back to their unexpected callers. "I believe you're acquainted with the gentlemen from the hunting party. However, one other visitor is here who you don't know. May I present Miss Shand of Edinburgh. Miss Shand, may I introduce Mr. Horatio Christie, Laird of Gleanstane and his daughter, Miss Letitia Christie."

"Lovely to meet you, lassie. Lovely, I say," he said in a booming voice. He tossed his top hat and gloves to Archibald before doing the same with his overcoat.

Sarah started to stand.

"No need Miss Shand. No need." Horatio took her hand in his meaty one, elevated it to his mouth, and pressed his squishy, wet lips to the back. "So are you with one of these reprobates who are up for the hunt?"

"No."

"That's her, Father. The woman I told you about." Letitia pointed at Sarah.

"So you ladies have met," said Robert.

"I found her on Gleanstane lands."

"Gordonsfield is similar to yours. I was wrong. Mine is closer to Edinburgh." Unable to concentrate on her food, Sarah snatched glances at the Christies. The young woman looked nothing like her father. Her blues eyes sparkled, and dimples formed on her pale cheeks when she smiled. Letitia maintained a straight face when making eye contact with the others, but lit up when she looked at Robert.

The housekeeper cleared the table. "Do you still play the piano, Miss Christie?"

"Why yes, Mrs. MacEwen, I do."

"Why dinnae you go o'er to the ballroom? I'll serve tea there."

"A fine idea. Come along everyone." Mr. Robertson stood and eased the women to their feet.

Sarah hung back, letting the others go ahead. Piano flourishes and Letitia's beautiful soprano voice soon drifted throughout the house. Robert waited at the door for her.

"So why the fuss over this woman playing and singing?" She kept her voice low.

"Well, er..., um...."

Was he uncomfortable because of what Letitia Christie said about her? The last thing she needed was to convince everyone she was barking mad.

Classical music grated on Sarah's nerves no matter how talented the singer, but she had to admit the woman had a beautiful voice.

"Come, Miss Shand." Mr. Robertson showed Sarah across the grand entryway and into the room behind the library.

Oak panelling covered the walls of the ballroom, and two massive chandeliers hung from the high ceiling. How did the servants light the candles in those fixtures? Two ornate silver candelabra sat on the instrument, and the flickering flames cast dancing shadows across Letitia's face as her fingers flew over the keys. Gigantic paintings, mostly of hunters with their horses and dogs, adorned the spaces between the heavily curtained windows.

Sarah found a chair as far away from the piano as possible. All the men were mesmerized by the music and voice.

The song came to an end and she fluttered her eyelashes at Robert. Did he realize what a massive crush the woman had on him?

"Ah, my Letitia possesses the voice of an angel, the voice of an angel, I say," Horatio said as made himself comfortable beside Sarah. "She sings *Gretchen Am Spinrade* by Schubert beautifully, don't you agree, Miss Shand?"

She nodded, trying to think of something safe to say. Every time she opened her mouth, something wrong came out. "So how long has Gleanstane been in your family?"

"My good woman, my ancestors took control of the lands during the uprising in 1745. Bloody Jacobite traitors."

Why didn't she pay more attention to her instructor in her secondary school history classes? The rebellions were on the curriculum in her advanced highers. "Didn't the Jacobites fight for Scotland. Return Bonnie Prince Charlie, make him King and escape from under the thumb of the English."

"Was nothing bonnie about him. Not a thing. You must be mad, woman thinking such a thing. Mad, I say."

Wonderful. Sarah had managed to put her foot in it again. Now the man reminded her of Blair and his mates when they watched football matches on the telly. Anyone who dared support a different team was the enemy.

"How could something for the betterment of Scotland be bad?"

Horatio roared. "You should be locked away in a madhouse for thoughts like those. Come, Letitia, we're leaving."

The room fell silent. "Why Father? My music hasn't disappointed you?"

"No, it isn't you. You were perfect as always. Perfect as always."

Mr. Christie took his daughter by the hand and stormed out. She batted her eyes at Robert one more time.

"What put him in such a foul state?" he said when he joined Sarah.

"I could ask you why Letitia kept looking at you like a lovesick calf. Anyway, I asked how long they owned Gleanstane. He told me the

Christies seized the property from the previous owners because of their supporting the Jacobites. He's not a fan of Bonnie Prince Charlie."

"A dangerous topic to discuss with Horatio. You're lucky he didn't take a swing at you."

"He said I should be shut away in the loony bin for suggesting it might have been a good thing had he been made King. You don't agree with him, do you? I mean the part about the mental hospital."

"No. Political views are personal. If everyone who disagreed with the pompous bugger was locked up, not many people would be left on the outside."

"But, I'm still afraid. After all, I can't remember where my house is."

"You're a little confused, but that doesn't indicate insanity. Don't worry; nobody will take you to the asylum while I'm around."

Sarah settled into the wingback chair facing the window overlooking Gordonsfield. The stars appeared brighter tonight but it was most likely down to the older single glazed windows. The housekeeper carried in a substantial platter of hot drinks, cheeses and oatcakes. "You wasnae in the ballroom when I got there. Help yoursel' to biscuits and cheese."

After Sarah chose what she wanted, Mrs. MacEwen took the tray to the other side of the room where Robert and the other men congregated in front of the hearth. She hated helping her mother serve after dinner snacks along with tea and coffee to guests in the B&B's lounge. Now she wished she were back. "Mum, I miss you."

Robert's grandfather approached Kenneth. "May I speak with you alone?"

"Of course, Mr. Robertson," he said following the Laird out of the room. About fifteen minutes later they came back, smiling.

The old man walked directly to Sarah. "Come, I have something I think you'll want to see."

"Could it wait until morning?"

"Now is best." He extended his hand to her.

Puzzled, she tagged after him out of the room.

"Kenneth, what did my grandfather want to discuss with you?"

"Not to worry, Robert. He's not sold off the family fortune or anything. Merely wanted to ensure his affairs are in order."

"The man is behaving a bit odd, don't you think?" said Ian.

Distracted, he turned around and said, "No, I don't believe so."

"No, my arse," piped up Benjamin. "He's acting like a young buck in love. Who could blame him? Miss Shand seems a lovely young woman.

By the way, how did you meet her? We've known your family for years my boy, and never once did any acknowledgement of Shands come up, let alone an attractive spinster."

"Robert tell me where did you become acquainted with such a charming and knowledgeable lass?" inquired Professor Ross.

"She is a most delightful lassie, smart, too, but she can be infuriating, not to mention extremely forward in her speech and actions at times."

"Methinks the lad doth protest too much. What do you say, Kenneth?" Benjamin asked.

The solicitor only smiled.

"What are you smiling about?"

"Alas, when it comes to the fairer sex, I'm a wretched failure. I find it best to keep out of matters of the heart."

What? What did he mean? Robert took a sip of his drink and looked over his shoulder at the library door. Unable to stand it any longer, he handed his single malt to Ian and ran out of the room.

Mr. Robertson knelt on the floor in front of the settle. He lifted the seat. Until that moment Robert never knew the bench held a secret compartment. "Granda, what are you doing?"

"Shush!" He drew out a parcel and unwrapped a substantial, uneven chunk of pink stone. "Come," he beckoned to both Sarah and Robert as he opened the front door.

The night air was damp, and a chill ran down Robert's back as he looked skyward. The wind blew the clouds around giving fleeting glimpses of the moon. His grandfather set the rock on the grass next to the laneway. Moonlight struck the rock when the thunderheads dissipated, and the mass began to glow a milky, bluish white.

"This fragment of moonstone has been in the Robertson family for generations. I forgot about it until this evening. The effect is most dazzling at night. Go ahead, Miss Shand, pick it up."

Sarah bent down and scooped the object off the ground. "The light appears to be coming from inside. I've never seen anything like it. Beautiful." She turned and held the chunk of stone out to Robert.

"Take it from her, laddie. It won't bite you."

He expected the rock's surface to be smooth, but the edges were rough and formed in layers.

"Interesting thing about moonstone," the old man said. "Supposed to protect travellers among other things."

"What other things?"

"Calms fever. Cures consumption and other blights. Most important of all, reconcile lovers."

"A-hem, so why would you be showing this to us, Granda?"

The old man smiled, took the stone from Robert, and went inside.

"What was that about?"

"I'm sure I do not know."

"I think the moonstone story is romantic," Sarah said as they walked to the front door.

Back in the great hall, Robert's grandfather returned the chunk of rock to its hiding place.

The old man stood and stabbed his index finger at Robert. "You're sullying the Robertson name by living under the same roof with an unwed lassie. Make an honest woman out of her for goodness sake."

"Our rooms are at opposite ends of the house, Granda. Nothing untoward is happening nor will happen. I'm a gentleman, and I'm quite sure Miss Shand is a prim young lady."

Sarah's cheeks reddened, and she lowered her head. Had he offended her with his comment about nothing improper going on between them? Did she want something to transpire? Robert blushed. He took her hand and met her gaze, so engrossed in the beautiful emerald green eyes he forgot his grandfather was in the room. He bent down to kiss her, but she pulled back and dashed away.

Sarah ran toward the back stairway sobbing, almost colliding with Morag as she burst through the kitchen door.

Inside the safety of her room, she leaned against the door and caught her breath. She turned and locked the door, secured the top and bottom bolt latches, and wedged a chair under the knob for extra measure. Robert's golden-brown eyes made her forget everything else, including being stranded in the past. He wanted to kiss her, and she was ready to reciprocate until an image of Blair and Niamh snogging flashed into her mind. How could she count on another man after what he had done to her? She threw herself face down on the bed and cried into the pillows.

Someone knocked on the door. "Miss Sarah, are you all right?" the young maid called.

"I'm fine. Go away."

"You dinnae sound it. Let me in."

Sarah dragged herself off the bed, shifted the chair from under the doorknob, and unbolted the door. "You might as well come in now that you're here."

Janet swept in, closed the windows, pulled the drapes shut and turned down the blankets. "You's been crying?"

"Yes."

"Something got you fair vexed. Do you want to talk about it? They tells me I listen good."

"No, but thanks for offering." The maid's kind gesture tempted Sarah to confide in her. Was it correct etiquette? So far, the Robertsons and their servants thought everything she did was inappropriate. "Janet, wait. I do. Have you ever been in love?"

"Aye, Miss Shand. I'm engaged to Peter Laurence. His family are crofters and run a small holding here on Weetshill. We're to wed next year."

"How did you know he was the one?"

"The one?"

"The man you wanted to marry and live happily ever after with."

"We came together at one of the Laird's harvest ceilidhs. Then we started courting. He always said I looked beautiful even after I worked and cleaned all day. I decided then he would make a fine husband and father."

"I see," she sighed.

That night, Sarah dreamt of moonstones. The precious heirloom glowed bright white in her grasp. Robert set the rock down then took her hands in his and kissed them before looking into her eyes and caressing her lips with his.

9

The next morning when Sarah left her room, she came face to face with the old man, bound in a white cloth up to his waist. "Mr. Robertson, what...?"

He said nothing but raised his hand and reached toward her.

Her head began to spin, and blackness consumed her. She came around when someone slapped the back of her hand and called her name.

Sarah's eyes flickered open. "Wh-what happened?"

"You fainted," said Janet. "Are you unwell?"

"I-I don't think so. Was Robert's grandfather just here?"

"No, miss. Let me help you up."

Soon Sarah was on her feet, smoothed out and on her way downstairs. After she walked into the breakfast room, Robert looked up from his food. "Are you all right, Miss Shand? You're looking somewhat out of sorts."

"I'm fine. Nothing, really," she said unsure if the statement came across convincing.

"I must apologize for my grandfather's behaviour last night. It was uncalled for."

"It's okay. I think the man wants to be a great-grandfather."

"But, he is. Margaret, has children."

"Oh." Not knowing what to say, she switched the subject. "Where are the others?"

"They're already out for the grouse. Angus took them at first light."

"And your grandfather?" Sarah dished up fried potatoes.

"He's not come down yet."

"Too bad. I like watching you squirm and blush." Sarah sucked the grease off the end of her thumb and smiled as Robert turned crimson.

"Archibald will bring the tea and coffee. Dougal says the Laird isnae feeling well this morning," Mrs. MacEwen said.

"Oh? Perhaps I should go to him."

"I's goin' to take some food to your granda, Sir," she said while she prepared a dish for the head of the household.

"Thank you. That is most kind."

The woman left out but soon came back, pale and breathless. "Come quickly. It-it's Mr. Robertson. He be terrible unwell."

Robert charged out the door, almost knocking over the butler and his tray.

"Miss Shand, we needs to find Angus. Tell him to fetch Doctor Burnett and Reverend Mitchell," she said shooing her out of the room.

Sarah froze. She liked the old man, and the panic in the housekeeper's voice scared her. Turning around gave her a start as the ghillie stood behind her. "I was supposed to find you," she gabbled. "How did you …?"

"I had a feelin' somethin' wasnae right when the mister dinnae come out wi' us this morning," Angus said.

"Robert's grandfather is unwell. Mrs. MacEwen wants you to bring the doctor and the minister."

"I'll gets 'em both here."

Sarah didn't want to stay downstairs alone, so she crept upstairs. At the Laird's bedroom door she held back, wondering if she would be welcome. "Can I come in?" She opened the door as she spoke. The housekeeper and Dougal stood beside the bed, and Robert sat on the opposite side, holding his grandfather's hand. Janet and two other maids cowered in a corner crying.

"Miss Shand, Sarah, is that you?" the old man wheezed.

She hurried to his bedside and knelt. "I'm sorry I caused you all this aggro since I got here. I never meant to."

"You didn't. You made me laugh. You demonstrated an interest in things in which my Robert couldn't care less. You remind me so much of my Lizzie, not in looks but mannerisms, things you do and say. I don't think I told you, but she liked the stone circle. Loved it enough, I took her there to propose marriage."

"I-I don't know what to say."

"Don't say anything. Promise me you'll stay here. My grandson needs a lassie such as yourself. Not that snivelling Letitia."

"But I don't belong here."

"You'd make this dying man's day. Make my Elizabeth happy, too. She's right beside me now, waiting for me. We're making the journey together."

Sarah's Granny Shand told stories about dead loved ones appearing to people who are about to die to help them cross over.

"You're not answering my question, dear girl. Will you stay on here at Weetshill with my wee Robert?" His voice weakened.

"All right. I will," Sarah said without hesitation.

"Thank you. This old man is ecstatic. I can go in peace now knowing you'll be here with my grandson."

She smiled.

"Now give me your hand. I have a gift for you." He nodded to Dougal who passed something to him. The old man sat the unknown object on her palm and wrapped her fingers around it. "I don't want you to look until after I'm gone."

Angus came in along with the physician and minister. Doctor Burnett strode to the bedside and put his stethoscope to the old man's chest. He beckoned Reverend Mitchell. The vicar was a short heavy-set man of about seventy, with white hair and a clean-shaven face. He wore a black suit and white dog collar. "Would you like to pray, Mr. Robertson?" he asked as he knelt beside the bed.

The old man nodded, and the minister took his hand and recited The Lord's Prayer.

Robert took his grandfather's other hand and stood silently at his side. He looked so sad. Sarah wanted to reach out to him, hold him, and take his pain away. Rather than do that, she turned and walked to the other side of the room, clutching the object the old man had given her.

"I love you, Granda."

The old man smiled up at him. "And I you, my lad. Tell your sister I'm sorry." He closed his eyes and took his last breath.

Sarah finally summoned the courage to open her hand, revealing a delicate brooch. The one in the picture of the Laird and his wife which fell off the wall. Robert came to her side. "Are you all right?"

Why was he worried about her feelings when it was his grandfather who died? The housekeeper shooed them out of her way when she turned to show him her gift. The woman thrust open the window, and shut the draperies, plunging the room into darkness.

"Sir," she said to Robert. "I's sorry, but I cannae wish you a happy birthday on the day your grandfather passed on."

Mrs. MacEwen blanketed the mirror and paintings with bed linens.

Afterwards, she assembled the maids and instructed them to do the same throughout the house. "Angus, good, you's still here. Find wee James. Send him to Kendonald wi' the mort bell from our chapel. Dougal, you fetch the Undertaker."

"I'll go to the moors and tell the men the hunt is over, shall I?"

"Yes, thank you."

"Can I do anything?" said Sarah.

"Miss Shand, you'll come wi' me to the MacDonald's."

"Why?"

"The missus will get the body ready for buryin'."

"Isn't that part of the Undertaker's job?"

"Nae lassie. He builds the coffin, brings it back here an' sees to gettin' the grave dug."

"I feel so stupid."

"No need. You ne'er had to deal wi' any o' this afore, have you? You wouldnae ken if you hasnae done it."

"Never been to a funeral."

"You be a lucky girl. Now you needs a cloak then we'll head o'er."

Wrapped warmly to protect themselves from the early morning dampness, they made their way toward Kendonald. "Do you remember when the picture fell the other day?"

"I do, and the last time that painting come off the wall was just afore the Lady perished."

The mournful clang of the mort bell broke the eerie silence, pealing three times before pausing and repeating the pattern to advise the community of someone's passing.

"The other day I thought I saw someone bound in strips of white material like a mummy. When I told Robert's grandfather, he said 'first the portrait and now this' or something like that."

"Poor wee hen. The painting falling is an omen of death." She made the sign of the cross over her body as she spoke.

"I assume the vision I had is another one?"

The housekeeper didn't answer but performed the religious symbolism again. Sarah shuddered and changed the subject. "You mentioned Robert's birthday is today? How old is he?"

"He be six and twenty."

"What? He doesn't look that old."

"And what about you, Miss Shand?"

"Nineteen this past January." Or was she? It was too much for her to comprehend.

Jackdaws and magpies squawked and chattered as if they, too, announced the death.

"Here we be." Mrs. MacEwen indicated a tiny slate roofed stone cottage at the side of the road. A nanny goat tethered in the garden kept the grass cropped short. She shoved the animal aside with her hip on her way to the door and rapped.

A slight woman possibly in her nineties answered. The lines in her skin formed deep chasms. She peered over Mrs. MacEwen's shoulder and stared through droopy, cataract-filled eyes. "You must be the lassie I heard about bidin' at Weetshill."

Senses tingling, Sarah remained quiet and stepped back.

"The Laird, he perished a short time ago," the housekeeper said, keeping her voice low.

"I'll fetch me bag and strykin beuird." Mrs. MacDonald disappeared into the cottage and returned with a board about six feet long and two feet wide.

"What's that for?"

"I lays the Laird's body out on it after I gets him washed an' dressed," the old woman said.

Sarah cringed. She hadn't been in this era long, yet this woman knew about her. On their way back to Weetshill, she felt the woman's eyes on her the entire time.

Once inside, the head servant turned to her. "You show Jean where to go. I gots other things to attend to."

Until that moment, Sarah didn't know the woman's given name. The gravity of the situation overrode the formalities of an introduction. She ushered Mrs. MacDonald to the old man's room. Curiosity got the better of her, and she asked. "How do you know who I am?"

"Small place. Gossip moves quick. An' there be somethin' about you that isnae right. I cannae say what, but I can feel it in me waters."

What did she mean? In her waters? "Find Mrs. MacEwen if you need anything."

"You're a strong lassie. I'm no as young as I used to be. No so easy to put the body on the beuird. You can stay an' help me."

"I-I can't."

"You's here now so let's gets it done. You roll the Laird up on his side, and I'll slide the beuird ahind him, then you can puts him back down."

Handling a dead body was not on Sarah's list of priorities. With shaking hands, she reached for the corpse. Just before she touched him, the bitter taste of bile rose in her throat, and she swallowed to keep from being sick. Helpless to fight her nausea any longer, she muscled her way past the woman and darted out of the room.

Once out of the deceased Laird's bedroom, she dashed for the chamber pot in her room and vomited. After her sickness subsided, Sarah went to the library. On her way, she met Dougal and another man on the stairs. "Mrs. MacDonald needs help. I can't do it."

"Would you tell Mr. Robertson the Undertaker has arrived?"

Flustered, she tried to avoid eye contact with the short, stout man. His dark headgear and black suit made his pale complexion ghostly.

The Undertaker tipped his hat to her and accompanied the valet while she continued through the great hall.

The door noiselessly shut when she entered the library. Robert sat in her favourite chair by the window, staring at the closed draperies, a beverage in his hand.

"Dougal asked me to tell you the mortician is here."

"Excuse me. I should speak with the man." He handed her his glass and left.

The door creaked open minutes later. Jean gawped at Sarah. "Me work here is done. I be leavin' now an' so should you. Sooner you leaves Weetshill the happier folk 'll be."

"You made your point. Since you're finished, you might as well leave."

"Hmph." She spun on her heel and hobbled out of the room. A few seconds later, the front door closed behind her.

Sarah pulled back one of the weighty pile curtains. The old woman limped up the lane.

Robert finally returned. "Mrs. MacDonald gone, is she?"

"Yes. Thank heavens. The old bird pretty much said she doesn't like me. I admit the feeling is mutual." She turned to face him. "I'm not sure why, but she creeps me out. She stared at me the whole time we walked back from her place."

"By now she's likely heard the gossip about an attractive spinster biding under the same roof as myself. I wouldn't be too worried."

Sarah nodded, offended at being referred to that way. The term made her think of an ugly woman who spent her life alone because no man wanted her.

"She is an unusual woman, but serves the Kendonald area well. Not only does she see folks out of this world, she sees them into it."

"You mean she's a midwife, too?"

"Aye."

Mothers entrusted the old woman to deliver their babies. Her long thin nose, gnarled hands, humped back, and distinctive limp reminded

Sarah of witches in fairy tales. Hansel and Gretel sprang to mind.

"This is what your grandfather gave me," she said as she pulled out her gift.

"Ah, my grandmother's pebble brooch," he said and traced over the surface with his index finger.

"So beautiful. What kind of stone is it? Never saw anything so unusual before, except in …." She pointed at the painting.

"I believe a banded agate, and yes, this is the same one she is wearing in the portrait."

"It's gorgeous but I can't. It should stay in your family."

"No, you keep it," Robert said. He took her hand and closed her fingers back around the delicate piece. "My grandfather gifted the jewellery to you. This morning, before you came into his room, he told me he wanted to give you something."

The gesture left Sarah speechless. One minute the old man wanted her out of his home, and now, he was passing down a family heirloom. "Thank you. I will cherish it always." A tear escaped from her eye. She turned, so Robert didn't see her face. "Oh, the clock stopped. Let me start it up again." She reached for the timepiece on the mantle.

"No, you can't."

"Why not?"

"Part of the death custom is to stop the clocks." He started toward her, but a knock on the library door made him turn in the other direction.

"I'm away, Sir," said the Undertaker. "I'll send the diggers to the kirkyard so they can make a start on the grave. Once I's back to me shop, I'll gets busy buildin' the coffin. I'll finish the funerary box an' bring it back here tonight."

"Much appreciated."

Sarah was lucky not to have ever lost a loved one, but if she never found a way back to her time, she would lose her entire family anyway. "So now what?"

"Today, carry on as usual. We'll decide on a time for the kistin when the coffin's brought back."

"Kistin?"

"Simply put, placing my grandfather's body in the casket."

"How can you be so calm? You're acting like nothing's happened?"

"I suspected this was coming for a while. Granda's been in ill health for some time. His isn't the first death in my family. My father perished when I was a young lad and my mother a few years ago. I want to ask a favour of you, Miss Shand."

"You want me to make myself scarce before, during, and after the service. I understand."

"Nothing of the sort. I would like you to be by my side these next days and again through the procession."

"What will people say?"

"To hell with what people say. My grandfather's dying wish was for you to be with me until after the burial." He balled his hands into fists.

Robert never swore in front of her before. "Will you let me think about it overnight, and I'll tell you tomorrow?"

"That will be fine."

Late in the afternoon, the housekeeper interrupted them. "Those o' us who can should gets an early night because the morrow will be a tiresome day."

"Mrs. MacEwen is right," Robert said.

Soon after the woman passed through the library, the butler entered and announced the meal.

"I'm not hungry, really." Sarah gazed down at her hands.

"You should eat."

Mr. Robertson's customary seat at the head of the table sat conspicuously vacant.

"Where is the hunting party? I thought they'd be eating with us again tonight?" Sarah picked at her ham, potatoes, and carrots.

"Off at Gleanstane. Angus arranged for them to stay with the Christies and finish their hunt there. Considering the circumstances, Horatio was more than happy to host them."

"Oh."

"Morag won't be pleased if your plate goes back to her kitchen with that much food left."

Sarah rose and walked to the huge fireplace. Even with the blaze, the room was cold, and she rubbed her hands together to warm them. "I'm not hungry. I'm too upset to think of eating." She turned her back to the hearth.

Before she could leave, the doorbell rang. "The Undertaker is here wi' the coffin, Sir," the butler announced on his return.

"Thank you, Archibald. Fetch the men to take it to my grandfather's room."

"Already done, Sir."

"Excellent."

"And the kistin?"

"Tomorrow. Nine o'clock. You'll advise Reverend Mitchell?"

"Aye, Sir."

Robert turned to her. "You'll be up and ready?"

"I'll set my ..." She was about to say alarm clock but stopped before her mistake slipped out. "I'll make sure Janet gets me up. You really need me at it?"

"Female friends and family members all come to help."

Sarah shivered. "Sounds very creepy and morbid. I don't think I can. I've never been to a funeral."

"You'll be fine."

"Hamish an' Callum say they'll do the first watch, Sir."

"The first what?"

"For the next few days and nights, everyone will take turns sitting with my grandfather's body."

The thought of the groom under the same roof all night added to her anxiety. Every time he was near, he stared at her like those icy blue eyes had X-ray vision.

10

A black mourning costume with accessories lay on the bed when Sarah woke.

Preceded by a soft knock, the door opened. "I thought I would come and help you, Miss Shand," said the young maid.

"I could use it. I'm nervous. Never heard of a kistin before let alone been to one."

"Dinnae fash. You'll be fine. Change into your frock, and I'll fix your hair for you."

Once dressed, she sat on the stool at the dressing table. Janet brushed her long hair and pulled her tresses into a bun near the top of her head. The few wisps of shorter hair hung in ringlets by her face.

"Should I wear the brooch Robert's grandfather gave me, or would it be in bad taste?"

"I think it would be braw."

"Would you help me put it on?"

Janet took the heirloom from her trembling hand and fastened the accessory to the neck of her attire. "There you be." The young maid positioned the plain, black felt hat on Sarah's head and secured the headgear with a long pin topped with a single black pearl. She gave her charge a black-trimmed, white handkerchief. "Here. You be ready."

Once Sarah was in the great hall she said, "I must leave you now, Miss Shand."

Robert stood when Sarah came into the breakfast room. "My mother wore that dress to my father's burial."

"I'll go find something else if you'd rather I didn't wear it."

"No, you're fine."

"You two best eat up whilst the food still be hot. Folk will be here soon," the housekeeper said on her way through. "Get plenty. You willnae has a chance later," she matter-of-factly said when she returned.

"Why?"

"The Laird had many friends. They will all want to come and pay their respects," Mrs. MacEwen said when she stopped by the door.

Sarah turned to Robert. "I have thought about your question. I'd be happy to be at your side today so long as it won't cause any problems."

"Thank you. It means much to me, and my grandfather would be delighted as well."

"How will you introduce me?"

"I'll do the same as I did with the hunting party and the Christies. You're a friend of the family from Edinburgh."

"Are you sure you want me here? I mean your sister lives there. What if she asks me questions I can't answer?"

"If I didn't want you here, I wouldn't have asked. Besides, I doubt Margaret will attend Granda's service anyway."

Sarah frowned. Why wouldn't his sibling come home? She hated the thought of a memorial, but not attending if one of her grandparents died, was unimaginable.

"We best eat, or we'll suffer the wrath of Mrs. MacEwen." Robert pulled his pocket watch out of his waistcoat but replaced the timepiece without looking. "There isn't much time before the kistin."

"This whole thing creeps me out. I don't want to be there."

"Please. I would like you to attend."

"Do you need anythin', Mr. Robertson?" the housekeeper probed.

"No, thank you. I'm off to wait for the others," Robert said. He raised his China cup and drank the remainder of his coffee. His finger tangled in the handle and the vessel clattered on the saucer.

"Coming, Miss Shand?" the butler asked.

"I'm scared, Archie. I don't want to be a part of this," Sarah almost said 'bizarre ritual' but stopped. "Besides, I think my being here will cause problems for Robert, and I don't want that."

"Dinnae talk daft. E'erything will be fine. Let's get you in there."

"All right. I can't put it off any longer." She took her time pulling on her black gloves, trying to delay the inevitable as long as possible.

"There's a bonnie lassie." He assisted a nervous Sarah to her feet and accompanied her to the library, already heaving with people, mostly women. She shrank back against the wall hoping to go unnoticed.

"You're here. We can start." Robert gave the minister the nod.

Reverend Mitchell preceded the assembled mourners to the old man's bedroom. Hamish and Callum, who had done the first watch with the Laird's body, exited to the hallway. The groom winked at Sarah as she walked by.

Despite not wanting to stare at his corpse, an unknown force drew her to it. Recalling her vision before his death, she shuddered. Clothed in a white linen nightshirt and stockings, he looked asleep rather than dead. The winding cloth covered his mid-section.

"You doesnae ken what's happenin' do you?" Mrs. MacEwen said.

She shook her head in response.

"After they place Mr. Robertson's mortal remains in the coffin, they'll fold down the windin' sheet past his feet. T'other end will be brung up over his head right afore the lid gets put on."

A wave of nausea washed over Sarah. She clutched the housekeeper's arm and swallowed to keep from throwing up.

"Then someone cuts a lock of hair and a small piece of the cotton to preserve it for the family." She explained and patted Sarah's hand as she spoke.

The explanation brought back the sick feeling stronger than before.

A saucer bearing a mouldy slice of bread rested on the corpse's abdomen and a plate of salt on his chest. The most disturbing sight was the coins on his closed eyelids.

Sarah jumped as someone tapped her on the shoulder. She whirled around to face Letitia Christie.

"Robert is mine. You'll not have him. Not ever."

"What you mean, yours?"

"We're arranged to be wed. Our parents agreed when I turned twenty-five, he and I would marry. So if you know what's good for you, you'll keep away from him."

Arranged marriage? Except for certain cultures, didn't that practice go out with the dark ages? The old man's comment about Robert needing a lassie like herself came back. Sarah began to understand what he meant.

Reverend Mitchell read a passage from the book of Psalms, and when he finished, the final act of the kistin took place. The women standing beside the bed arranged the deceased Laird's body in the coffin.

Picking up the candles that burned by the bedside all night, the housekeeper led the procession to the ballroom. The coffin's lid leaned against the wall behind three chairs positioned to hold the casket. Fresh tapers flickered in candelabra on tables at both ends of the plain wooden box.

The enshrouded paintings sent a chill up Sarah's spine. Robert stood at the side of the room, and she joined him. Letitia glared at her as she passed.

The room heaved with people, and although still early in the morning, the whisky flowed freely. People toasted the Laird's memory and recalled his past.

"Mrs. MacEwen said there wouldn't be a chance to eat today, but look at all the food." Sarah pointed to a buffet loaded with a magnificent feast.

"Not for us, but for the folks who will be coming to say farewell to my grandfather. Some of them travelled a long way."

A humidor full to bursting with cigars, pipes, and tobacco pouches sat on a table by the door.

"I hope anyone who smokes is courteous enough not to light up indoors," Sarah said.

"Why would you say such a thing?"

"Doesn't matter. Here probably isn't the place to bring this up but I need to get this off my mind." She tipped her head to him.

"What is it?"

"Well, during the kistin, Letitia mentioned an arranged marriage between you and her."

"You're right. Here is not where we should discuss it," said Robert. "Let's go to the Athenaeum. You look like you've seen enough of this room for one day." He offered her his arm.

"Yes, please." She couldn't resist giving the Christie girl a smug look as they left.

He steered her into the crowded, noisy library and decanted a single malt for each of them. "I must go speak to these folks. I won't be long."

Sarah started toward the women assembled on the one side of the room. They stared at her, then turned and gossiped amongst themselves. Feeling uncomfortable with everyone's eyes on her, she grasped the crystal decanter and walked to the far corner where the men from the hunting party stood huddled. These men were virtually strangers, but she was more comfortable with them, especially the professor, than anyone else in the room.

"Any of you care for a refill?" No sooner was the question finished, four hands thrust their glasses towards her. She poured a dram into each and set the decanter on the desk.

"I was saying it won't be the same coming for the grouse now Mr. Robertson is gone," said Kenneth.

Letitia trailed behind her father and sat in Sarah's favourite wingback chair. She batted her eyelashes at Robert as he spoke to Horatio.

"I'd much prefer to be here at Weetshill even given these unpleasant circumstances. One more night at Gleanstane will do my back in for certain. I'm not sure which is worse, the damp or the lumpy bed," Ian complained.

"Did the Christies score all their money during the Jacobite Rebellion?"

"I don't believe so, despite Horatio's claims," said the Lord Provost.

"Old Horatio used to be quite the gambler," Benjamin said. "I seem to recall him winning a prize thoroughbred in a game of cards."

"I forgot about that." William raised his glass to his lips.

"Is there a Mrs. Christie?" asked Sarah.

"No. The woman passed on some years ago. A delightful lady she was. Kind and gentle," said Kenneth. He paused then continued. "Generous, too, much to Horatio's chagrin. She gave to the church and the parish poorhouse."

"Letitia was a mere adolescent; I think about twelve, at the time of her mother's passing, if memory serves," William said.

"Horatio and his daughter haven't been the same since her death. Unhappy souls are still grieving," replied Kenneth.

"Oh," muttered Sarah. Even though she didn't particularly like the girl, she couldn't help but take pity on her, losing her mum at such a young age.

"I hope these gentlemen aren't boring you," Robert said when he joined the group. The daggers from Letitia's eyes stabbed Sarah's back, so she turned and fired her own.

"Your grandfather. He's aged so much from our last visit. I couldn't believe it was John," said the professor.

"I agree. Declined considerably since mine as well," Sarah interjected, hoping to convince the men she was a friend of the Robertsons.

Archibald entered the library. "Excuse me, Sir. Reverend Mitchell would like a word wi' you. Where would you like to talk wi' him?"

"The dining room, I think."

"I'll stay here so you and the minister can speak in private," she offered. "Soon after I arrived, Robert's grandfather took me around and showed me the family portraits."

"Do you know Margaret?" Benjamin asked. "You're both from

Edinburgh."

"N-no. It's a big place. What's Robert's sister like?"

"Ah, a fine lassie. She's not been home since she ran off long before her mother's death," he said. "I always found that a bit strange. She loved to listen to our stories about the city and the hunt when she was younger."

After their meal, the housekeeper carried a large tray of refreshments into the room. "Here, help yourselves to oatcakes, cheese and bannock."

"You keep feeding me like this, Mrs. MacEwen, I'll be as big as this house."

"A strong wind would blow you away. You is but skin and bone."

"I need to lose about a stone."

Robert grinned sheepishly.

"Why are you smiling like the cat that got the cream?"

"Am I?"

"Yes, you are."

"I-I thought you're bonnie the way you are."

"Thank you." Sarah's cheeks flushed. "Er, will you answer my question now?"

"Which query would that be?"

"I asked you before if there was anything to what Letitia Christie told me during the kistin."

"Och, that one. I'm afraid, yes it is true. The agreement was made by our parents many years ago. An alliance between the two families, if you will. We're to wed at Hogmanay."

Sarah's heart dropped. "Do you love her?"

He didn't answer.

"Dinnae sit up in here too late. You both need your rest. The morrow will be another long day," Mrs. MacEwen said before leaving and pulling the door closed behind her.

"Don't worry. We won't." They said in unison. They looked at each other and laughed.

He smiled at her. "Thank you, Sarah. May I call you that?"

"Yes. After all, it is my name.

"It feels good to laugh." Robert's laughter turned to tears, and he buried his face in his hands. "What will I do without him? I miss him so much."

She knelt on the floor, pulled his head down on her shoulder and patted his back. His entire body convulsed with sobs.

"Let it out. This has been bottled up inside you for too long." She gently stroked his head and tried to soothe him with her voice.

Robert looked at her through tear-filled eyes, then wrapped his arms around her and mashed his mouth on hers. Although surprised, she kissed him back. His lips were soft, yet firm and tasted of the single malt he consumed. Seconds later, he pulled back, but his eyes remained fixed on her emerald green ones, and his hands gripped her shoulders.

Neither one said a word as they stared into each other's eyes. Only the crackling fire broke the silence. Sarah was sure her heart pounded loud enough for him to hear and wondered if his beat as vigorously. His face was etched with sadness and something else she couldn't read. The yellow glow of the paraffin lamps softened his features in contrast to the effect of the dancing flames.

"Sarah, I should be remorseful ...." Robert still maintained eye contact with her.

"You're all right. I'm not sorry."

"Please, pardon my behaviour."

Her experience with Blair outweighed her desire to stay in his arms, and she pushed him away. The last thing she needed was another man who was involved with someone else. "Nothing to apologize for."

"Yes, there is."

"Okay, I forgive you." Anger surged through Sarah at Robert's endless apologies, but she didn't want to feel that way. Not now. She wanted to feel the way she did when their lips met. "I kissed you back, didn't I? My handprint would be on your face if you offended me by it."

"So long as you're not angry with me."

"I'm not."

Archibald came in to check on the fire. "Should I put another log on, Sir?"

"Just let it die down. We'll be retiring soon."

"Very well," the butler said and left the room.

"I'm going to bed now. I can't keep my eyes open. Are you staying down here?"

"Yes, I think I will linger for a while. Good night, Sarah. Sleep well."

"The same to you." She closed the door behind her, leaned against the wall, and ran her tongue over her mouth, still shivering with excitement from their encounter. During their relationship, Blair Frenched her thousands of times, but none affected her this way. Not even when he pushed her jumper up and fondled her breasts. It made no difference. Robert belonged to someone else, so the sooner she forgot that kiss, the better.

Robert served himself a dram and held up the tumbler. The crystal refracted the light from the paraffin lamps. The amber liquid glowed orange no matter the angle. The brief spell of intimacy and Sarah refused to leave his consciousness.

Why had he kissed her? Promised to another, it was the last thing he should do; the pact made between their parents within a year of their births. Expressing affection of this sort with anyone else, especially a woman he barely knew was wrong. Even though they were to marry before the year's end, he never once thought of kissing his bride-to-be.

A prim and proper young woman would not allow him to kiss her. Sarah's actions were not. Still, she kissed him back, and he was glad. Her mouth was soft and sensual.

His thoughts filled with Sarah, he set his glass on the coffee table and went off to his room. The orange glow of the fire bathed the room with light and shadows as the flames danced over the logs. He put on his nightshirt, hung his clothes neatly over the quilt rack, and sank into his soft bed.

Until a few days ago, Robert had every intention of marrying Letitia Christie, notwithstanding the fact he didn't love her and knew he never would. Duty bound him to keep the promise his parents made with the Christies. Then Sarah barged into his life and ignited his flames of physical longing.

Attempts to force her from his mind were unsuccessful. Every time he closed his eyes, her emerald green eyes, soft skin, the fragrance of the toilet water she used, and her sweet, silky lips haunted him. He sighed deeply and rolled over.

11

Robert was receiving guests in the ballroom when she took her place beside him the next morning.

"I thought you wouldn't be here today after last night."

"I promised you I would be by your side, and I'm not one to go back on my word."

Letitia sat in a far corner of the room. Sarah made eye contact with the Christie woman, and her gaze dropped to the floor.

One by one the mourners passed by to express their condolences. The recognizable figure of Jean MacDonald limped through the crowd. She ignored Robert but berated his companion in front of everyone. "I told you afore; there be somethin' about you, lassie. Still dinnae ken what it is, but you doesnae belong here."

"Madam, this is not the time or place," he said. "I'll thank you for keeping your thoughts to yourself. Any more bad things from you about Sarah, I mean Miss Shand, again, you will be asked to leave. Do I make myself clear? I believe you owe her an apology."

Rather than comply, the old woman turned and left.

Not long after Jean MacDonald's departure, the Christie girl disappeared, too.

Shivering, Letitia wrapped her cloak snugly around her. Already cold and damp, a steady drizzle fell adding to the chill.

Once she reached her destination, she pounded on the door of the modest stone cottage. "Mrs. MacDonald, please let me in!"

After a few minutes, a flickering light shone through the chinks in the closed shutters. Shuffling footsteps from inside grew louder as the occupant came closer.

The door creaked open, and the old woman stood with her gnarled hand on the edge. "Miss Christie, did you follow me from Weetshill? You shouldnae be out in this weather. You'll catch your death," she said. "What gots you so vexed?"

Letitia muscled her way in, pulled her hood down, and shook the rain out of her hair. She stripped off her cape and thrust the garment at the old woman. "That horrible girl who is staying at Weetshill."

"Och, dearie me. Miss Shand. I kent she was trouble from whenst I first laid eyes on her," she said as she ushered her to the sitting room.

"Yes. She's the one. Since her arrival, Robert's ignored me. He's only interested in her." Letitia collapsed on the settee.

"He does seem fair fond o' her," she said as she draped the cloak over the arm and sat down on the nearby nursing chair.

"He shouldn't be. We're arranged. I'm the one he's going to marry." She pulled a lace-trimmed handkerchief out of her black velvet drawstring bag and dabbed her eyes. "I should be by his side during these difficult times. Not her. I wish she'd go back to wherever she came from," she said wringing the delicate fabric between her fingers. "I first encountered her at that dreadful stone circle," Letitia agonized. "Near where Mother planted those beautiful roses she received when I was born. She took me many times before she passed on."

"I ken the rose garden you speak of."

"Well, this woman claims her family are the rightful landowners. She's not wed. Doesn't wear a ring, and she's living in the same house as my betrothed."

"This doesnae bode well, child. An unmarried, unchaperoned young lassie bidin' wi' a bachelor? I cannae bear thinking of it."

"Nor me. Why is this woman so besotted with the ancient monument and the ground around it? The place means nothing."

"That's where you be wrong, Miss Christie. Back in the day, they held rituals there, and now, witches may be amongst us. Maybe she is one of them kent to cavort amongst the stones?"

"Could be. That place gives me the shivers, and so does that woman. We need to dispatch her to where she belongs. The other night when Father and I ate dinner with the Robertsons and the hunters, Miss Shand used her left hand the entire time."

The older woman's face turned white. "Corrie-fisted you say? That be a sign of the devil." She patted Letitia's knee with a gnarled hand. "I'll fix us a brew. Hot an' sweet is what you need."

"I need more than tea. I need that awful girl out from under Weetshill's roof."

"Dinnae worry that pretty face o' yours. We'll work it out betwixt us."

"I'm not sure we can," Letitia grieved.

"Poor hen. This Miss Shand, wi'out a doubt, charmed young Mr. Robertson."

Letitia's eyes brightened, and she dried her cheeks. "As in cast a spell on him?"

Jean nodded.

"You are a genius. Now I know how I can rid myself and my Robert of this person." She dropped to her knees in front of the old woman and took her gnarled, arthritic hands in her own.

"Miss Christie?"

"Who possesses the power to place someone under an incantation? A witch. You said sinister rituals happened at the stone circle. She is most fond of the place."

"Somethin's been nigglin' at me about the lassie, an' findin' out she be corrie-fisted, too."

"Now you know what it is." Letitia sprang to her feet. "I need your assistance for this to work. Will you help me?"

"Och, aye."

The following day, prior to the service, Mrs. McEwen clipped a lock of the Laird's hair and a small corner from the winding fabric. Before the pallbearers sealed the coffin, the assembled mourners filed by and touched the deceased. Robert stopped to kiss the forehead of his grandfather's body; his eyes moist. Sarah wished she could hold him and comfort him, but the timing was inappropriate. She reached out as she walked past, but couldn't make physical contact with the wrapped form.

"If you doesnae touch the body, the sight of the corpse will haunt your dreams for as long as you live," a woman behind her confided.

Putting her hand near a dead person, let alone touching one, was the last thing she wanted to do. If anything, doing that would give her more nightmares than not. Sarah lingered by the door. The undertaker screwed the lid on the coffin. Robert draped the mort-cloth over the casket and, with the men from the hunting party, lugged the cist to the altar area of the mansion's chapel.

Sarah sat with the Christies. She longed to be next to Robert. He looked so sad and vulnerable on his own.

Reverend Mitchell had begun the service when the door opened and slammed shut. Sarah spun around in her seat worried about who entered. A woman in black with a veil over her face stood at the back.

"My dearest Margaret," he said as he rushed to her side. "I didn't think you would come."

"It's risk-free to return now, so I came as quickly as I could, Brother."

"Please," he said as he escorted the woman to the family pew at the front of the chapel.

Letitia stood and embraced Robert's sister when they reached the second row. The woman's veil moved, and Sarah glimpsed her face. She was a feminine version of Robert with the same golden brown eyes and dark curly hair.

The skirl of bagpipes began in the distance.

The pallbearers ferried the casket to the waiting horse-drawn hearse, drawn by a jet black team wearing matching black plumes in their bridles. The mourners trailed Reverend Mitchell outside and lined up behind him. Sarah took her place behind the Robertson siblings along with Letitia Christie and her father. She peeked around Horatio's bulk occasionally only to receive one of Letitia's dirty looks.

MacPherson's Lament grew louder as they approached the churchyard. The minister, with his head bowed, tolled the mort bell in a rhythm matching the beat of the music.

Soon, the hairs on the back of Sarah's neck bristled. A flicker of movement in the woods caught her eye. Jean MacDonald peered out from behind a tree. How could she tell Robert? No way she could without causing a scene, so she sucked in a breath and walked onwards, trying not to show her apprehension.

At the kirkyard, Angus, looking uncomfortable in what had to be his best brown tweed suit, played the pipes. He continued to play laments as the men filed through the cemetery gate.

Sarah started to follow, but Robert put his hand on her arm.

"You can't come in. You must stay out here with the other women."

He took his position by the grave. She couldn't shake the feeling someone watched her. Reverend Mitchell finalized his committal service, and as the coffin descended into the ground, the strains of Amazing Grace drifted over the mourners.

At the end of the ceremony, Robert joined her and the others outside the churchyard. "Are you all right, Miss Shand?"

"No. I saw the MacDonald woman lurking in the woods, staring at us when we came. I'm frightened."

"Are you sure it wasn't just your imagination? It is a sombre occasion. Perhaps your mind is playing tricks on you." They turned to make their way back to the great house and found themselves face to face with Mrs. MacDonald. Sarah stifled a scream.

"Ye's evil," the old woman spat. "Ye's an evil murderin' witch."

Everyone stopped and stared.

The old woman was relentless. "I kent I felt somethin' about you in me waters, and now I ken. You placed a spell on the house so they cannae see you for what you really is. You'll pay for this, lassie. Mark me words. You will pay. You should be burned at the stake or dooked in the river. Ye ken that be what they do wi' witches."

Angus stepped forward, pipes under his arm. "I dinnae ken where you get your ideas from, woman, but you's talkin' daft. Sarah is nae more a witch than the rest o' us."

"She's got you under 'at same spell. She'll kill you. She'll kill all o' you. She killed the Laird sure as I'm standin' here! She didnae touch the Laird's body afore they put the lid on his coffin. Had she done, his corpse would hae bled. Hasnae you watched her? She's corrie-fisted. You ken what 'at means. She's evil. Evil like the devil, hisel'. I ken she done it because I found this empty bottle on the floor near his bed," she said holding up a small glass container.

Sarah moved closer to her accuser. "Robert told you earlier today this was not the time to cause a scene. We've just buried his grandfather. Can't you show a little compassion? I had no more to do with Mr. Robertson's death than the minister or the doctor did."

"Mrs. MacDonald, I think you should leave. You caused sufficient upheaval for one day. Angus, please escort this woman away from here," said Robert.

The ghillie snatched her by the arm and led her away. "Take yoursel' out o' here; you bletherin' skite. Step on Weetshill lands again, and you'll be sorry," Angus bellowed as he shoved her up the path, and stood guard until she vacated the area.

Sarah ran to him. "Thank you so much for getting rid of her."

"Me pleasure, Miss Shand. She willnae be back anytime soon, but I will keep watch." The gamekeeper accompanied them back to the mansion.

"I'm scared. What did she mean when she said the corpse would have bled if I touched it?"

"Don't worry. There is an old superstition if a murderer touches the victim's dead body, it will bleed."

"Oooh...," Sarah shivered. "Are you sure the old crone isn't dangerous?"

Before he could speak, Angus answered her. "She's as daft as the day is long, but I dinnae think she's that."

"You're positive?"

"I cannae think she came up wi' the idea on her own."

"What was Mrs. MacDonald's performance in aid of, Letitia?"

"I don't know what you're talking about." She turned to walk away.

Margaret grabbed Letitia's arm, twisting her around. Something had changed in the Christie woman since the last time she saw her. Haunted eyes stared back at her, no longer full of life as they were when the two girls played together as children. "What's bothering you? Is this down to my brother and the young woman Mrs. MacDonald berated in front of everyone? Who is she anyway?"

"It is too terrible for words." She bowed her head as she spoke.

"We've been friends for a long time. You can confide in me. You must realize that by now."

Letitia sniffled and said, "She's some harlot from Edinburgh who thinks her family owns Gleanstane. I first encountered her at that ghastly stone circle. Now she's staying under the same roof as my Robert, and I think she's turned his head. He's hardly paid me any attention since that Miss Shand arrived."

"Hmm, is that so? My perfect brother isn't so perfect in the end," she mused. "I think I need a wee chat with him."

The hairs on Sarah's arms raised as she broke out in goose bumps. Chilled through, she couldn't stop shivering no matter what she did to warm up. Robert took off his coat and draped the woollen garment over her shoulders. "Let's get you inside before you catch your death."

She shivered again, and he held her close to him. The heat radiating from his body warmed her, and she encircled his waist with her arms.

The housekeeper met them at the mansion's front door. "I put e'eryone in the ballroom, Sir, so you'll has the library to yersel'."

"Thank you, Mrs. MacEwen. That is exceedingly kind. Are Mr. Christie and Miss Letitia in there as well?"

"Only him. His daughter dinnae come back wi' him."

"Oh, I see," said Robert rubbing his chin.

"Your sister isnae back yet either. Perhaps they's having a wee blether. They hasnae seen each other in years."

"Most likely the reason."

"You poor thing. Let's sit you in front o' the fire." Mrs. MacEwen clucked over Sarah. "Archibald an' Dougal are seein' to the other folks in the ballroom," the servant said as she seated her in the armchair closest to the hearth.

"Will everyone please stop making such a fuss over me? I just got a chill."

"Don't put on a brave face. I know perfectly well you're distraught." Robert said sternly. He pulled the stopper out of the decanter and served them each a whisky. "Drink this. It will help calm you and heat you up," he said as he gave her a glass.

"She needs tea. Hot and sweet. I'll fetch some," the housekeeper stated. She exited the room as Robert's sister swept in.

"Ah Margaret, you're here. I can properly introduce you to Miss Shand."

"Call me Sarah," she said as she extended her hand in greeting. "I'd like to think we can become friends.

"I hear you are from Edinburgh? What part of the city are you from?" The woman didn't take her hand.

Sarah swallowed. She wasn't familiar with it even in her own time. The grounds for the Royal Highland Show near the airport was the extent of her knowledge. "L-Leith," she said not knowing if the town even existed in the year 1886.

"I don't remember ever meeting your family, but never spent a great deal of time in that area. What is your father's name?"

"James."

"What does he do for a living?"

She couldn't say he was a farmer since they supposedly lived in an urban setting. "H-he deals in livestock," said Sarah, her voice quaking.

"How did you and my brother meet?"

"Sister, please, enough questions. You're making Miss Shand uncomfortable."

"She's all right. I don't mind. I bumped into Robert at the Edinburgh Exhibition when he and your grandfather visited earlier this year. I was too busy looking at all the electric lights and backed into him."

Margaret looked at her sibling. "Why didn't you tell me you were coming to the city? I would have made arrangements to see you."

A doleful expression appeared across her face as if she was about to cry.

"We were only on a day trip to the exhibition and had train connections to make. I'm sorry. We should have come to call on you. We were wrong not to, and I apologize."

Odd, Robert and his grandfather were in Edinburgh but didn't see Margaret. One of the hunters commented about the woman running off before her mum perished and not coming home afterwards. There was far more to her than anyone was saying.

"I spoke with Letitia after Granda's solemnities. She told me about encountering Miss Shand at the stone circle."

Sarah braced herself before speaking. "I was wrong. The area is so similar to my home. You can't hold that against me."

Margaret smiled. "Really? I wasn't aware of one of those in Leith."

Another mistake. How could rural Aberdeenshire resemble the area surrounding the port town? Granted, Robert's selection of her hometown when he introduced her made it impossible to maintain the ruse. If Sarah remained at Weetshill, even if only until she could find her way back to the twenty-first century, she needed to befriend Robert's sister. "Here take mine. Mrs. MacEwen was going to make me a hot drink," she said and held out her glass.

Kenneth poked his head into the room. "Miss Margaret, could I speak with you alone? I won't keep you long."

"Certainly," she said, "Excuse me."

"I don't think she likes me," Sarah said when the door closed.

"You must understand. My sister and Letitia are childhood friends. It will take time for her to warm up to you."

"Like that's gonna happen. There's nothing between you and me, so what are they worried about?" she said as she flopped back into her chair. "Why did Jean MacDonald accuse me of being a witch? I never did anything to her. I only ever saw the woman when we went to get her after your grandfather died, and the few times she was here between then and now."

"I don't think she came up with the idea on her own. And with Miss Christie not returning, I suspect her involvement."

"Huh?"

"I think perhaps she was involved in the scheme."

"Miss Letitia isnae pleased with young Mr. Robertson spending time wi' you," Mrs. MacEwen said when she came back with Sarah's tea. "She be jealous and might be wantin' you gone."

"So she's enlisted the help of an old woman to accuse me of being a witch? What will that prove? You don't think the villagers will swallow her story? What about the bottle she flaunted claiming she discovered it under the bed?"

"Cannae be, Miss Shand," the housekeeper said. "Afore and again after Jean tended to the Laird, the maids give that room a good sweep. They would have found anything out o' place."

"B-but if people believe the old crone, where does that leave me? She and Letitia, the pair of them are completely unglued in the head."

"They could well be, as you said," Robert agreed.

She paced in front of the hearth. "God, I don't understand any of this. It's a bloody nightmare."

"All the gates are secured, Sir," Angus said when he came into the room. He turned to Sarah. "You'll be safe here, lassie. The bletherin' skite willnae get near you. I'll be makin' me way back to mine for the night now, Sir. Good night all."

"I'll lock an' bolt the door ahind you." Mrs. MacEwen followed the ghillie. She came back a few minutes later.

"That's Angus away. Archibald a'ready saw the others off. He's secured the front door an' the rest o' the house."

"Look, whether she came up with the idea on her own or not, Jean MacDonald thinks I'm a witch. I think she'll try to do something to get me out of the way."

Robert put his arms around her. "Whatever she believes, we'll keep her away from you. I'll make sure of that," he said. "Why don't we call it a day, too? You need a good night's slumber. I'm sure you'll feel much better in the morning."

"I hope you're right. Good night." She wished she could spend the night with him but tried to force the thought from her mind.

The butler poured Robert a steaming cup of coffee when he walked into the breakfast room the next morning. "Here you be, Sir. I'll fetch the newspaper and post straight away. Callum is back frae Duninsch now."

He turned away from the sideboard when the rustle of skirts came up from behind. Disappointment washed over him when Margaret stood in the doorway instead of Sarah. "Sister, what are you doing up so early? I thought after your long trip; you would have rested longer."

"I couldn't sleep. No sense in tossing and turning by myself. So tell me, Brother where did you really meet Miss Shand. I don't believe she hails from Edinburgh, and she isn't from Leith, if she is telling the truth about her father being a cattleman. The place is a fishing town. There isn't a cow or farm in sight." She walked to the coffee pot and poured a cup.

"She explained that to you last night. We met at the exhibition."

"And based on one chance meeting, you invited her to stay under Weetshill's roof?"

"N-no. Granda found her a delightful young lassie and said she reminded him of Gran. He wanted to see her again. I think he knew his time on this earth was nearing its end. She only just arrived a couple of days before Granda's death." While not entirely accurate, his words held a shred of truth.

"Why is she wearing our beloved late mama's clothes and our Gran's brooch?"

"I offered Mother's things to you when I wrote you of her death, but you refused them. You refused to come home. I couldn't let them go to waste in the wardrobe so I told Miss Shand she could wear them. She didn't think she would be staying this long and didn't bring enough clothing, not to mention she had no suitable attire for such an occasion with her. Granda gave her the brooch on his deathbed."

"Of course he did," Margaret responded with a bemused smile. "You don't lie any better now than when you were a wee lad."

Robert looked at his shoes. "W-we're not lying."

"After the interment yesterday, I caught up with Letitia. Something is tormenting the girl. I'm not sure what, but I'm certain it's something to do with her - Miss Shand - being here."

"Your imagination is getting the better of you." He, Margaret, and the Christie lass often frolicked with one another as children, but she changed as she matured. She no longer laughed, and she always looked sad. Their parents put them together at parties when they grew older. He despised the fact he couldn't choose a partner for himself. She was impossible to dance with, holding herself so stiff and rigid it was like sweeping around the floor with a caber. Robert's mind wandered to the day he danced with Sarah. "Whatever is wrong with Horatio's daughter isn't down to us. Something about her has been off for years, since soon after her mother's death."

"Letitia is my friend, and you and this Miss Shand are humiliating her. You two are to wed this year."

"Don't remind me," he sighed.

Margaret guided him to the table and took a seat beside him. "What's that tone for?"

"Difficult to explain."

He started to stand, but she immediately pushed him back down. "Arduous or not, I want to hear."

"I don't love Letitia. I never loved her, but rather than suspend the deal our parents made; I was willing to go through with it. Until now ..."

"What do you mean, until now?"

"Well, this is where things get complicated."

"Hmm, no doubt."

"Until Miss Shand, I never felt so alive. Happy at the sight of someone first thing in the morning, and sad to see them go the last thing at night."

"You're saying you are in love with this harlot."

"I don't know. She makes me feel in ways I did not think possible. And, she is not what you called her. She's a respectable young woman," Robert said, his voice becoming louder with each word.

"I think you doth protest too much."

"I'm going to call on Horatio later to discontinue this ludicrous agreement."

"What?" Margaret dropped her fork, and and the silver cutlery clattered on the China plate.

"You heard. Never have I felt anything for Letitia. Why lead her on? It's the best thing to do for both of us."

"She loves you."

"That doesn't make my decision any easier."

"But ..."

"You were arranged in marriage to a candidate our parents contracted for you before our father's death?"

"He was an old man. A mean old man. At least you're bound to someone your age who loves you. I envied you."

"Nevertheless, you didn't go through with it. You ran off, met George, and fell in love. You didn't want to endure a loveless marriage, so why should I?"

"I understand. Really, I do, but I always thought you would abide by the terms."

Robert looked at Margaret. "Are you implying that I have no backbone and can't make up my mind?"

"I didn't say that."

"You implied it. I don't love Letitia, plain and simple, and the sooner I nullify the contract, the better."

12

Robert went back to the library and unlocked the small metal box containing the important family documents. He rifled through deeds, bills of sale, and contracts until he found the one he wanted. He unfolded the brittle paper and tucked the written agreement in his suit jacket.

In spite of the misty rain, he walked to the Christies instead of going by carriage. He needed the extra time to come up with the words he would need for his meeting with Horatio Christie.

Gleanstane House was a massive stone building with a round tower above the front door. Robert stood on the gravel drive, gathering his courage before turning the doorbell key.

The door creaked when the elderly butler pulled it open. "Good morning to you, Mr. Robertson. How can I be of assistance to you today?"

"I need to speak with Mr. Christie. It is of the utmost importance."

The servant shuffled to a nearby closed door. "Mr. Robertson is here, Sir," he said as he opened it a crack.

"Very well, Carlyle. Show him in."

The butler stood outside the drawing-room door and bowed.

Horatio strode across the room to meet his guest. "Good to see you, Robert. Good to see you." He extended a meaty hand.

Manners dictated Robert shake the man's hand, so he complied rather than be rude. The imposing old furniture, always gleaming and immaculate when he came to Gleanstane as a little boy with his father was now shabby and dust-covered. The colourful patterned wallpaper had faded and was peeling in a few corners. A musty odour lingered signifying the room hadn't been aired out in years. The picture of Horatio, Philomena, and Letitia as a smiling little girl stared at him through dirt and cobwebs. Mrs. Christie had been an attractive woman. She had blue eyes, not as brilliant as his Gran's or Letitia's. She styled her blonde hair in a huge knot on her crown, and ringlets fell down the back of her neck to her shoulders. Both parents gazed at their daughter with expressions of pride.

"What brings you out here today?"

"A matter of extreme importance."

"Oh, sounds to me like a conversation we might need a dram to get through." Horatio rang a bell to summon the butler. "Whisky, Carlyle."

While the servant poured the drinks, Robert paced back and forth trying to find the words he needed to say. He drained his glass in one gulp.

"This is fine single malt. I say, fine single malt. To be consumed slowly and savoured, not gulped down like a drunkard in a tavern."

"So sorry." He lowered himself into a faded, plush red chair that appeared on the verge of collapsing.

"Another drink for my guest, Carlyle. Now suppose you tell me what's got you in such a state of vexation."

Robert stiffened. "Well, Horatio. It, it's this arranged marriage."

"Och, you merely have cold feet. Cold feet, nothing to worry about my lad. All grooms become nervous as the wedding date approaches."

"It is not my nerves, which is why I must tell you this now." Robert rose and walked to the window, keeping his back to his host. "I understand the obligation through the pact you and your late wife made with my parents, but I'm sorry, I cannot go through with this marriage." He turned to face Horatio's wrath.

"What are you saying, you can't go through with it?" Mr. Christie's eyes narrowed, and his face became redder by the moment. "By all that his holy, man, choice doesn't enter into the equation. You must." He slammed his meaty fist down on the desk, the only sturdy looking piece of furniture in the room.

"Let me explain."

"I thought you were a man of your word, Robert, and here you go breaking it to a sweet, innocent lassie like my Letitia."

"Sir, please. This was never my pledge, but my father's and mother's."

"Why did you not protest until now? What has made you willing to break my daughter's heart?"

"I don't love your daughter." There, he said it out loud. Sweating profusely, Robert waited for the man's reaction. He pulled a handkerchief out of his breast pocket and dabbed it over his face.

"What do you mean you don't love her? She's a wonderful lassie. What's not to love?"

"I'm sorry, Sir, but I don't love her. I can't take part in a marriage with no feelings whatsoever for the person who would become my wife."

"You would learn to in time. I know you would, Robert. She will make you an excellent spouse."

"I never would. I'm sorry, Sir, but I would be betraying my emotions if I was to marry Letitia."

"So you are letting your heart rule your head."

"I'm not," Robert answered, louder than he expected. The volume and tone of his response shocked him, and he knew his timbre shook Horatio as well.

"Well, if it isn't my girl, who is it? With whom are you in love? Who then, Goddammit?" The veins in his neck bulged and his eyes grew dark and menacing.

Until now Robert had never been fearful of Horatio Christie, but he looked the man square in the eye. "There is no one else."

"It's that slip of a Miss Shand who is staying at Weetshill. You a bachelor and she a spinster sleeping under the same roof? It doesn't look good, I say. It doesn't look good."

"I don't like your implication, Sir. Nothing untoward has gone on, nor is going on between us. She is a friend of the family from Edinburgh. She arrived a few days before my grandfather's death and only stayed on for the funeral. The locals would have nothing to gossip about if he were still alive because she would be home by now."

"Well, I'm not standing for this. I tell you I won't. You will marry my daughter. Your parents agreed to a binding indenture with Philomena and me, and by all that is holy, you will live up to the terms. You will, or I will drag you in front of the magistrate for breach of contract."

"It can be nullified with relative ease." Robert tried to sound confident, but the beads of sweat on his forehead said otherwise.

Horatio went to his lockbox. After two unsuccessful attempts and much mumbling, he opened the vault and pulled out his copy of the document. "Here. See for yourself," he said thrusting the sheet into Robert's hands.

Robert shook the paper open and slammed the agreement down on the desk. "Read right here," he said, pointing, "this clause explains how I can avoid what would be a farce of a marriage. All I need to do is repay you for the value of the endowment."

"My good lad, this is the amount of the dowry." He jabbed his finger on the page.

Robert bent down and read the fine print. Two-thousand, five-hundred pounds. He raised his head. Horatio wore a smug expression on his face. "Don't worry. I'll see you get your cash. Every last penny of it."

"Bah! You'll never come up with that kind of money. You have to come up with the funds before Hogmanay, the day the nuptials are to take place. I guarantee you won't," he said with a triumphant laugh.

Without answering, Robert turned and left the room. Despite the bravado he displayed to Horatio Christie, he had no idea how to raise such an exorbitant sum, but he had to find a way. Until Sarah crashed into his life, he would not have considered breaking the arrangement. People didn't fall in love that fast, did they?

Sarah was in the library with a Jane Austen novel when Margaret found her.

"Do you know where my brother went?"

"No clue. Why?"

"I'll tell you then. He's gone to Gleanstane to wriggle out of the deal to marry Letitia."

"Are you sure?"

"Yes. I spoke with Robert at breakfast, and he told me was going to call on Horatio."

"Well, his choice. The last time I looked, he was a grown man capable of making up his own mind." She put down the book.

"I don't think I like your attitude."

"Don't you want him to be happy?"

"Of course I do."

"We're both in agreement on that score." Sarah stood and walked to the window. Turning around to face Margaret, she said, "Do you think he would be with Letitia?"

"I-I don't know. She loves him with all her heart and soul. I don't want to see her hurt."

"Robert isn't breaking the arrangement to upset her. He's doing it so she can move on and find someone who will love her in return."

"And none of this is down to you, I suppose."

"No."

"I don't believe you. He told me before meeting you he never felt so alive."

Sarah's cheeks burned. Did he really feel that way about her, or was his sister making it up to determine her reaction?

"You are hiding something. I don't know what, but I will find out."

The old floorboards creaked behind him. Robert turned as Letitia approached from the foot of the staircase. "I need a word with you," he said before begging, "Can you ask your father to cancel this pact, please?"

"I will do no such thing."

"It isn't fair to either one of us to be trapped in a loveless marriage. You should find a man who will love you with all his heart and soul. You have the right to that much."

"Ours wouldn't be, Robert. I love you enough for both of us, so no, I will not ask him to do it."

He grabbed her by the shoulders. "You were behind Jean MacDonald's outburst at my Granda's burial."

"Me?"

"Yes, you. That old woman isn't intelligent enough to come up with the witch idea all on her own. I can envision you two together plotting and conniving. You deserve each other."

"I did it for you, Robert. For us. I love you. I always have. I see the way Miss Shand looks at you and how you look at her. She's turned your head, that harlot."

"You stupid, stupid, girl. Do you honestly think I would marry someone like you?"

Letitia's bottom lip quivered. "But we're arranged."

He let go of her. "When I take a wife, it will be for love, not some foolish arrangement. I never loved you, nor could I ever, you vindictive, immature..., I can't say the word but only because I'm a gentleman. It sure as hell doesn't stop me thinking it." He walked away. His fingertips brushed the doorknob, and he stopped and turned. "You are spoiled and selfish, Letitia Christie. Your father should have spanked you and spanked you often to beat that selfishness out of you."

Robert slammed the door behind him and inhaled a lung full of fresh air. The mist had turned into torrential rain, driven by a cold north wind. The drops stung his face like thousands of tiny pinpricks. He pulled his collar up and strode away from Gleanstane House, wishing he had requested the carriage and driver now.

Weetshill was a most welcome sight when the tops of the chimneys emerged over the hill.

"Sir, you's drenched. Let me take your overcoat," Archibald said when he came in the front door.

"Thank you."

A familiar voice resounded in the entryway, and Sarah lingered by the library door. "Margaret said you went to the Christies to break the contract. Is that true?"

The butler came with Robert into the room and stoked the grate. In no time, the fire crackled, eliminating any chill, real or imaginary.

"Yes." He returned the document to the box and locked it.

"Our presumptions about who was responsible for old Mrs. MacDonald's outburst at Granda's funeral were correct. Before I left Gleanstane, Letitia confessed. She claims your presence threatens her. Frightened as long as you were here, her marriage to me would never take place."

"What made you decide to do it?" Sarah sat and stared at the floor.

"I never did feel anything for Miss Letitia," he explained. "Then once I let my guard down and got to know you, I knew my grandfather was right."

Blushing, she said, "How did her father take the news? He thinks the sun shines out her ass."

"Miss Shand!" Robert smiled at her. "Not well at all, I'm afraid. He has threatened to haul me in front of a magistrate, but he doesn't stand a chance of that happening. There is a clause that will nullify the indenture with no repercussions."

"How?"

"I compensate Horatio for the amount of the dowry he would have provided Letitia when we wed."

"That simple?"

"Yes and no."

"Huh?"

"There will be some formalities, but raising the money is the problem. Such a sizeable sum and I need the funds before the year's end. I would much prefer sooner than later."

"I feel like you're in this mess because of me."

"Nothing to do with you, although I must admit before you came along, things were quiet and orderly."

"I never intended for you to break the contract."

"The only thing you are responsible for is opening my eyes to spontaneity, laughter, and fun, like when Granda played his fiddle, and we danced. Those were things grievously lacking before your arrival."

"I think you're doing the right thing," Sarah said. "Best get this business out of the way now if you're not going to be happy. Too many

94

marriages end in divorce these days." She bit her tongue. Was it even legal back then?

"To be sure. Scotland had more than a hundred divorces last year." Robert walked to the hearthside. "My biggest concern is where I'm going to obtain the money?"

"What kind of ransom are we talking about?"

"Two-thousand, five-hundred pounds."

Sarah recalled her parents moaning over the fact their last big family vacation cost twenty-four-hundred. An equivalent sum certainly had to mean more than that in the 1800s, but how much? She gulped. "Can you raise that amount of money?"

"I think so. I'm going to Aberdeen tomorrow. I'll try to borrow the necessary funds from the bank."

13

"Father, why does Robert hate me so much? Why does he want to hurt me?" Letitia mewled as she burst into the drawing room.

"You're a fine specimen of a young woman. Any man would be happy with you as his wife. Any man."

"Anyone but him."

"Come my dear girl." Horatio patted his thigh beckoning his daughter to sit.

She started for his lap but stopped. "No. It doesn't seem right, me sitting on your knee. I'm not a wee girl anymore. I love him. I always have. I dreamt of our wedding day for such a long time."

"Ah, my sweet Letitia. Everything is all right. That Robert Robertson will rue the day he betrayed Horatio Christie. Mark my words," he said as he smiled.

"You're scaring me, Father. I've never seen you so angry," she said as she knelt beside his chair. "I won't be marrying Robert, will I? He can nullify the arrangement. I heard. I was eavesdropping at the door."

"He'll never raise the money, my beautiful lassie. Never raise the money."

She cocked her head to one side and looked at her him. "Money, Father?"

"Yes. I made sure your dowry would be substantial enough they could never raise it when the agreement was drawn up. The contract would be guaranteed."

"Did you think I would never be able to find a man on my own? Is that why you arranged my marriage?"

"No child. Not at all."

"Did you think Robert would try to weasel out of it?"

"Was the last thing I expected. The last thing. The Robertsons are a wealthy family. After I'm gone, you would be well provided for, as would your children and grandchildren."

"You're not dying, are you? I couldn't bear to lose you, too." A tear ran down her cheek.

"No. I'm healthy as a horse. Just wait until Hogmanay, and you'll see, you will become Mrs. Robert Robertson," he said, wiping the moisture away.

"Did you hear the distressing things he said to me, Father?"

"No, I did not."

Embellishing in all the right places, Letitia replayed her encounter with him. An evil smile spread across her face. Not only would Robert rue the day he crossed her father, but he would also rue the day he jilted her.

Horatio stood and took her in his arms. "There, there," he purred. "You will marry Robert. I assure you."

She wriggled out of the man's grip in time for Carlyle to announce Margaret's arrival. She wiped her eyes and left to join her friend.

"Have you been crying?" Margaret asked.

Letitia nodded and blew her nose into a delicate, lace-trimmed handkerchief.

"All down to my brother, no doubt," she said hugging the girl.

"Let's go to my room where we can speak in private." She saw the way to the stairs.

Once inside the bedroom, Letitia closed and bolted the door behind her. "We won't be disturbed now," she said as she showed her guest to a chair by the inglenook.

"I thought I should tell you that Robert is talking about borrowing the money from the bank to buy his way out of your arranged marriage. I for one, pray he's unsuccessful. I'm not fond of that Shand woman."

"Me, too. I love your brother with all my heart even though he hates me so much."

"There is one thing about remaining a spinster, though."

"What?"

"You don't have to perform your wifely duties. You do know what that means, don't you? I remember being unsure what would take place when George and I married."

Letitia became quiet. She walked to the cheval mirror in the corner and stared at her reflection. She turned and said, "You must give your word you will never repeat this to anyone."

"Whatever is wrong?"

"Just swear to me you'll never breathe any of this to another soul."

"All right. I swear."

Bending down, she whispered in Margaret's ear, "I did it before many times and still do on occasion."

"What? With who?"

"Shh. Not so loud. I can't tell you, but please tell Robert I will be a fine wife for him because I'm prepared."

"I-I don't know what to say."

"Even if he wriggles out of our arranged marriage, I have a plan. I'll ensure he never marries that Shand woman."

14

The front door closed and Sarah went to the foyer to discover who was there. She caught a fleeting glimpse of Margaret running up the stairs. After a few minutes, knocked on the woman's door. "I saw you tearing through the hall and thought you were perturbed. Can we talk?"

"What do you want?"

"Not to be enemies. Letitia is your friend. I'm miserable about being stuck in the middle of this whole mess. I never intended to hurt anyone."

"I'm sorry, but I find that very difficult to believe," Margaret said as she pulled the door open a crack.

Sarah bulldozed through before the woman had a chance to change her mind. "Honestly, I didn't. Robert and I didn't meet in Edinburgh at the exhibition either."

"I knew as much. Go on."

"This is going to sound crazy, but he found me injured on the doorstep. No idea how I got that way or how I ended up here. He brought me in, and everyone looked after me. Your family is wonderful."

"Really. You might not be so quick with your words if you knew the things that I do."

"What do you mean?"

"I'd rather not say just now."

"In the beginning, your grandfather thought I was a gypsy or thief who would abscond with the family silver. Once we got to know each other, and just before he passed, he asked me to stay on here. He was a wonderful, compassionate person."

"He's obviously mellowed in his old age. I avoided the place for years because Granda wasn't the kind old man you describe."

"Something else is bothering you," Sarah said. "Why don't you tell me?"

"I'm beginning to wonder if the arranged marriage between my brother and Letitia is a good idea."

"Why do you say that? Not so long ago you wanted to see them together. What changed your mind?"

"Something Letitia said today."

"Robert told me she was behind Mrs. MacDonald's outburst at your grandfather's funeral. What do you think she will do now that he is breaking off the arrangement?"

"I don't know, but I think you two should be careful."

15

"Good morning, Mr. Robertson." The National Bank of Scotland manager greeted Robert with a firm handshake. "Come into my office, and we'll discuss your urgent business my clerk informed me of."

"Well, Mr. McGregor," he said, reviewing the nameplate on the man's desk. "I need to obtain two-thousand, five-hundred pounds."

"That shouldn't be a problem given we've had reputable dealings with the Robertsons of Weetshill in the past. Now just what do you need the money for?"

Robert took in a deep breath and exhaled before beginning. "Well, I require the funds to buy my way out of a marriage contract. I don't love the girl and would be doing her an injustice if I went through with it feeling the way I do."

The man stared, his brow furrowed. "I'm sorry," he said after a lengthy pause. "We cannot support financing for such a frivolous venture."

Dejected, Robert forged on toward the railway terminal but stopped at the Bank of Scotland on the south side of the road. After his previous rejection, he had nothing to lose. This time they would accept his application. Again, his request for a loan was turned down.

Robert wandered along Union Street oblivious to his surroundings. In time, he ended up in front of his solicitor's place of business. With no appointment, would Kenneth be available? He hoped his friend could spare him some time. He ascended the narrow stairway to the lobby where the clerk banged away on his typewriter keys. "I don't suppose I could have a moment of Mr. McIntosh's time, could I?"

"I'll check for you, Sir. Can I say who is calling?"

"Robert Robertson of Weetshill."

A few minutes later, Kenneth stepped into the space. "Oh dear, things didn't go at all well, did they?"

He shook his head.

"Come in."

Robert accompanied him into his office and slumped into one of the chairs facing the desk.

The solicitor took out two glasses and a decanter and sloshed some into the waiting vessels. "I think we'll need a wee dram before we conclude this business," he said handing him a glass. "Now suppose you tell me what happened?"

Mouthful downed, he began. "The manager denied my loan request. He told me the justification was too frivolous. Marry the girl, and get on with life."

"Did you only try one?"

"No. I tried the Bank of Scotland as well with the same results."

"I told you not to tell them the real reason you needed the funds."

"It didn't seem right to lie."

"And as your solicitor, I shouldn't have suggested you do."

"I could sell a parcel of land. That should realize more than enough money to cover the dowry. Would you attend to that for me?"

"Of course, but let's not be hasty. Put old Horatio off for a while longer. A quick sale is one thing, but you want your full asking price paid."

The men sipped their drinks slowly. This malt was different from the usual whisky kept on hand. This one had a wonderfully peaty, smoky taste with just a hint of fruit.

Wheels crunched on the gravel drive. Sarah dashed to the front door. The expression on Robert's face when he exited the carriage told her things did not go well.

"I tried. I honestly did. Two banks and they both turned me down."

"I'm sorry. Is there something else you can do? Can I help?"

"This is my mess, and I'll find a way out."

"I want to." The words spilled out so naturally, but she needed to stay out of the situation. More than once, she told herself not to fall in love with him, but it was too late. She already had.

"I decided to sell some acreage to raise enough cash to pay off Horatio. I hate the idea because Weetshill has been in my family for generations. Still, I must sidestep this farce. I asked Kenneth to take care of the transaction for me when I saw him today."

"No. You can't sell off the land. I won't let you."

Before he could reply, Archibald entered the room. "Mr. and Miss Christie for you, Sir."

Horatio burst into the library, not waiting for an invitation, with Letitia following behind. She gave Sarah a hateful look when she slinked by her in the anteroom.

"Well Robert, my boy. Have you got that money yet?"

"No."

"What's taking so long? I say, what's taking so long?"

"It is a sizeable sum, Horatio, and not that easy to obtain."

"Just remember, my lad, the funds must be in my hands by thirty-first December, or you must honour the contract."

"You'll have your payment in plenty of time, don't worry."

"Can I offer anyone a drink?" Sarah offered as she walked to the table where the Robertsons kept the decanter and glasses.

"What are you doing, letting her wait on you like a servant?" Horatio demanded.

"First off, I couldn't stop her if I tried, and secondly, unlike you, I don't treat my servants like slaves. I'm not going to drag Archibald in here to do something I can do for myself or Miss Shand for that matter."

Letitia's bottom lip quivered. "Father, I want to leave."

"Very well, my dear." He rubbed her shoulder and turned back. "You haven't heard the last from me. Not heard the last."

Robert opened the library door. "I'll see you both out?"

16

Two days later, a letter by special delivery came from Robert's solicitor's office. He dashed to the breakfast room where Sarah stood at the sideboard holding a plate. "Kenneth's messenger just arrived with this. You remember I contracted him to execute the sale of a portion of the acreage on the other side of the burn." He read further and his excitement faded. "The property didn't fetch as much as we desired. It's still not enough to discharge my debt to Horatio. My inheritance from Granda won't be available for some time, Kenneth says. Maybe not until after the New Year and if that's the case, I'll be forced to go through with the marriage to Letitia."

"How much did you get?"

"One-thousand, five-hundred pounds. Now, what do I do? I'm still well short."

"Well short of what, Robert?" His sister said as she strolled into the room.

"I sold a parcel of land, but the transaction didn't realize enough money to pay off Horatio."

"And you need?"

"Another thousand."

Margaret looked Sarah in the eye and talked low. "Will you swear whatever you're hiding won't destroy Robert?"

Sarah's eyes widened, but she nodded.

Turning around, she swept back out of the room. She returned a few minutes later, clutching a handful of pound notes. "This should be enough to get you out of the mess."

"How, Sister? Where did you get this money? Does George know?"

"This has nothing to do with my husband. After the committal, Kenneth took me aside and gave me a package containing a huge amount of cash and a letter from Granda. He apologized for mistreating me after Father's death and said he understood why I ran off rather than go through with a marriage to a man I didn't love. He said he provided the funds in that manner so the money would not become my husband's. It would be mine to do with as I pleased. Well, I want to help you."

"But I thought ..."

"Something is off these days with Letitia. Perhaps it's best if you don't go into the arranged marriage. I won't stand in your way of happiness. Just be careful is all I ask."

Robert threw his arms around Margaret and hugged her. "Thank you. I will repay you once Kenneth settles Granda's will. With interest."

She smiled. "I'll make sure you do. Now say you'll take it."

Why had his sibling, so determined for him to go through with the arrangement, changed her mind to the point of lending him money? She had never kept secrets from him before, but now was doing her best to avoid him and couldn't look him in the eye for any length of time.

Sarah had remained silent. She finally broke into the conversation. "Does this mean a trip to Aberdeen? I assume there are contracts you need to sign for the land sale and that kind of stuff."

"I'll ask Kenneth to bring the money and documents here." Robert held Sarah close. Her body came into contact with his and stirred feelings that until now remained buried. Her scent reminded him of the springtime meadow after the rain when everything smelled fresh. Then it occurred to him. "The messenger. I left him standing in the hall."

Robert sprinted out of the room. "I'm so sorry to keep you waiting like this. I need you to tell Mr. McIntosh I need the necessary paperwork brought here and if possible for this evening."

"Yessir, Mr. Robertson. I'll pass your message to him."

After tipping the courier, he sighed with relief. If all went to plan, Kenneth would arrive that night, and by the next day, the ridiculous arrangement would be over.

On his entrance to the breakfast room, he said, "The sooner Horatio Christie is out of my life, the happier I'll be."

Archibald placed a fresh pot of coffee on the sideboard.

"Mr. McIntosh will be arriving later today if everything works out," Robert said. "Can you make up a room for him, and tell Morag we'll be one more for our meal tonight, please?"

"Everything will be as you wish."

About seven-thirty that evening, the solicitor arrived at Weetshill. "Your message surprised me. I have the money from the sale and the documents. But you're still one thousand pounds short."

"No, Kenneth. The cash you passed on to Margaret from Granda – she agreed to lend me enough to pay my way out of the marriage contract. I promised to repay the funds to my sister with interest. Perhaps you can draw up a document to that effect whilst you're with us?"

Robert summoned the butler. "I apologize for being such a bother, but can you send word to Horatio I would like to see him tomorrow morning at his earliest convenience."

"Sir, I will, and, Sir, you're not a bother."

17

Over breakfast the next morning, Robert told Sarah of the decision he had come to the night before. "I would prefer you stayed away while I conduct my business with Horatio."

"I'm all right with that. I don't want to be there anyway. I'll make myself scarce. Go for a walk or something."

Kenneth looked up from his food. "An excellent idea. The old bugger can be quite the blowhard."

Robert stood and pecked his sister's cheek when she entered the room. "Thank you again for the loan. Everything is in order. Horatio should be here within the hour."

"I hope things go well for you, although I can't imagine Letitia's father taking the situation well. I'm going to take my meal to my room," said Margaret.

"What is bothering her?"

"Not sure. Your sister mentioned Letitia said something the other day that bothered her but never went into the gory details. I'll leave you to it," Sarah said leaving them at the table.

The door had only just swung closed behind her when Archibald announced Mr. and Miss Christie's arrival. "Miss Christie? Why did she come with him? This business is going to be unpleasant enough as it is."

"The lassie is devoted to her father, Robert. You have to give her credit for that," Kenneth answered.

The men followed the butler to the library where the solicitor took a seat behind the desk. Letitia sat in a chair by the sofa, staring at her folded hands. She looked up at him once through red-rimmed eyes but quickly turned away.

"Well, Horatio, I think you'll find things in order. The two-thousand, five-hundred pounds and the release contract requiring your signature," said Mr. McIntosh.

"This is blasphemous, blasphemous," he bellowed as he leaned forward and watched the notes disbursed, one by one.

Robert found himself counting along silently. He trusted Kenneth but worried a mistake would drag the whole thing out longer. The man laid the final note on the desk's surface and with the count correct, relief washed over him.

"You can sign right here, Horatio." Robert's legal representative indicated the place on the document. "However; before you do, we'll require impartial witnesses. That leaves out everyone in this room. What about your butler, Robert? Would he sign? And perhaps your coachman, Mr. Christie? Once we have the signatures, we can put all this unpleasantness behind us."

Letitia made a choking noise and fled from the library in tears.

After what Sarah deemed was a reasonable length of time for the men to finish their business, she went back to the house. The young Christie woman flew toward her in a streak of scarlet and black as she rounded the last corner of the driveway, nearly knocking her to the ground.

Why in the world had she come along? If she were in the girl's shoes, she wouldn't want to be within a mile of the transaction.

"Wait, Letitia, please."

"You can be happy. The deed is done. Robert paid my father off. Counted every last pound with me sat there in the room."

"Those insensitive gits," she said, grabbing Letitia's arm.

"Let go of me."

"In a minute. Hear me out first. I didn't come to Weetshill intent on breaking you two up. Sometimes those things happen. I'm sorry to see you hurt in all this."

"I don't believe you."

"Believe what you want." Sarah loosened her grip. "They should never have done that contract business in front of you. You didn't need to witness it. Why on earth did you come with your father? I wouldn't have come if I were you."

"This is all your fault."

"Letitia, please. You're unfair."

"Unfair? That's rich coming from you. You, who bewitched my

Robert, dare to talk about fairness. He may be out of the contract, but he'll never marry you. I'll see to that. You're going to regret this, both of you." She wrenched her arm free and dashed away.

Sarah slammed the library door behind her. "You bunch of insensitive galoots. Letitia is in bits because of your little performance."

"You'll not speak to me in that tone," Horatio roared. "I say you'll not, you vulgar woman."

"Oh sit down and be quiet," she snapped. "Why did you bring her along anyway?" She whirled to face Robert. "And you? Why did you count the money in front of her? She didn't need to witness that. You made her feel like a cheap cut of meat."

"You got what you wanted. Got what you wanted, lassie. My Letitia's torment is all down to you." Horatio stormed out in a huff.

"Not what I wanted. It was what Robert wanted," she shouted after him.

"Sarah, please," he said as he touched her arm.

She recoiled at his touch. "I thought if anyone had suggested Letitia leaving, you would have been the one. She would listen to you; you know she would."

"I'm sorry you find this situation so upsetting. I thought you would be pleased."

"I'm thrilled about you being released from the arrangement. Not so about the fallout." Sarah stared out the library window. Horatio Christie's carriage pulled away. "If Letitia does anything stupid, I'll never forgive myself, but I am happy you're not forced to go through with that insane contract."

"I suppose you think I'm cold and callous."

"Never. Not the sharpest tool in the shed maybe, but not cold and callous," Sarah said as she slumped into the wingback chair.

18

Teardrops burned Letitia's eyes. Her father sold her like an animal at the Duninsch Mart. Marrying her disgusted Robert to the point he bought his way out of the contract. That Shand woman turned him into an uncaring man.

She paused by her mother's rose garden to catch her breath. Something Jean MacDonald told her about rituals taking place there in the past came back, and an idea came to her.

Letitia couldn't let Sarah win, at least not this way. She had hoped it would not come to this, but the time came to put her plan into action. One way or another Robert would never marry her. Once the discomfort in her side was gone, she moved on toward the MacDonald cottage.

Fighting back her tears, she battered the door with her fists.

"Miss Christie, what brings you here?"

She squeezed past the old woman and into the vestibule.

"You's been cryin'."

"I've never been so humiliated in all my life."

Jean ushered her into the modest sitting room. "Och, what has you so vexed, child?"

"You're aware Robert Robertson, of Weetshill, and I are in an arranged marriage agreement."

"E'eryone in these parts kens."

"He's paid Father the amount of my dowry, so he doesn't have to marry me. He's free to wed her," Letitia keened.

"How do you ken that be why?"

"Why else would he want to nullify the contract? She's bewitched him. Surely, she has."

"Lets me fetch you a cup of tea. It'll put the world to rights."

"I don't want it. I want to make Sarah Shand miserable. I'll make her rue the day she thwarted me. Just watch."

"I dinnae think I like what you is sayin'." The old woman set the tray on the rickety table.

"Poison. I need some. Please, you must help me," she appealed falling to her knees and clutching the old woman's skirt.

"Miss Christie? You isnae talkin' sense."

"I never made more sense in my life." Suddenly Letitia calmed. "This is the last time anyone will humiliate me."

"You is makin' me scairt. I doesnae like what I's hearin'. Gettin' the folks of Kendonald wondering about that Shand lassie is one thing. Killin' someone is another."

"But, you must help me."

"I dinnae have to do anythin'. I think it be time you was leavin'."

"If you don't, I'll, I'll go to Police Constable Skinner and tell him about your dear departed husband. How his death wasn't natural." Letitia stood and stared down at Jean.

All the colour had drained from the old woman's wrinkled face. "How do ye ken?" she asked, her voice trembling.

"Mummy suspected something suspicious, and she told Father and me before she passed on. With your reaction just now, I think she was right. So are you helping me, or am I going to the police?"

Jean was thunderstruck at the notion her secret was known, primarily by Horatio Christie. That man looked down at everyone who wasn't his social equal like something scraped off the bottom of his shoe.

She needed her past to stay buried along with her husband. He had been worse than a wild animal and would have killed her with his fists if not for the poison she snuck into his food.

"I dinnae like this, Miss Christie."

"Why should this time be any different? You did it before and without remorse. Now get me what I asked for," she raved.

The old woman hobbled off to the kitchen to the cabinet where her box of supplies were housed. This scheme was something she wanted no part of, but she couldn't risk Letitia going to the police. Carefully, she opened the lid and took out a small vial, poured half the contents into another, and topped it up with water before replacing the stopper. She shuffled back to the sitting room and handed over the diluted poison. "I dinnae has any part o' yer scheme. Remember that."

"How much do I need for a fatal dose?"

"Jus' a couple o' drops. Now be on your way. I doesnae want to see you here at my house again."

"Don't worry. You won't."

Later that night, Sarah pulled the covers up to her chin. Not able to sleep any longer, she lay and waited for the mansion to fall silent for the night. So many things happened since her arrival at Weetshill. Not all good. Jean MacDonald's outburst at old Mr. Robertson's funeral fuelled the gossip she knew had spread throughout the community about her and Robert. Now with the marriage contract broken, was the course of history altered? Was there to be a Robertson-Christie heir who would now never be born?

In her family history, she couldn't go beyond her great-grandparents who fell in love during the war when her great-grandfather lodged in this very house.

The *Back to the Future* movies and the changes in Marty's life because of things he did when he was in the past came to mind. Same with episodes of *Doctor Who* and *Star Trek*. Time travelling characters were forbidden to interfere with life and therefore change the future, but sometimes entire families were wiped out because of the alteration of ancestors lives. What if she already harmed her family without knowing?

Letitia's warning 'he'll never marry you. I'll see to that. You're going to regret this, both of you' echoed through her head, too. Dawn neared, and she made a decision. She had caused enough disruption to Robert's life, and had to leave. Leaving Weetshill was Sarah's only choice – if only to protect Robert from harm.

The sky revealed the first hints of morning light as she hurled back the covers and tiptoed to the window. She put her hand on the icy cold glass. No matter how much she wanted to go away with nothing more than what she came with, she would freeze to death without a winter cloak.

Sarah dressed and crept downstairs to the library. She pulled out a sheet of paper and readied the mother-of-pearl handled stick pen. The writing instrument was harder to use than expected and great blobs of ink smudged across the page until the nuances of the implement were determined. She wrote Robert a letter and left the note on the desk.

The door latched behind her. To her horror, the housekeeper was already up and working.

"Where are you off to this time o' the mornin'?" Mrs. MacEwen asked.

"J-just going for a walk. I couldn't sleep last night and thought the fresh air might help," she lied as she closed the front door. By the time they discovered she had left, she would be far away.

At the pasture where the ancient monument stood, a winded Sarah heaved in a lungful of air. She completed her trek to this special place in less time than usual. Unable to explain why the stone circle and the ley line intersecting it had transported her back to the past. With any luck, she could find her way back to 2010 where she belonged before she caused any more trouble.

A flash of scarlet, the same colour as the gown Letitia wore the previous day, glimmered in the soft pre-dawn light, as she crested the peak. Sarah scrambled over and discovered the Christie woman sprawled on her back on a fallen stone. "Oh my giddy aunt, what have you done?"

She knelt next to Letitia's body. The woman's eyes were opened wide, and an empty glass vial lay on the ground beside the rock. A sniff of the open vessel revealed a medicinal odour like the laudanum she had taken. She felt the girl's neck and found a faint pulse, but the woman was not breathing. "Don't you dare die on me," she said, before beginning mouth-to-mouth resuscitation.

"By all that is holy, what are you doing to the lassie?" a gruff voice roared.

"I'm trying to save Letitia's life." Sarah gasped between breaths. "Who are you?"

"Thomas Sievewright, ghillie for Mr. Christie." He prodded her with his walking stick. "Noo clear off," he said snatching her by the arm.

"Up yours." Shaken free from his grasp, she resumed artificial respiration. "I'll be black and blue thanks to you. Should have you done for assault, but that isn't going to help her. Stand back and let me finish." She stopped and felt for a pulse again. It was stronger now.

A stir, followed by a gasp, and Letitia vomited. Not wasting any time, Sarah moved her on her side and tore a strip from her cotton petticoat. She used the rag to clean inside her mouth so she wouldn't choke.

Sarah pulled her off the boulder and rolled her into the recovery position, then removed her cloak and laid it over the girl to keep her warm.

Letitia's eyes fluttered open. "You. Did you save me? Why?"

"Shh. Don't talk. Just rest. No man is worth taking your life. Trust me, I know. When my boyfriend left me, I tried to top myself, too." She turned to the ghillie. "I need to find Robert and Mr. Christie. Can you stay here with her?"

"No, you're comin' wi' me." Tommy grabbed her arm and dragged her down the hill.

"Let go of me, you big oaf." Sarah fought to escape his vice-like grip.

"I willnae do no such thing. Not wi' what I seen you doin' to Miss Letitia."

Sarah kicked at his legs, but her skirts hindered her movement. "I was saving her life. She would be dead if I didn't know what to do."

Margaret was already at the table when Robert entered the breakfast room. She looked up at her brother as he took his seat. "So the deed is done."

"Yes, and unfortunately, Miss Christie witnessed it."

"Oh, wonderful. How could you?"

"Pardon me, Sir. A visitor to see you," the butler said. "I put her in the library."

Letitia. Margaret jumped up and dashed to the other room. Instead of her childhood friend, the wrinkled face of Jean MacDonald greeted her. "What are you doing here?"

Robert went after his sister and stepped past her. "This had better be good."

"A-aye, Mr. Robertson. I ken I isnae to be here, but I couldnae stay away. Miss Christie. She isnae right in the head. She came to me lookin' for poison."

"Go on," he said.

"I dinnae ken where to go. I think she might be goin' to harm Miss Shand. I had to warn you. I tol' her me tellin' e'ry one she be a witch was one thing, but killin' I wouldnae be party to."

"And did you give it to her?"

"A-aye but I watered it down so 'tain't so strong."

"Did you go to the village Police?"

"I-I thought I should tell you first."

"I appreciate that but go now. Tell Constable Skinner what you told us."

"An' if I's wrong?"

"We'll deal with that contingency should it arise."

Margaret dropped into the wingback chair by the window as the old woman left the room. "Oh Brother, this is terrible. Letitia said she had a plan to remove the Shand lassie from your life. What if she planned to poison her? I should have told you sooner, but I never once thought it would come to this."

Robert reached over and patted the back of her hand. "I think you're overreacting. Sarah is still snug in bed. In the meantime, Mrs. MacDonald is off to speak with the local constabulary."

"I do hope you're right. Letitia's desperate enough to do almost anything," Margaret said standing. She walked to the desk and picked up a smudged sheet of paper. After scanning the note, she held the stationery out to him. "I think you had best see this."

He skimmed over it before collapsing in one of the chairs in front of the workspace.

Robert,

My heart is breaking as I write this. I would love to stay here at Weetshill since everyone has made me feel so welcome. I hate to break my promise to your grandfather, but I'm thinking of everyone's best interests.

I caused you way too much trouble since I got here and I think I should leave so your life can go back to normal.

Robert, you've been a good friend to me. You deserve better than me and my baggage. I will miss you so much. I fell in love with you, and that makes this even harder.

Please, don't try to look for me. I need to disappear from your lives so you can move on.

You are all dear to me, and I hate to leave you this way.

Sarah

19

Jean MacDonald left the house at the same time the Christie's carriage pulled up. The old woman bowed her head and scurried past the man like she was terrified of him.

"Now what?" Robert mumbled. "Show him in here, would you Archibald?" He returned to the library.

Within minutes, an extremely pale Horatio Christie stood in front of him. "Have either of you seen my Letitia?"

"Why do you ask?"

"She's not come back since she darted off. These past few weeks have been hard on the lass. Not like her at all, and with you and that Shand lassie," he said waggling his finger at Robert, "rubbing her nose in it at every opportunity, it's no wonder."

"There's no need for that. I'm sure she wants to be alone. She'll be back. Just give her some time. She might even be home waiting for you now."

"She hasn't slept in her bed. I'm trying not to think this, but what if she's done something daft?"

"Jean MacDonald was here a while ago vexed over a visit she had from your daughter last evening. There was talk of poison and killing."

"Letitia wouldn't harm a fly, let alone kill anyone," Horatio gloated.

"I told the woman to go to the police and tell Constable Skinner everything she told us."

"I couldn't stand if anything happened to my little girl. She's all I have left."

"I'll help you look for her," Robert offered.

"Excellent idea. Excellent. It's so not like my Letitia to do anything like this."

"Is your coachman waiting for you?"

"Of course he is. What kind of a damn fool question is that?"

"I merely implied if you had dismissed yours, I would get mine to drive us."

"Quite alright, Robert. Quite alright. I'm worried. Very worried."

"Then there is no time to waste."

Horatio's driver took them to Gleanstane House.

"Has she come home yet?"

"I hasnae seen Miss Letitia since yesterday, Sir, when you and she went off to Weetshill," said Carlyle.

"Where on earth could she be? Where?" Horatio took a handkerchief out of his breast pocket and mopped his brow."

"Why don't we try the stone circle?" Robert suggested.

"She wouldn't. She detests that place. Told me so, herself many times."

"Didn't your wife plant a flower garden near it?" He put his hand on Mr. Christie's arm.

"Ah, my Philomena, God rest her soul, planted some roses up there years ago. Maybe you're right. Maybe my Letitia is there."

"You stay here in case she comes to the house. I'll go look for her."

Robert sprinted up the steep incline from the house to the top of the hill. The sound of a person moaning emanated from within the area as he neared the ancient monument. An upright stone supported Letitia, and a familiar cloak enveloped her body. He knelt beside her. "What happened?"

"I wanted to die, so I took poison," she slurred.

A small flash of light from an empty glass vial glinted in the sun as Robert leaned over her. He snatched the bottle and shoved it into his pocket before bundling Letitia into his arms to carry her home. "You're going to be all right. I'll take you home and send for Doctor Burnett."

"Sarah, she … she saved me."

On their arrival at Gleanstane house, the butler pulled open the door, and Robert carried her inside.

"You found her. Dear God in heaven, what on earth has happened to her?" Horatio prattled.

"She needs medical attention, but I'm sure she'll be fine."

"Carlyle," Mr. Christie shouted, "Get that damn coachman to find the doctor."

"Sir." The servant shuffled off to fulfil his orders.

He steered the way to his daughter's room.

She moaned, and her eyes fluttered open when Robert laid her on the bed.

"My Letitia, my beautiful Letitia," Horatio wailed. "What did you do?" He began to pace. "Where is that physician? Why isn't he here yet?"

"Your coachman just left. It will take some time to travel to his surgery and bring him back here."

Mr. Christie pulled a chair to Letitia's bedside. "What were you thinking, my sweet girl? What?"

"I need, need to see Miss Shand," she moaned.

"Why?" Robert moved nearer to her bed.

"Need her. Kissed me. Breathing."

"What nonsense is she talking? What?"

The girl made no sense in her semi-conscious state, but if Sarah had been at the stone circle with her, where did she go? He wanted to press her for more information, but in her weakened condition, Robert didn't dare. "Now that Miss Letitia is going to recover, I must return to Weetshill. Please keep me apprised of her recovery. He took out the vial and deposited it on the nightstand. "When the physician arrives, show this to him."

Mr. Christie scowled but nodded.

"What's taking the man so blasted long? The coachman should have been back with him by now," muttered Horatio.

"Father, hold me please."

He sat on the edge of the bed and cuddled Letitia. "Everything will be all right. I'll make sure they never hurt you again."

She felt protected encased in his strong arms. It had been a long time since he held her this way.

More than two hours later, Carlyle announced the physician's arrival. "Shall I show him in?"

"Of course, you fool. Send him in here now, I say. Send him now," Horatio ranted. "What the blazes took you so long? My wee girl could have died waiting."

"I'm sorry, but I do have other patients. As it happens, I was at the Cooper steading attending to a worker who had a bad accident. I got here as quickly as I could." The doctor examined her then sent the butler for whisky. "Hmm," he droned as he checked her. "You're a fortunate girl.

You could easily be dead. What did you take?"

"I-I don't know, came from Jean MacDonald," she murmured.

Horatio pointed to the vial Robert had left on the nightstand. Doctor Burnett examined the bottle and sniffed inside.

A tiny amount of liquid remained in the bottom, so he poured a drop on his thumb and touched it to his tongue. "Definitely laudanum here and perhaps something else. This concoction could have been lethal. Who found you?" He asked after she groaned.

"Leave her be, man. Let the wee girl rest," Horatio barked.

"Father, it's all right. Miss Shand, but I only saw her for a moment when she covered me up with her cloak. It had to be her."

"Why are you defending that woman, child? Why I say?"

"You're fraught, Mr. Christie, but you're not doing her any benefit upsetting her." Doctor Burnett mixed the spirit into a glass of water, propped Letitia up and held the vessel to her lips.

She sputtered and coughed. "Please Father, you must believe me. Miss Shand saved me."

After Robert left Gleanstane House, he went back to the stone circle hoping to find Sarah. He shouted her name repeatedly but to no avail. "Where are you?" He scoured the vicinity around the ancient monument, but there was no trace of her. He tried one last time, but again, received no reply. Where did she go? She vanished from his life as quickly as she crashed into it.

20

"Let me go," Sarah shouted, trying to yank her arm out of Tommy's grasp.

"Nae. The only place you's goin' is to the Police."

"But I saved Letitia Christie's life. That must count for something." She kicked at him and when she failed, drove her heel into his instep.

"You shouldnae done that," Tommy snarled at her and jerked her hard by the arm.

He forcibly dragged her until they stopped in front of the station house.

"Constable Skinner. I'm glad you's here. You wouldnae believe the things this lassie was doin' to Miss Christie up to the stone circle."

"A-hem." The policeman cleared his throat, slid his glasses down and looked over them and said, "Go on Tommy."

The lawman was in his mid-forties, with a thick, dark moustache, a long thin nose, and a giant mole on the left side of his face.

"Hunched down over her, and kissing her ... on the lips, she was."

"Of course I was, you stupid old git. I was doing mouth-to-mouth. Without my intervention, she'd be dead," Sarah snapped.

"Bringin' folk back tae life. If that isnae witchcraft, I dinnae ken what is," the old grizzly ghillie answered.

By now the room heaved with people. From where did they all come? The street was empty when he dragged her here.

"What are you goin' to do about her? With what she's done to Miss Christie," Tommy said.

120

A sea of faces, flailing arms, and pointing fingers surged forward. Sarah backed away until she was against a wall. The policeman blew his whistle. "Calm down people. This commotion isn't doing anyone any good. Now out!"

Everyone slowly filed out but Thomas Sievewright. He remained behind, conferring with the officer. She couldn't hear their exchange, but periodically, one of them looked over at her. The ghillie took out a folded sheet of paper and slid it across the desk to the man.

"Very well, Tommy. Thank you. I'll take it from here," Police Constable Skinner said then turned to Sarah. "All right then, lassie. Let's go for a little ride."

"Back to Weetshill? I have to go back and tell Robert and Mr. Christie I found Letitia."

"Right this way. I'll take you back where you belong." He ushered her through the building and out the back door. "Up you get." He held open the door of an enclosed carriage for her.

The interior was narrow with boards for seats on either side. She started to speak to him, but he slammed the door shut. There was no handle on the inside. Sarah pounded on the wooden surface. "Let me out of here." The scrape of a padlock slipping through the hasp and latching echoed through the confined space. "I demand you release me," she screamed.

"Calm down; we're just taking a wee journey."

The only light came through two small barred windows at opposite ends of the carriage. She climbed up and gripped the metal bars. "Why are you doing this to me?"

Constable Skinner whistled, and the box pitched backward, knocking her to the floor.

Sarah dragged herself back to the seat to get away from the stench of stale urine. The scent of sweat and different body odours lingered in the cramped space. She rubbed her arm where it hit the bench when she fell.

Her worst nightmare came true. She was on her way to the mental institution. Sarah kicked the wall. "You're not going to get away with this," she hollered. "Robert will find me. He won't let you do this to me."

"Not if he doesn't know where you are."

Mrs. MacDonald stood on the Kendonald constabulary steps and drew a deep breath. The door opened as she reached for the knob, and Thomas Sievewright stared down at her. "I needs to see the Police Constable. He be in?"

"Why do you need him?"

"Miss Christie come to me last night for poison. I think she was goin' to harm Miss Shand, but I dinnae ken for sure. I's seen Mr. Robertson an' he said I should come here."

"Go on home, you daft old biddie. You hasnae business with him." He bent down and glared at her. "I wouldnae be causin' trouble for Miss Letitia or the mister if you ken what's good for you. I'll be watchin' you, and if you set one foot here again or tell anyone about the poison, you'll live to regret it," Tommy growled.

Jean clutched her chest and shuffled off to her house. She pushed the door shut behind her, and latched the central lock and the one at the bottom. Despite the door not being overly high, it required her to stand on her tiptoes to slide the bolt at the top into the casing. Once the entrance was secured, she hobbled from one room to the next, closing and latching the shutters as she went.

"Has Miss Shand come back yet?" Robert asked when he got back to Weetshill.

"She hasnae, Sir," said Archibald.

"Where could she be?" He hadn't meant to speak aloud.

"I'm sure I doesnae ken."

Robert shouldered his way by the butler and went upstairs to the room Sarah used during her stay. He rapped on the door, but no one answered. He stepped inside, but the empty room remained the same as in the years since his mother's death up until Sarah's arrival.

Something white on the floor caught his eye when he walked to the window to look out over the property. Robert bent down and gathered up a woman's nightgown. He lifted the cotton garment to his face. Her scent lingered. He dropped to the ottoman by the end of the bed, leaned over and buried his face in the soft cloth.

He couldn't bear to think of her lost and bewildered, wandering around the countryside looking for a family and home that didn't exist. Robert sighed, "Please God, keep Sarah safe."

The police carriage came to a standstill, and Sarah held her position at the back, hoping she could make her getaway when the door opened. She stood on the bench and peered through the bars when it didn't.

The smell of cow manure wafted through the vents. They had to have stopped at a farm to feed and water the horses.

On the off chance someone was out in the barnyard, Sarah kicked and hammered on the door. "Please help me. Get me out of here," she shouted. "This man kidnapped me." Footsteps squelched in mud, and then someone pummelled it from the opposite side.

"Shut up."

"I need the loo," she lied. She would hide in the barn if the cop let her out. That was one good thing about growing up where she did. She knew all the best hiding places.

"What?"

"I need to pee. If you don't let me out, I'll wet myself."

"Drop your drawers and go then. You won't be the first." He laughed.

A few minutes later, the wagon jerked into motion again. Dejected, Sarah slumped in the corner, those dreaded words, 'not if he doesn't know where you are' echoing in her head.

It bounced over the rough road, jostling and shaking her like a rag doll. The daylight dimmed, making her more and more claustrophobic. Cemetery vaults were more spacious than this.

They had left around ten in the morning, and now the ambient light coming in the high windows grew fainter. With no food since the previous day, her stomach ached with hunger. Exhausted, physically and mentally, she nodded off.

The carriage came to a sudden stop, jolting her awake. The door flew open, and the policeman hauled her out and heaved her over his shoulder like a sack of potatoes.

"Put me down." She slapped his back and kicked at him.

"No."

Sarah raised her head and tried to look around. A big dark building that could have been Weetshill stood in front of them. Had he taken her back to Robert?

"Bring her in," a female voice said.

Not Mrs. MacEwen's voice, but someone else's. Not Robert's home either. Skinner took her to the asylum.

21

Sarah pounded on Skinner's back with her fists and swung her feet in the air. "Put me down. Why are you doing this to me? I didn't do anything."

Metal clanging echoed as he shouldered her down a long, dark hallway. Creaking door hinges soon replaced the racket.

"Stick her in here. We'll de-louse her in the morning," the woman said.

Police Constable Skinner tossed her on the bed and backed out, closing the door with a loud snap as the latch took hold.

A faint light shone through a small, grimy window near the ceiling. She squinted as her eyes grew accustomed to the gloom. The only furniture was a narrow bed with no sheet or blanket.

Sarah worked her way along the wall to the door, rubbing the palms of her hands on the cold, plaster surface. Like the carriage, this door had no knob or handle on the inside. She was at the mercy of the powers that be until someone decided to let her out.

She walloped and kicked on the door as hard as she could and screamed, "I'm not crazy. I don't belong here." Sarah paused while waiting for a response but there was none. "Let. Me. Out. Do you hear me?" she began again. "Contact Doctor Burnett at Kendonald. He'll tell you there's nothing wrong with me."

"What makes you think he dinnae has you brung here?" a deep male voice taunted.

"Then get hold of Robert Robertson at Weetshill. He knows me. He'll tell you the truth." She smacked the door with the palm of her hand one last time, then pressed her cheek to the cold metal surface and wept.

"Haud yer wheesht or I'll gie you a skelpit lug! You willnae get anyone here to believe you." The man punched the opposite side of the door sending the vibration through her head.

"You lay one hand on me, and I'll see you done for assault." Sarah kicked the door one more time and backed away.

She found her way back to the bed, laid down and stared at the ceiling. Would this be her existence from now on? A shred of sanity remained, but wouldn't for long in this place. Drained, she drifted off into a restless sleep.

A key slid into the door lock making Sarah jump. The light from the small window told her it was early morning. Maybe she could surprise the person entering and escape. She sprang off the mattress and flattened herself against the wall next to the door.

"Take her to the baths. She needs de-lousing," the female said.

"Aye, Matron." A burly man accompanying the housemother grasped Sarah's arms.

His voice was the one tormenting her through the door the night before. He dragged her to a dank room with a tub filled with hot water. No matter how hard she tried to shake her arm free and extricate herself from his grip, she was unsuccessful.

A heavyset woman came in carrying a scrub brush. "Get in and warsh."

"I'm not using something for washing floors!"

"I'll do it if ye doesnae."

If Sarah controlled the thing, it would be easier than if someone else did. "All right but I'm not bathing with you here."

"I isnae leavin'."

The de-lousing was humiliating enough but made worse by having to strip down in front of a total stranger. She turned her back to the woman, undressed and climbed into the washtub. Strong chemical fumes burned her nostrils as she sniffed the rising steam. Under the attendant's watchful eye, she washed with the brush. "Are you happy now?"

No reply. Before Sarah had a chance to react, a hand yanked her head back, and metal blades snapped. She sprang to her feet and turned to face the attendant. The woman stood open-mouthed with a lock of hair in one hand and an enormous pair of scissors in the other. "What do you think you're doing?" she demanded, rubbing the back of her head.

"E'eryone who comes here gets their hair chopped."

"I'm not everyone." Sarah scampered out of the bath and lunged at the woman. She knocked the scissors out of her hand and kicked them across the floor. They skittered to the edge of a grate, teetered briefly, and fell through. After a long time, a splash echoed from the drain.

"Well since ye wouldnae let me near you with them, then I'll has to dunk yer head." The woman seized Sarah's wrist and pulled her arm up behind her back. She dragged her back to the tub, forced her down, and plunged her head beneath the water.

"What the hell are you playing at? You trying to drown me?" She coughed as she tried to stand but was held firmly by her shoulders.

"Yer hair. We need to de-louse it, too. Ye willnae lets me cut it, so we has to do it this way."

"I don't have lice."

"So ye say."

The woman snatched Sarah by the hair and streamed cold water over her head. One whiff of the undiluted liquid and the stench was unmistakable. "Why are you pouring kerosene on my head?"

"Only way to kill the cooties." The employee worked the fuel oil into Sarah's scalp and bound her head in a towel when done. "Leave it there," she ordered, "and get out now."

Sarah snagged the piece of scratchy wool and wrapped it around herself. Her clothes were gone, replaced by flannel drawers, a white chemise and blouse, black skirt, and a purple jacket. "What did you do with my clothes?"

"Burned 'em. Cannae be too careful wi' lice."

Sarah put on the institution's gear and started to unwrap the towel from her hair.

"Ach, leave that there. Ye cannae take it off. Now come!" The woman grabbed her by the arm.

The chaperone took her to a room filled with long wooden tables. Sarah's escort pushed her on a narrow stool, snapped her fingers, and pointed.

Someone placed a bowl of runny oatmeal in front of her, and the hunger pangs returned. She picked up the spoon in her left hand, but quickly transferred the cutlery to her right, not wanting to attract any more attention.

Robert walked into the breakfast room and slumped into a chair. He hadn't eaten since noon the day before, but he had no appetite. Even the delicious smells from the chafing dishes on the sideboard didn't entice him.

"Good morning, Sir. Coffee?" Archibald asked.

"Please." His eyes remained fixed on the door.

"Naught to eat?"

"Not now."

The door opened, and he hoped Sarah would blow in like her usual breath of fresh air. Disappointment washed over him when it was Mrs. MacEwen.

"Any word on Miss Shand, Mr. Robertson?" the housekeeper asked.

"Nothing as yet."

"Here is the newspaper and post," the butler announced as he put it on Robert's right.

"Thank you." He opened the paper and scoured every page for a clue to Sarah's whereabouts but found nothing. "Have Dougal bring my coat. I'm going for a walk." Robert left the room without touching his coffee.

"Sir."

The valet waited by the front door, an overcoat and scarf over his arm and a pair of leather gloves in his hand.

Robert's destination was unknown. The only thing he knew for sure was he had to escape from Weetshill. Now with both Sarah and his grandfather gone, his home was nothing but a hulking, cold house. He walked until he ended up at Gleanstane. He was about to walk to the top of the hill when Thomas Sievewright closed in.

"Who goes there?" The ghillie called out and quickened his pace. "Mr. Robertson. Sorry to hear about your grandfather's passin'. What brings you here?"

Robert swallowed and said, "Miss Shand who's been staying at Weetshill. She's fascinated with the stone circle here. I thought, perhaps, you might have seen her." He gave the man Sarah's description.

"Hasnae," he said, shaking his head.

"You don't mind if I go sit a spell, do you?"

"Nae. Why you'd want to is beyond me."

While Robert sat on one of the fallen boulders, he realized why she loved the place so much. It was perfect for quiet reflection. He lingered about an hour recalling his childhood having fun here with his sister and Letitia, before deciding to leave. As he stood, a woman's voice called, 'Sarah, where on earth are you? We're worried to death.' That voice. Miss Shand's mother? She mentioned hearing the woman calling her, but why could he hear her and not see her? Sarah said she heard the sound, but not knowing where her mum was, terrified her.

Once, he saw the fleeting images of a chubby, freckle-faced girl and an old woman sitting in the spot he just vacated. He had always thought they were ghosts and now wondered if her mother was, too. Maybe the entire family were dead, and she didn't remember or was hiding it from him. Why?

Kendonald spread out along both sides of the road. Robert hastened toward the hamlet. At the Y-junction, the police house was visible. Perhaps the local bobby could do something in his official capacity to help find Sarah.

On the wooden pavement in front of the granite building, he hesitated for a moment before walking up the path to the door and letting himself in. "Hello. Is anyone about?"

"Right with you," a voice hollered from elsewhere in the house.

Soon Police Constable Skinner appeared from the back. "Ah, Mr. Robertson. Good to see you. What can I do for you today?"

"A friend," he began. "She's been staying at Weetshill."

"Och," the policeman spluttered.

"Well, she's vanished without so much as a by your leave."

"Hmm... and this friend's name?"

"Sarah Shand. Long brown hair, bright green eyes, beautiful. Stands about this tall." Robert held his hand up.

"Haven't seen anyone fitting that description."

"Will you at least make some enquiries?"

"Aye, if it will put your mind at rest."

"Thank you." He walked to the door, shoulders slumped, and stuffed his hands into his coat pockets. The action took him back to his childhood, and he hesitated for a moment before leaving. "Did Jean MacDonald come here yesterday?" he said, turning around.

"Not seen her in weeks," Skinner responded.

Robert shut the door behind him. Why didn't the old lady talk to the constable as she had promised? Something was amiss. He wanted to believe the man had told him the truth, but something about his mannerisms gnawed at him. In his position, he'd been sworn to uphold the law. Surely, he wouldn't break it.

On his way home, Robert stopped by the woman's cottage. The place was locked up and the shutters closed and latched from the inside. He pounded on the door and called out, "Mrs. MacDonald. Robert Robertson here. I need to speak with you." No one came, but he thought he heard the shuffle of footsteps in the house.

After breakfast, another employee took Sarah into a spacious sitting room. She was the only one with her head bound in a towel. Some of the women were nearly bald, while others had long tangled locks. All clad in identical clothing. A few looked at her, some sat and stared off into space, and some muttered to themselves.

A loud bell clanged, and the inmates filed down through to the dining hall. Sarah chose a chair with its back to the wall away from everyone else. Someone plopped a plate containing a boiled potato and cabbage, stringy beef, and a slice of bread in front of her. Pitchers of water and pots of weak tea sat on the table. She took hers black. This stuff tasted hideous. There was no milk or sugar, but she doubted the flavour would improve. Still, the dishwater they fobbed off as pekoe was her safest option since boiling the water would kill any bacteria.

After she ate, the burly attendant reappeared and dragged her down to the baths for another kerosene treatment. Her scalp still burned from the first round. The fumes were stronger this time, but at least they didn't dunk her in a tub full of the diluted chemical. Had people popped their clogs from inhaling the vapours? Much more of this barbaric treatment, she would have no hair left.

The brawny helper from earlier took her back to the day room where she tried to occupy herself without looking crazy. She walked to the window, but the only thing visible was a stone wall. Another woman, with short, unevenly cropped hair, and blank, beady eyes imitated Sarah's moves, unnerving her. A man with a long crooked nose, pronounced harelip, and few teeth came over. "Do you want to play with me?" he said, his tongue protruding through the gaps in his lip and mouth. She ran away from him and sought out a place where nobody would notice her. Saved by the clang of the call to eat, the workers marched the patients off for tea. The remainder of the day adhered to a similar pattern – day room and trying to keep from dying of boredom.

A third chemical dousing came later that night. Afterward, a servant took her to a sizeable dormitory and assigned her a bed.

Gradually, other women filed in and put on their nightgowns. Sarah snatched the one laid out on her bed, wadded up the garment and threw it away. She curled up on top of the covers and cried herself to sleep.

The following morning, Sarah woke to someone jabbing at her.

"Come. Time to get up."

She opened one eye, groaned and rolled over.

"Now, lassie, I isnae tellin' you again." This time the person squeezed Sarah's arm and brutally hauled her to her feet. "You's comin' wi' me."

Half asleep still, she couldn't keep up with the woman's pace and stumbled down the corridors in tow.

"Here. Superintendent's office." The female attendant shoved her in then slammed the door shut.

The desk and chairs reminded her of the ones in the library at

Weetshill as did the shelving units, but that was all. The books were all big and thick with titles like *Surgical Anatomy*, *Physiology of the Brain*, and *The Handbook of Medical Entomology*. Anatomical charts hung on the walls not lined with bookcases, and a human skull sat on the corner of his desk.

He turned away from the window and looked at her. "Sit down."

He was a broad-shouldered man in a dark suit. His white hair, moustache and beard gave him a distinguished look.

"I trust you slept well last night? I'm very sorry about the night of your arrival. You must understand, we need to keep new patients away from the others until there is no danger of an infestation. From the notes here; you attacked the woman who had been assigned to de-louse you."

"She tried to cut my hair. What did you expect me to do?"

"Having your head shaved is far less severe than the regimen you're receiving. You'll be able to wash your hair with soap and water later today."

Sarah would have preferred real shampoo and loads of conditioner, or better yet, an oil treatment to end the burning. She craned her neck in an attempt to read the open file on his desk. To her dismay, the handwriting was impossible to decipher, so she merely nodded in acknowledgement.

"Constable Skinner from Kendonald brought you, I see. Apparently, many villagers lodged complaints against you."

"Such as?"

"Practicing witchcraft, partaking in an unnatural act of a sexual nature, assaulting the man who took you to the police, and attacking one of our workers."

"I was ...," she started then stopped. Would even an educated man of the time know about resuscitation techniques? "I was trying to save a person's life, and your worker came at me with scissors and tried to cut my hair," she finally said. "Who filed the complaints?" Sarah had her suspicions. Letitia Christie topped the list, followed close behind by Jean MacDonald and the Christies' ghillie.

"I can't tell you. But the physician's signature is right here." He spun the sheet around and showed it to her.

The old Scots script was hard to read. The writer didn't put much pressure on the page, and some letters were barely visible. Still, there was no mistaking the name – Dr. Josiah Burnett. The location of his practice was also noted. Kendonald. Sarah couldn't believe he signed the order to have her committed. When he came to treat her after her arrival at Weetshill, he seemed such a nice man. Why had he turned against her like that?

"You'll be kept under observation here in the central building for a few days, and if all goes well, you'll move into the asylum for women next door."

The Superintendent scribbled something in her case notes, but his handwriting was illegible.

He rang a bell, and the woman from before rushed into his office. "She can sit in the ladies' day room until they serve breakfast. I want her watched closely for the next twenty-four to forty-eight hours. There isn't anything specific in her file, but she may come to be violent."

"She did an awful lot o' screeching when she got brought in."

"I think we best keep a close eye on this one. She could make trouble."

About mid-morning, a female employee arrived at her side. "Come. Time to wash your hair." She took Sarah's forearm.

"I can walk by myself," she seethed, shaking the woman's hand off.

"Cannae abide that." She firmly clenched Sarah's upper arm instead.

"Do what you have to do." She sighed as the two continued to the bath area.

"Water comes from the hand pump aside the sink, and there be a cake of soap to use."

"No hot water? You're making me wash my hair with cold?"

"No tellin' what you lunatics will do. Had an inmate throw a kettle of water over one of our attendants. Scalded the poor soul."

"I'm not a lunatic," she fumed.

Before taking the towel off her head, she removed her jacket and blouse. The dampness of the room gave her a chill, and she broke out in goosebumps.

The woman shoved her down over the wash basin. Sarah bit her tongue to keep from screaming she was capable of washing her own hair. After the scissors incident, the staff watched her closely. She would do her best to be a model patient and hopefully obtain a transfer to the women's hospital. If she didn't have to take on a man the size of a lorry, she would stand a much better chance of escaping.

The water was freezing, and the soap got into her eyes, but she gritted her teeth and kept silent. The woman scrubbed her head so hard it throbbed, but the stench of kerosene remained.

Robert ambled down the path to the stables where the groom attended one of the horses. Finally, he called out to him. "Can you come here, please?"

Hamish tied the lead to the fence and walked toward his employer. "The pony, she's better today, Sir. No near so lame. That liniment worked."

"I'm delighted, but I'm looking for Angus. Do you know where he is?"

"On the moors. Said somethin' about checkin' on the game."

"Thank you," Robert said as he pulled his collar up around his ears. The wind in the hills could be bitter, even in late August. He wished the gamekeeper would be easy to find. Luckily, he caught up with him before he reached the top of the hill.

"The stag's been aboot."

"It's good, isn't it?"

Angus nodded. "We's got another huntin' party comin' in this week. To gives them a good day o' sport, we need game for them to stalk."

"Yes, you're right, but I'm not up to hosting them. Would you ask Horatio Christie to contact me about the group staying with him?"

"I will, Sir."

The men walked together in silence while the ghillie checked tracks.

Robert kicked at the pebbles on the path. "Angus, I need your advice."

"You wants advice from me?"

"Yes. I have no one else to turn to now my father and grandfather are both dead. It's about Miss Shand. How do you know you met the lassie you want to spend the rest of your life with?"

"You jus' ken, I reckon."

"She is so different from any of the lassies I've known in the past."

"That she is, Sir."

"Despite these differences, there's something about her."

"She's pleasin' to look at."

"She is stunning. Also headstrong and feisty." Robert hesitated before he spoke choosing his words carefully. "How did you know Isabel was the one for you?"

"I jus' did."

"Still, there must have been something."

"E'ery time I saw her, it made me happy to be alive."

"Anything else?"

"She liked the animals, and she dinnae shy away from havin' to clean carcasses."

"So that is what made you know she was right for you."

"Och, aye."

"I think I'm falling in love with Miss Shand. And if she ever comes back, I want to ask her to be my wife, but how do I go about it?"

"Jus' ask her."

"I can't just blurt it out."

"Do you love her?"

"I think I do."

"An' does she love you?"

"I think she does."

"Then jus' ask her. Dinnae beat about any longer. She willnae thank you."

"I'm petrified she'll say no. Were you scared before you asked Isabel?"

"So scairt I hardly ate or slept for a fortnight. Took me that long to get up the courage."

"And were you two happy?"

"Very, Sir," Angus said as he bent down and plucked a blade of grass.

"I don't mean to be selfish, but I do need advisement."

"Do you think you can spend the rest o' your life wi' her and be content? Do you think she'll be willing to stay with you and be the Laird's wife?"

"I certainly hope she can."

"I cannae tell you if it be right or wrong. If you love Miss Shand and she loves you, and you think she'll make you happy then it be braw."

22

After a long three days in the main building, the housemother came for Sarah. "Come with me," she ordered.

"Where are you taking me?"

"If you don't want to go to the women's asylum, you can stay here."

"I don't want to spend a minute longer in this place than I need to."

The new accommodations resembled a large house. The heavy oak front door contained a leaded glass panel. Inside, the hallway was bright. Pastel flowered wallpaper adorned the walls. The ceilings, while not as high as Weetshill's, were at least ten to twelve feet. A large, winding staircase stood along the side wall. Surprisingly, it was homely.

The jackets of the female employees' uniforms were identical to those in the central hospital except for the colour. Here they were green. In the primary building, they were navy blue. Regardless of which section of the institution the patients were housed, they wore purple. Sarah needed to get her hands on one of the worker's coats. Once in her possession, she'd put it on inside out under hers, and tack a few stitches in to hold it in place. At the perfect moment, reverse the two layers and walk out of the loony bin without a backward glance. But, that meant finding one her size, and so far the attendants were much bulkier than she was.

Sarah found a place to sit near a window in the day room, hoping none of the other patients would notice her.

While she tried to think of a way out of her prison, somebody bumped into her wooden rocker. She turned to yell at the person but stopped when a youngster no more than eight years old stood in front of her. An overweight woman with dirty hair and wild eyes lunged for the little girl. The child jumped back, cowering behind Sarah's seat. In a mass of flailing arms and legs, Sarah and her chair toppled to the floor.

Out from the bottom of the pile, she got between the big woman and the small girl. "Leave her alone, you nutcase. She's just little. Pick on someone your own size," she yelled and pushed the woman.

Even though she and her sister fought and bad-mouthed each other, the event reminded her of their days at the Kendonald Primary School. Rachel had been small for her age, and she had rescued her younger sibling from bullies more than once.

"What's your name?" She asked the tiny, wide-eyed girl.

"J-J-Jenny."

"I'm Sarah. Why was that woman attacking you?" She smoothed the girl's dark, matted hair.

"I-I-I d-d-dinnae ken."

"She gives you any more trouble, you find me. I'll see she doesn't harm you again."

The words were barely out of her mouth when the hefty woman tackled her, "She's my doll, nae your'n," she screeched. The inmate glommed her and smashed her head against the floor.

"G-get off me," Sarah laboured as the enormous woman's weight crushed her ribcage. The small girl screamed.

What sounded like a dripping faucet right by her face turned out to be Jenny wetting herself. Before the growing puddle spread any further, members of the staff pulled the woman off and helped Sarah to her feet.

Woozy from having her head bashed, she couldn't stand without assistance. A female employee righted her chair and sat her down.

Dazed, she tried to focus on her attacker, but her vision remained blurred. Two, no three, no two people stood before her.

The patient screamed, "Let me go," and attempted to escape from the attendant holding her back. Finally, two more employees, men this time, came with a straight jacket, bound the woman, and took her away.

Once the excitement abated, a worker snatched Sarah by the arm and said, "Come on. We're going to the matron's office."

"Suppose you tell me what that was all about?" the head of the institution said as she sat behind her desk.

"I have no clue. That woman attacked a kid. I didn't start it. When she rugby tackled my chair and tipped us over, trying to get to a little girl, I ended up on the bottom of the heap. What was I supposed to do? Sit back and watch her beat the child?"

The administrator peered over her glasses at her, the same way

Granny Shand looked at her and Rachel when they misbehaved. "Whether you did or not, the incident goes on your record. Three times and we send you back to the other building. Any further bother, and you go back into the cell. Do I make myself clear?"

"Crystal," she grumbled. "Why is she in here? This doesn't seem to be the place for a small child."

"Isn't your business. I suggest you go back to the day room and stay out of trouble."

Sarah stood and leaned on the desk. "I saved the girl from a beating and for my efforts, got a right rollocking. I think I deserve to know."

"Don't threaten me, lassie." The matron rose and took a few steps forward, so she was practically nose to nose with her.

"She stutters, and she wet herself. Big deal. Little one was probably scared mindless. Certainly, no reason for being here."

"More to it than that."

"Tell me, then. She seems like a super kid. Just had a rough go of things."

"She's got the falling sickness. Brought here and left when she had her first fit. By the way, your threat is number two."

Someone dumped Jenny in the mental hospital because she had epilepsy. One of Sarah's schoolmates from The Gordon Schools suffered from the disease. Admitted to the Scottish Epilepsy Centre at Quarriers Village, her medication was regulated. The most recent time Sarah saw her, she was living a normal, healthy life.

After her trip to the matron's office, she sat by the window and contemplated her situation. Extra care was needed if the woman was true to her word. The last thing she wanted was to go back to the central building. She worried about Jenny. Was she all right?

At four o'clock, the supper bell clanged, and the patients made their way to the dining room. A scan for the child proved fruitless. She hoped the attack on her didn't bring on more seizures. At least, the woman who started the fight wasn't in the room.

Later, when they announced lights out, the matron ushered her to her room. Punishment for her involvement in the brawl in the day room or her protection?

Changed into her asylum issue nightgown, Sarah crawled into bed, trying to find a comfortable position that didn't bother her sore ribs. It took a long time, but eventually, she drifted off.

The blankets moved, and someone joined her. She jerked awake and sat up, terrified of what she might find. Jenny snuggled beside her. Sarah covered them both up and put her arm around the small girl. They remained in the same position all night.

When Sarah woke the next morning, Jenny's hair was matted worse than before. "Let's make you look good and smell nice."

"M-me?"

"Of course you, silly," she said as she held out her hand in invitation. "I bet your hair is beautiful when it's brushed and styled."

"N-n-no! J-Jenny doesnae want that," she objected when Sarah tried to brush the matted hair.

The job would be so much easier with real shampoo and conditioner. "Do you want to look pretty?"

"L-l-like S-S-Sarah?"

"Yes, like me." The two words used in conjunction with each other weren't ones that came to mind. Blair's unfaithfulness sealed it for her. She forced a smile. A memory was dredged to the surface bringing along the taste of chips. Vinegar was her mum's go-to when she ran out of conditioner.

Sarah beckoned an attendant. "Have you seen the state of this wee girl's hair? I can't get a comb through it."

The woman shrugged.

"Can I have some vinegar? Not much. About half a cup at most."

"What do you plan on using that for?"

"To put in Jenny's hair so I can untangle it without hurting her," she replied adding 'too much' under her breath. Short of shaving the child's head, she could not think of anything else that would help.

After a long wait, someone brought a small cup of the requested liquid to her. Sarah gave the petite girl a rag to hold over her eyes and instructed her to lean over the tub. She wet her hair again with water, then applied the vinegar and rubbed the acidic solution in from the scalp to the ends.

"Owwww."

"I'm sorry, sweetie. I'm not hurting you on purpose. Whoever let your hair get into this mess should be ..."

"Should be what?"

Sarah turned around. The woman scowled at her. "How about a good hiding to start with?"

"Crazed thing wouldn't let anyone near her until you came along."

"She's not crazy. Where I come from, you could be arrested for child abuse."

"Hmph," she snorted and stomped away, and turned back when she reached the door. "You're getting mighty close to number three. The only reason you're not already there, is we don't have time to deal with that one." The woman nodded toward Jenny.

Eventually, all the tangles disappeared. The protests became less frequent after the application of vinegar. Even the simplest tasks were difficult nursing sore ribs. Working through severely matted hair didn't help. Sarah discovered a heart-shaped birthmark when she tied Jenny's hair into a French braid. Her grandmother had told her they called birthmarks on the neck stork bites or angel kisses. "Come on; we better go for breakfast."

"J-Jenny p-pretty?" she asked, her eyes sparkling.

"Yes. I'll show you in the mirror." But there was no looking glass anywhere.

By the time they got to the dining room, the morning meal was no longer available. Sarah raised a fuss and got a bowl of oatmeal for the little girl.

After Jenny had eaten her fill of the asylum's cooking, she took her to the day room. "Let's play I spy with my little eye."

"Wh-what's that?"

"Well, we look around and find something then describe it. Here, I'll go first and teach you."

She nodded.

"Hmm, I spy something that is green."

"I-is i-it th-the t-table?"

The child didn't know her colours. She would need to learn them before they could go any further. "No, sweetie. Green is the colour of the jackets the staff wear and the grass."

With a great deal of patience, she got her to recognize the fundamental ones. On her turn at the game, she ensured she adhered to only those objects.

The little girl seemed to enjoy it. The lifeless eyes that stared at her in the beginning now sparkled with life.

Sarah was tired of only getting fresh air when the windows or doors opened. Her opportunity came the following day when an attendant took her to the airing court.

Finally, an employee who was about her size and wearing a green jacket. If she got her hands on one of those pieces of clothing, her plan was already in place. There was no way she could run away and leave the youngster behind.

"Young Jenny is fair fond of you. Must be something mighty special to win her over. She doesnae normally take to folk."

Sarah inhaled and said, "Obviously, you didn't hear. She was getting a pounding from one of the adults, and I intervened."

"We're pleased you took such a shine to her and she to you. That wee girl had been quite the handful before you came along. Most days we had to let the bairn run wild because we couldn't take the time to chase her."

Flattered by the attendant's comments, Sarah blushed.

The airing court had become overgrown by brush and weeds. "Too bad they don't clear this and plant fruit trees and a garden."

"'Tis a fine thought, but we hasnae anyone to do the work or take care of it. We're already short staffed." The alarm bell blared, cutting their conversation short. "Can you keep Jenny out of trouble? I must go."

"Where is she? I didn't see her this morning."

"S-S-Sarah," a small voice called.

She turned, and before she could react, she was flat on her back with the young girl sitting on her giggling wildly.

A steam engine's whistle blew as Sarah lay on the ground. The noise distracted her. She crawled out and sought the source of the sound. Black smoke belched from the stack. A gust of wind relayed the conductor's voice announcing the boarding calls. Now she waited for an Aberdeen train announcement to figure out which direction it travelled.

Looking after the child made the time in the asylum bearable. Did Jenny suffer seizures after lights out? Sarah had not seen her have another one since the day of the brawl with the huge patient. Even her speech impediment was much improved.

After the attendant's comment about how the staff appreciated her help with Jenny, they did not watch her as closely when she was with the little girl.

One day, when they were out in the grounds unsupervised, she disappeared behind a clump of hydrangeas near the wall. A moment later, she poked her head back out and gestured to Sarah. Behind the bushes, was a semi-rotted door about two feet high, secured with a rusty chain. Jenny removed the manacle and pulled the door open.

A root cellar? Her grandparents had one, but she was never allowed to enter it. It was dark and underground and dangerous. Wasn't this too far from the building to serve that purpose?

Once in, she beckoned Sarah to follow. She had to crawl on her hands and knees to fit through the small opening. Inside, the room was big enough to stand in, but in the dim light from the open door, not a thing was visible. "What is this place?"

"T-they b-bring dead people here."

That explained why the door was so small. It didn't need to be large to slide coffins through.

She grabbed the little girl by the hand and yanked her out. "Why would you take me inside there?"

Jenny started shaking. It was the beginning of a seizure. She pulled the little girl to the ground and held her tight.

The convulsion ended, and Sarah bundled her into her arms and rocked her back and forth. "Are you all right? I'm sorry I yelled at you."

"G-go b-back in," she insisted. "D-dead p-people c-can't hurt you, they only smell b-bad."

Why was it so crucial she went back inside? She shrugged her shoulders and crawled into the crypt, feeling her way along the wall until she reached the far end. She brushed her palms over the entire rough surface and discovered another wooden door. This one was about her height. She located a knob and turned. The portal opened about an inch or two. A chain on the other side prevented it from opening further. Sarah strained to look through the crack and spotted grass and blue sky – freedom. The wood creaked and groaned as she pushed against the door. Like the one behind her, this one was rotten. With some effort, she might be able to force the thing open or break it down. She found her escape route.

She backed into something as she retreated deeper within the chamber. With trepidation, she turned and ran her hands over a stack of coffins. Chills down her spine made the hairs on the back of her neck bristle, and she scrambled outside.

Sarah wrapped her arms around her and said, "Thank you for showing me how to get out of here."

"J-Jenny come too?"

It would be hard enough to flee on her own, but she couldn't leave the little girl behind. "Yes, you can come."

"L-let's g-go n-now!"

Breaking out right then was tempting. "Not now. I need to work some things out. In the morning after breakfast, I promise." They could escape right after they ate, and no one would miss them until lunchtime. By then they could be miles away.

"Busy place tonight, isn't it?" Angus said to Callum as they crossed over the threshold of the public house.

" To be sure. I dinnae think there was this many folk in Kendonald."

"Oh, Tommy frae Christie's be here. We'll join him," he said as he signalled the barman.

The tavern was alive with people. Most nights, there might only be a handful of men in enjoying a quiet drink after a long day's work. Tonight it thrummed with excitement.

"Oi, what's all the strushan?" he said as he pulled out a chair and sat.

"I dinnae ken."

Something in the ghillie's reply bothered him. He was about to ask more questions when Callum brought over their drinks.

"Been talk of a young lassie having been packed off to the asylum a while back," he said as he distributed the whiskies and took a seat.

"Tommy? Ken anything aboot that?" Angus figured he knew the lassie's identity but needed confirmation.

"N-nothing."

"What a load of shite. You know exactly who was took. What say the three o' us take a walk over the road and have a talk with Police Constable Skinner?"

"I cannae."

"Start talkin', Tommy," the Weetshill gamekeeper said. "We both ken 'at you ken." He nodded to his companion.

"Well ... she ... she be Miss Shand. She isnae right in the head. I found her kissin' Miss Letitia on the lips at the stone circle up at Gleanstane."

"She's had a bump to her heid, nowt else. No need to lock her away," Callum said.

"What about the things Jean MacDonald's been sayin'," he lowered his voice as he spoke.

"Crivvens, Tommy. That old bat isnae more than a bletherin' skyte. Daft as the day is long, she is. So keep talkin'," Angus bellowed. "Where was she taken?"

"I cannae tell you."

He stood, towering over the seated ghillie. "You'll tell me, or we'll be takin' a walk to the police station.

"L-L-Ladysbridge."

"That isnae even in this shire," said Callum.

Angus gulped down his dram. "We needs to get back to Weetshill and tell the Laird." He turned to Thomas Sievewright. "How could you, man? No tell a soul what's happened to Miss Shand. You shoulda told young Mr. Robertson straight away. Save all this nonsense."

It was late when the men returned. A lone lamp glowed through the windows. "Should we tell him tonight?" Callum asked.

"Sooner he kens, the better."

The door was locked and bolted. Angus hammered on it with his fist.

"Whatever is the matter?" the butler said.

"Is - he the mister - still awake? We saws the light in the library."

"I believe he's still in there."

"We gots news for him," Callum spoke up.

Archibald ushered them into the room. Robert was comatose on the sofa, a couple of days' stubble on his face. A glass lay on its side on the floor, surrounded by a spreading wet spot. The nearly empty decanter sat on the coffee table.

"Wee Robbie, you's got yourself into a' awful state. I ne'er thought I would see you like this," Angus said as he knelt by his employer's head. "I needs you to wake up. I has news. Good news."

Robert groaned but did not open his eyes.

"I ken where she is," he shouted, trying to rouse his sleeping employer.

"W-what?"

"Miss Shand. They's took her to the asylum o'er by Ladysbridge Station."

"B-but ... I asked. No one knew a thing. I don't understand."

Callum stepped forward. "I was getting the drinks in at the Kendonald Arms, and there was talk o' a young lassie bein' taken away mair than a week ago."

Robert propped himself up on his elbow. "And?"

"Come to find out Tommy Sievewright knew all along. He talked when I said we'd take a walk to have a chat with the police constable," Angus said.

"I asked after her. Skinner claimed he knew nothing."

"I wouldnae be so sure. The Christie's ghillie didnae want us to talk to him," Callum added.

"We must go to her." He jumped up. "Come, we must get her out."

"We'll leave at first light, Sir. It's too late to be settin' off tonight."

23

The following morning on her way to breakfast, Sarah sought out the little girl, and they entered the room together. "Make sure you eat lots," she whispered. "It could be a long time before we get the opportunity."

Jenny raised her head and nodded.

While she ate, Sarah stashed dried slices of burnt toast in her pockets. They would at least have this if they couldn't find any food on their journey.

Their meal finished, she left the room first and waited in the entryway for the small girl. "You go to the place you showed me and wait for me. I'll be there as soon as I can. Run."

Once Jenny was out the door, Sarah walked out behind her, hoping to attract as little attention as possible today. With her luck, this would be the day their actions would be under a microscope.

A noise from behind scared her, and she hid behind a tree as two men advanced from the wall.

She examined her surroundings, ensuring no one was about and started down the hill. When she spotted her fellow escapee, she put her finger to her lips and said, "I wondered where you got off to."

Sarah waited until the men left. Once they were gone, she urged Jenny to hurry. Outside the crypt, she said, "We need to hide in here until I can batter down the door. Will you be all right?"

The little girl nodded.

"I promise everything will work out and I'll be right there beside you. All I need you to do is swear you'll manage in there until we escape. We'll be separated if we're caught." Sarah hoped no one heard the racket when she tried to demolish the wood.

A single carrion crow swooped down from a nearby tree landing on the top of the wall. The bird was soon joined by another and then another. Their squawking and cawing filled the air. "Shut up, you stupid birds," she muttered, hoping their cacophony would not attract attention.

Before entering the tomb, she reached down and grasped the chain, thinking she could use it in self-defence if someone discovered them. A pungent, sour odour that had not been there on her first foray into the place saturated the cavern as she crawled into the unlit space.

Sarah had almost worked her way to the door to freedom when she stumbled over a bundle on the ground. The hideous stench overpowered her. There was no mistaking the rancid stink of decomposition. The crypt was empty before. How many more corpses were in here to trip over? She scrambled to her feet, and her hand brushed the fabric covering the cadaver. It was one of the scratchy wool blankets from all the beds. Did they bring them back and re-use them after disposing of the bodies? She bit down on her lower lip to keep from screaming. "We probably should go back to the asylum before they come for the body and catch us."

About to turn and crawl back through the small door, male voices resonated beyond the outer one. Sarah clapped her hand over Jenny's mouth and held her breath.

The click of a key in a lock startled her. She clutched the little girl and pulled her into the corner behind the stack of coffins, hoping to remain hidden. "It will be all right."

The door opened, and the light blinded her. Again she covered the girl's mouth with her hand. Something with many legs crawled across Sarah's face, and she willed herself not to brush the creature away, or worse, scream. They were so close to getting away, yet on the verge of being discovered. Her heart thumped so hard she was sure whoever was on the other side heard it, too.

The men dragged the remains out, and the blanket fell away from the corpse's face. The deceased was the big woman who attacked them. Was this how the asylum disposed of troublesome patients?

"Another fine specimen," a man said.

"We aim to please."

"I assume I'm providing you with an adequate supply," a familiar voice said. The Superintendent.

"Here's your payment. Can I count on you to provide another corpse soon?"

"But remember, you don't know from where you're obtaining the bodies. The council won't take kindly to finding out they're coming from here. With a decent stipend, I wouldn't have to do this in the first place. There won't be any more for you if I'm dismissed."

After what seemed like hours, the door slammed, and the lock clicked. Was the wooden door rotten enough to shatter? The clatter of horses' hooves faded away, and she rammed her shoulder into the surface.

Several attempts later, the door frame cracked. The opening widened enough for a little person to squeeze through, but too small for Sarah. "You go, and if I can't get out, run away as fast as you can."

"B-but d-don't want to l-leave S-Sarah."

"Stay tight to the stone fence. I'll tell you when it's time to go." Sarah leaned into the door so that Jenny could crawl out. "There's my brave girl," she said then pressed her lips to the child's forehead. "Move away from the door, so the wood splinters don't hit you."

She flung herself against it again and again, but the chain held fast. Pain sliced through her arm like a knife, worsening every time she slammed into the door. Not ready to give up yet, she kicked at the lower part, but it still wouldn't budge. Finally, she collapsed against the wall, exhausted. "I can't get out," she gasped. "Run." Then a loud bang startled her, followed by another. With one final whack, the corner of the door below the cable disintegrated, and Jenny stood there holding a big rock in her hands.

"J-Jenny g-get S-Sarah out." She put it down and helped Sarah scramble through to freedom. They made it.

Robert woke early, kicking himself for not looking harder for Sarah before. He was sick as he imagined the hell she must be going through.

Turning up the paraffin lamps, he peered into the mirror over his washstand and didn't like his reflection. Unshaven and unkempt, this was not the way he wanted her to see him.

Shaving brush lathered, Robert spread the white, creamy foam on his whiskers. Carefully wielding his straight razor, he managed to shave without cutting himself. He dried his face, and the pressure exerted intensified his headache. An after effect of the previous night. He wished he had, what was it Sarah called it? Oh yes, Paracetamol.

Robert turned down the lamps and crept downstairs so not to wake anyone. The grandfather clock in the great hall chimed five o'clock as he tiptoed past.

"Mr. Robertson, you is up early this morn."

The voice startled him. "Aye, Morag. I didn't expect you up at this hour."

"Much work to do in a day. Needs to get started. Come, let me fix you somethin'."

"I-I don't have time."

"Come."

Robert was fighting a losing battle. He schlepped along behind the woman into the kitchen. Since he was a boy, this was the first time he infiltrated the cook's domain. Morag had allowed him and Margaret to come in when she baked special sweets around the holidays.

"Sit. I mean, Sir, please sit down."

"Don't worry. I won't think badly of you for ordering me about."

"I dinnae ken what you has got on for today, but must be somethin' important to get you up this early."

Angus walked in through the scullery door. "You're lookin' much better than the last time I saw you. Are you ready for the off?"

"I cannae abide the pair o' you goin' off without a hearty breakfast."

"We don't have time," Robert protested.

"You'll both eat. Won't take me but a moment to get some food on."

He looked at the ghillie. "I think we're here for a wee while."

"Dinnae fash, Sir. There be plenty o' time."

"Are we going by train?"

"Be faster wi' the horse and carriage. Wi' all the stops it makes and the strange path it takes."

"You're probably right."

The cook quickly prepared eggs and fried bread, and brewed coffee. "Here you be. I ken it be summink important you must attend to," she said as she sat the plates in front of them.

"I think we should stop by Dr. Burnett's on our way," Robert said.

"If you wish, Sir. You doesnae think he had somethin' to do with all this, do you?"

Until suggested, he never entertained the idea. "Of course not, but he might be able to help us get Sarah out of that terrible place." Why did Police Constable Skinner deny knowing where she was? Was he in cahoots with them?

"Best o' luck to you," Morag said when the men left.

The doctor's surgery was on the way to Kendonald, so Angus steered the horse that way. Fortune smiled on them because when they got there, the man was home.

Robert related the news of Sarah's whereabouts to the physician. "I wondered if you knew anything," he concluded.

"When did you say it happened?"

"Most likely the day Letitia Christie tried to take her own life."

"Hmm…, yes that day. I was at the Cooper steading from sun up until I went to Gleanstane. One of their workers was grievously injured when he fell from the hay mow. Unfortunate soul landed on a pitchfork which is why it took me so long to travel back to attend to Miss Christie."

"So you knew nothing of this," Robert reiterated.

"No. Miss Shand was confused after a head injury, but I never thought she was insane. I wouldn't have anything to do with having her committed. Miss Letitia swore that it was Miss Shand who saved her. I'm inclined to believe the girl, no matter how distraught she was."

Sarah checked right and left for traffic, but no one was out - either walking or in carriages. She turned back in the direction they came from, too, in case someone watched from the cap of the wall. "Come. We've got to run." She took the child's hand. They dashed across the roadway and into the field. "Thank you for coming up with your ingenious plan to get me out," she complimented as they ran.

The station stood ahead of them. They could hide in the brush and wait for the trains to come in. Once the conductor called for a train bound for Aberdeen, they could tag along behind it down the tracks. The burn flowing between them and the depot came as a complete surprise. At the bank, Sarah skidded to a stop and put her other arm out to keep the child from falling in.

The stream was narrow, but it was about four feet down to the water from where they stood. "Come on; we'll go around by the road. Will be safer." She checked over her shoulder again to ensure no one gave chase. On the route leading to the Ladysbridge Station, Sarah found them a place to hide behind a stack of ties.

The familiar chugging of a locomotive, followed by the hiss of steam came from the far side of the building. Finally, the conductor's call came. "All aboard for Bridgefoot, Golf Club House, Banff Harbour and Banff," he declared. The engine pulled away from the platform, and they lingered until the last carriage disappeared around the bend.

This rail line didn't exist in Sarah's time. How close would they get to Weetshill if they kept to the tracks? At least now, she had an idea of the way to go. "Come on, this way." She took Jenny's hand, and they started for what she thought was the direction of the Huntly Road.

Once she reached the town, she could make her way to Kendonald easily. From there, it was a short walk to Robert's home.

"I-I'm scairt," she whimpered.

"I'm scared, too, sweetie." Sarah bent down and cuddled the little girl.

"W-what if they c-catches us?"

"I'm going to do my best to make sure they don't. Come on. The sooner we're away from here, the better."

Every time the clopping of horses' hooves clattered in the distance, she grabbed the little girl's hand, and they took cover in the bushes along the road. Sarah tried to make their breakout fun for her, so she didn't freak out and suffer a seizure. "Would you like me to teach you a game?"

Jenny nodded.

"I'll teach you how to play the game hide and seek. I'm going to close my eyes and count to ten. While I'm doing that you go into hiding, then I try to find you. Do you think you can do that?"

"Y-yes."

"I'm going to start counting. Just don't go too far away. Then once I've found you, you can count, and I'll find a place to disappear," Sarah said as she shut her eyes and began. "... eight, nine, ten. Ready or not, here I come," she yelled and opened her eyes. "I wonder where she could be," she said aloud.

She turned around, but there was no trace of the little girl. How far could someone that size go in such a short time? Maybe this game wasn't a good idea after all. A tug on the back of her skirt made her look over her shoulder. Jenny wore a wide, cheesy grin on her face. "Were you there the whole time?"

"Y-yes."

"My turn now. You close your eyes and count to ten then try to find me."

The excited youngster closed her eyes and covered them with her hands. "O-one, f-four, s-six..."

It was clear the child didn't know the correct numerical sequence. Could she make a game out of teaching her that? In the meantime, Sarah hid behind a nearby oak tree. "Come look for me, I'm hidden," she called.

"I-I f-found you. Th-that was easy!"

"If we hear anyone coming, we're going to hide, too. Won't that be fun?" she added, to prevent frightening the child.

Their game continued for the next mile or so, and Sarah counted for both of them. She wished she knew where she was related to Kendonald. She only knew the route from the village. Right out from the police office, then another right at the Huntly Road. But after that, she didn't know.

Without a watch, there was no way of knowing how long they walked. The workers burned her comfortable boots along with the rest of her clothes when she arrived at the asylum. The pair the refuge provided her with pinched in some places and chafed in others. Sarah sat on a fallen log, pulled her footwear off, and wiggled her toes. She tossed them into the bushes.

Their asylum-issue outfits were conspicuous which would draw unwanted attention to them. They needed something else, but for now, they couldn't stop.

She tugged at Sarah's skirt. "I-I'm h-hungry."

"Me, too." A farmhouse stood in the distance with a meadow between them and it. Maybe they could find something to munch on there. "Just a bit further." She tried to ignore the rumbling in her stomach even though they didn't leave until after the morning meal. Then Sarah remembered stuffing toast in her pockets. She reached in but found nothing but crumbs. Compartments turned inside out, she shook the bits into her hand and licked her palm. Jenny mimicked her, and they managed to obtain a minuscule amount of nourishment.

Laundry flapped on a clothesline near the stone cottage. The colourful array of articles whipped in the wind. Some minor modifications were required, but Sarah could make them work.

She became more worried the closer they got. As she pondered a way of getting the items off the line without being noticed, the distant clopping of horses' hooves grew louder.

"Quick. We must hide." She took Jenny's hand and led her to the dry stone dyke along the road. She boosted the little girl across the barrier then scrambled over herself.

"Th-this is f-fun."

Fun? After the horse and carriage clattered by, she peered over and sighed with relief. Back against the stones, she closed her eyes. An apple was thrust into her face when she opened them. "Where did you get that?"

The small girl pointed to an orchard.

"You didn't take that off a tree did you?"

"N-no."

"Good." The farmer wouldn't object to them taking some windfalls, would he? The trees remained heavily laden with ripe fruit. She took off her jacket, and the two of them harvested as many apples as they could.

"Hey, you. You there," a man shouted. "Be off."

Sarah turned in the direction of the angry voice. The man brandished a shotgun. "Quickly, we've got to get out of here." A blast shattered the silence as they tumbled over the dyke, and the fruit they had gathered spilled on the ground. They retrieved what they could and ran.

"C-can we do it again?"

"Great. I created a pre-teen tearaway."

Further down the road, they came across another clothesline full of laundry. No one was nearby, so Sarah left the little girl by the fence and crept across the fields. Looking around, she pulled the pegs off a few pieces and raced back to the wall. Jenny's dress was too big, so she rolled up the sleeves and the middle, tied the belt around the little girl's waist, and hoped it would stay hitched up.

Once she had the little one clothed, Sarah put on the items she had snagged for herself and stuffed their uniforms under a straggly holly bush. She hoped they would be far away before someone discovered the garments

"St-stealing is b-bad."

"I know, sweetie. We're only borrowing these things. Once we're back at Weetshill, I'll have them laundered and taken back to their rightful owners. And if they're not fit to wear again, then I'll have Robert send the family money so they can replace them."

They followed the track until they came to a T-junction with a more travelled road. The position of the sun indicated they'd been walking for well over an hour.

Robert fidgeted on the carriage's driver seat beside Angus. Sixty minutes later they reached the crossroad, and they still had a minimum of another twenty miles to travel.

"Can't you make this creature go any faster?"

"I cannae run her all the way to Ladysbridge, Sir. She'll drop dead afore we're halfway there. If Miss Shand is there like we's hearin', she'll be there when we get there. Best to take our time."

"You're far more knowledgeable when it comes to animals than I am. I trust your judgment."

Angus snapped the reins again bringing the mare to a gallop, and they moved along quickly for a time. They were almost at Bogniebrae when he pulled back and slowed her to a steady walk. "She needs a rest and water, Sir."

"Very well."

The ruins of Bognie Castle stood in the field to the east.

"We'll stop in here. See if we can water the auld gal afore going on." Angus turned into the laneway further up the road. A young man was busy mending a fence. "We're on our way tae Ladysbridge," he called out. "Could our animal drink and rest here afore we carry on?"

"Aye. Water just over there." He directed their attention to a trough outside the barn. "You got any crazy people in there?" The farmhand eyed the men with suspicion.

"No. Why do you ask?" Robert descended from the carriage.

"There was a wagon stopped a few days back with a woman inside screamin' her head off."

"Was it tall and narrow with bars on the back window?"

"A Black Maria. Aye."

"Skinner, and yet when I went to him, he claimed to know nothing," Robert said through clenched teeth. "That … that bastard." His temperature rose in anger, and he balled his hands into fists.

The horse rested and drank. Angus took a feedbag out of the box on the back of the brougham and held it while the mare ate.

"Thank you for your kindness," he said. As they passed the young man on their way out the driveway. "Come, we've no time to waste."

"J-Jenny t-tired."

They had travelled quite a distance, so no wonder she was exhausted. "Here, climb up on my back," Sarah said. "Now put your arms around my neck and hang on."

Sarah piggy-backed the small child for the next mile or so, and the longer she walked, the heavier the little girl grew. She searched for landmarks known to her in the future, but saw none, and wondered if she had gone the wrong way.

The crumbling structure of Bognie Castle stood in farmland off to the left. The stormy sky showed through three rows of window openings in the only whole wall. Sarah came here on a primary school trip when she was about eleven years old. Nothing changed in the years between 1886 and her time. Relief washed over her. She knew where she was.

Robert climbed out of the carriage, checked his pocket watch, and strode to the door of the asylum building. He raised the ring on the lion's head knocker and struck the plate four times. No one answered, so he rapped again. Still no response. It wasn't until he used his fist that the locks released and the door opened.

A short, sour-faced woman with grey-streaked hair greeted them. "What can I help you with?"

The men muscled their way through the door, barely giving the woman a chance to get out of their way. "We're here for Miss Shand," he said. "I understand she was admitted a few days ago."

"You need to see the Superintendent. Wait here, please."

Robert turned to his ghillie. "I can't bear to think of her being in this place."

"Nae much longer now, Sir. We'll be takin' her away wi' us."

A tall man in a dark suit joined them. "I'm Mr. Nelson overseer of this institution. How may I be of assistance, gentlemen?"

Robert repeated the purpose of the visit. "The lassie should never have been brought here."

"Miss Shand? Do we have a Miss Shand here, matron?"

"No, Sir." The woman twisted a handkerchief in her hands. "We did, but we discharged her to the Asylum for Women."

"And where is that? We've travelled a long way today, and we're not leaving without her," said Robert.

"Would you show them the way? I must return to my paperwork."

"This way, gentlemen." She guided the men out the front door to another structure that looked like a substantial private home. "We can only have so many patients in the central building or need to have a doctor on staff. Well, we can't afford that, so we built the women's sanatorium instead."

On the porch, she turned the doorbell key. Its shrill ringing could have awakened the dead, but no one came in answer.

Robert reached past the woman and tapped on the leaded glass window. After a lengthy wait, an employee opened the door.

"Whatever is going on in here?" the matron demanded.

Women in uniform dashed from one room to another. Doors slammed, and people shouted. He stepped into the vestibule and looked around. Even though it seemed like a homely place, he still hated to think of her imprisoned there. He couldn't deny his feelings any longer. He had fallen in love with her.

"Oh Mrs. Nelson, one of our patients is missing," the worker lamented.

"Which one?"

"The new girl, Sarah, the one who got beat protecting the child. She's only been with us a few days."

"You let her get beaten?" Robert shouted.

"We went to her aid as fast as we could. She's not the only one in here. We have thirty-nine other patients to watch."

"How long do you suspect she's been missing?" Robert's rage neared the boiling point.

"Best as we can tell after breakfast. The last place anyone saw Miss Shand was in the dining hall, but no one's seen her since," the employee bawled.

"You haven't raised the alarm?"

"No. I wanted to locate her without all that fuss."

"How could you be so careless? She could be anywhere by now," Robert snapped.

"The bairn cannae be found either. D'you think she might be with the Shand lassie?"

"We've got more important things to worry about than that child and her fits."

The matron's tone came across cold and uncaring. He turned and started towards the door, crushed having missed Sarah by a matter of hours. Now she was out there all alone, and he might never find her. Even worse, maybe she wouldn't want to be seen? It could be, she blamed him for her ending up in the asylum. Soon after her arrival at Weetshill, he'd promised her she would not be sent there.

24

"If only we had come yesterday. Now Miss Shand is gone, and we may never pinpoint her whereabouts."

"We'll do our best. Where would you like to start?"

"Ladysbridge Station."

"She willnae have money, Sir."

"We have to begin somewhere. Perhaps someone will recall seeing her in the area?"

Angus turned the horse and carriage around, and they started back to the main road.

Despite his inquiries at the railway stop, no one saw anyone fitting Sarah's description the day she escaped. Dejected, Robert schlepped back to the carriage. By now, Sarah could be far away from here. If she found her way back to Weetshill, he vowed on his life to protect her. "We best make a start for home, Angus. But drive slowly. We'll keep watch for her on the way."

The carriage creaked and bounced along the pothole-ridden road. Robert scoured the landscape for any trace of Sarah. In some places, thick hedgerows completely obscured the view of the surrounding countryside.

They had travelled about a mile and half when something caught Robert's eye. "Stop the carriage, Angus." He leapt out and scrambled to the bushes and pulled out a pair of women's boots. "She's been this way." Upon keener inspection, his shoulders slumped. "These aren't Sarah's."

"She wouldnae have her things, Sir. They'd take them away frae her there. Only have what they give her."

Robert took heart from the ghillie's words, knowing if the footwear bothered her feet, she'd get rid of them. The thought of her walking great distances in stocking feet angered him almost as much as the events that were responsible for her commitment.

"Looks like rain, Sir. I'll put the top up," said Angus.

"Thank you." He clutched the button tops to his chest. While there was no proof she had worn them, there was none to the contrary either.

The ghillie made the adjustments. "Here you go, Sir. You best get in," he said as he opened the brougham's door.

Robert boarded. No sooner was the door closed, the rains came in a torrential deluge. Sarah would catch her death if she were out in this storm.

Sarah hoisted Jenny over the dry stone dyke along the road, and they ran to the ruins.

Oblivious to the few spatters of rain, the little girl wandered around the remains. "Wh-what's this place?"

"A castle."

"Wh-why is it f-falling d-down?"

"The people who lived here hundreds of years ago might have set it on fire."

"Wh-why b-burn your h-house?"

"To keep it from falling into enemy hands or the enemies burnt the family out."

The intervals between raindrops shortened, and the deluge started. With the child in her arms, Sarah scampered through one of the lower windows into an alcove in the end wall.

With Jenny situated at the back of the recess, she sat in front of her, shielding her from the rain. Mind and body exhausted, she rested her forehead on her knees and began to bawl in gut-wrenching sobs.

"D-d-dinnae cry." She stroked her hair as she spoke.

Sarah took a deep breath and exhaled slowly. Her emotions got the better of her, and she had to be strong for the little girl.

After an hour or so, the downpour passed over, and the sun peeked through the clouds. "The rain has stopped, finally. Let's go."

Robert lowered the window and called out to Angus. "Go towards Huntly. I don't know how familiar Miss Shand is with the country roads, so she's apt to keep to the ones she knows."

"The sky is clear now, Sir. Would you like me to put the top back down? Make it much better to see."

"Please do."

The ghillie brought the carriage to a halt at the edge of the gravel.

Robert scanned the fields, hoping for some sign of her. The bright afternoon sun forced him to shield his eyes with his hand. She had vanished into the mist. The boots, which may not have been hers, were the only indication she might have travelled this way.

"Do you want me to go into Huntly, Sir?" Angus asked when they stopped at the Aberdeen Road.

"No. Just take us directly home, but keep to the main roads."

Before the Y-junction in Kendonald, Robert tapped his ghillie on the shoulder. "This sounds daft, but drive up past the stone circle at Gleanstane. Miss Shand doesn't always behave logically, so she just might be there."

"Aye, Sir."

They approached the ancient monument. "Would you stop for a moment, please? I want to get down and have a better look."

Angus reined in the horse bringing her to a halt.

Robert climbed out and walked across the windswept field. The place was as lonely and desolate as when he first visited after Sarah's disappearance.

He picked up a small rock, ran his fingers over its rough surface, and tucked the pebble into his pocket.

"Miss Shand isnae with you?" the butler asked.

"No, Archibald. We were too late. She left before we arrived."

"Gone?" The housekeeper asked as she came from the dining room. "What do you mean, Sir?"

"According to the administration, she escaped after breakfast with a young girl."

"And you been lookin' for her on your way home?"

"Of course, we have," Robert snapped. "I'm sorry, Mrs. MacEwen. I didn't intend to do that."

"You's all right, Sir. You's worrit."

"Where can she be?"

"I dinnae ken, Sir." the butler said, "but I pray she'll be safe and sound. The house is empty wi'out her. Even though she makes my hair stand on end, I miss bein' called 'Archie.'"

"Me, too, Archibald." Robert's voice trailed off as he stared out the window in the direction of the place Sarah referred to as Gordonsfield.

Margaret swept into the library. Her brother's furrowed brow and constant drumming of his fingers on the sofa told her he was agitated. "You were away early this morning. What was so urgent?"

"Business I had to attend to," Robert answered.

She sat beside him and put her hand on his arm. "You have my deepest sympathies," she said. "I'm aware you're missing Miss Shand, but I have to say this. If she thought anything about your feelings, she wouldn't have up and left the way she did."

"Sarah did what she thought was best. She wanted to make sure everyone here was safe. The men went to the public-house last night and had an interesting chat with Thomas Sievewright whilst they were there. After some persuading, Tommy told them Constable Skinner took Sarah off to the insane asylum over by Ladysbridge in Banffshire. Angus and I went to fetch her, but she had already escaped." Robert eyed his sister with suspicion. "I can't help but think it has something to do with Letitia. Can you tell me what is wrong with her? Even before her attempt on her life, she's been acting strangely. Not at all like the young girl we both frolicked with as children."

Margaret turned away.

Robert stared at her. "You do know something. Tell me, please. Why did you suddenly agree I should be out of the marriage contract?"

"I'm not aware of much. About the time you first went to see Horatio about terminating the arrangement, Letitia told me she would be a fine wife to you because she was 'prepared.' Then she rambled on about performing 'wifely duties' many times and having a plan to keep you and Sarah from getting married. I think she's sick. I'm worried about her."

"I have to wonder if she had anything to do with Sarah's being committed. Perhaps she's having a mental breakdown and needs to be in hospital, herself. Why don't you go visit her and see if you can find out what happened?"

Before Margaret reached the Kendonald Road on route to Gleanstane, a light rain began to fall. She regretted not taking the time to grab her cloak. Surely, her friend had nothing to do with Sarah's commitment, but the tone of Letitia's voice and the look in her eyes contradicted the woman's words.

"Oh, Miss Robertson, do come in," Carlyle greeted her. "Miss Christie is in her room. Do you need me to show you the way?"

Eyeing the aged butler, she replied, "No thank you."

"Very well."

Margaret rapped on the woman's door before opening it. "May I come in?" she asked.

Laying her embroidery in her lap, Letitia raised her head. "Kind of you to come."

"I just hope you don't think badly of me for not coming sooner, but I thought I would give you a bit of time to rest and heal."

"I'm glad you came." Teardrops spilled down Letitia's cheeks.

"Oh, you poor thing. Tell me why you are so upset."

After blowing her nose, she stuffed her handkerchief inside her sleeve. "I-I thought Sarah was my adversary. Thought she took my Robert away from me."

"What are you saying, Letitia?"

"S-Sarah rescued me."

"What?"

"I tried to kill myself. I drank poison because I wanted to die. I don't know how long I lay on the ground up there. I attempted to make it look like Sarah was involved because she likes the place. I wanted her blamed for my death, but my plan didn't quite work. Tommy was supposed to find me. He walks over that hillside at first light every morning. I wanted him to see me."

"He knew you were going to do this?"

"No. At first, I only drank a bit of the poison, but when I didn't think it was working, I guzzled the whole bottle. Sarah came along well before he made his morning rounds, and she found me instead. I remember waking up and seeing her covering me up with her cloak. It was cold that morning, and I would have frozen without the warmth of the heavy wool. Then back here I heard Doctor Burnett talking about what an exceptional job someone had done keeping me alive," she chattered. "Sarah told me she had thought about killing herself once because a man left her, and no man was worth it. I'm not sure what she did, but she saved my life."

Margaret's eyes moistened. "You're certain it was her?"

"Y-yes. Miss Shand was right. As much as I adore Robert, I'm glad now I didn't die."

"And now you're free to find someone else who will love you."

"I doubt if that will ever happen."

"I found a man who loves me, so you could, too," Margaret said, rubbing Letitia's upper arm.

"Is your marriage a happy one?"

"Yes. George is a respectable merchant in Edinburgh. He is a wonderful husband and provider."

"How did you meet him?"

"I was working as a nanny not far from the castle. I had taken the children on an outing to the Princes Street Gardens. I sat on a settle watching the kiddies play, and a tall gentleman asked if he could join me. An adult conversation was something I had been sorely lacking, so being able to speak to someone about my age was a godsend. We chatted that afternoon and agreed to sit together in this same place the next time I came back. We talked about the theatre, our favourite plays and actors. On one of our meetings, George got down on one knee and asked me to be his wife."

"I so wanted to marry Robert. I love him with all my heart."

"I know you did."

"Not only that but Father prepared me for marriage."

"What are you talking about?"

"He did what all fathers do. He taught me how to perform the wifely duties. It's, well they're unpleasant, but I learned well and am exceptional at them, so he tells me. I would have done it for Robert."

"What? You mean he ... it isn't right! Surely, you realize that." Waves of nausea threatened to overpower her.

"Your father died when you were little. Of course, you wouldn't be versed in such matters."

Margaret slumped into the chair. "Please come back to Edinburgh with me for a while. You need some time away from here. You can stay with George and me and the kiddies."

"No. I mustn't leave Father."

"But ...." She wanted to slap some sense into her friend, but it would not help. She needed to convince her to liberate herself from under this roof – even for a short respite.

The bedroom door flew open and in burst Horatio. Had he been listening at the door the whole time? "Get out of my house," he bellowed. "I don't need you filling my wee girl's head with silly notions and taking her away from here." He grabbed Margaret's arm and shoved her toward the door.

"Father, please. Don't make Margaret leave."

"No one from that family is welcome in this house ever again," he roared.

"Sister, whatever is wrong?" Robert said when Margaret stepped across the threshold.

Ignoring him, she stormed past him into the library and poured a large drink. She downed the liquor in one gulp and supported herself against the table as her breathing slowed to normal.

He came to her side and helped her to the sofa. "Something has you in an appalling state of vexation. Tell me."

"Letitia said some things I can't bear to think about."

"Tell me, please," he begged. "Does it have anything to do with Miss Shand?"

"I can't tell you what she said, but I don't believe her involvement in Sarah's being committed. She told me Sarah saved her."

"Yes, she mumbled something along those lines when I first found her and again after I had taken her back to Gleanstane."

"Excuse me; I'm going to my room. I'm too flustered to even think about what I heard, let alone talk about it."

Robert squeezed his sister's hand. "You can tell me."

Margaret shook her head and darted out of the room, leaving him more confused than he already was.

Sarah's feet ached more with every step. Her exhausted body screamed for relief, but she didn't dare stop.

After stumbling and falling, Jenny's knees and hands were scraped and bleeding. Even though she cried and wailed, at least she didn't have a seizure. "We'll rest for a while," she said as she comforted her.

For the child's sake, she wished they could accept a ride in a passing carriage, but after her experience at the local police house, she trusted no one. They hid in a small grove of trees, and Sarah examined her hands and legs. A thorough cleaning and application of antiseptic cream were required, but that would have to wait. There was still one apple left, so she polished the piece of fruit and offered it to the youngster.

They were about halfway between Huntly and the Kendonald Road. Jenny needed to rest. She made the little girl comfortable and bundled her in the jacket they'd used to carry the apples.

Extra vigilance was required when they got to closer to the village. No way they could be seen. The road past the stone circle would bring them straight through the hamlet and along the Christie's land. The last person she wanted to run into was Thomas Sievewright. There was the footpath to the churchyard, but she dismissed the idea because there were too many houses nearby.

Robert's home was off to the left soon after the roadway veered away from the railway line. If they could get a little farther now, they could finish their journey under the cover of darkness.

"Time to wake up. We're almost to Weetshill. We'll be safe there."

Jenny stirred but didn't awaken. A few extra minutes of sleep would not be of any consequence at this juncture.

Again, the sky clouded over, and the temperature began to drop. Sarah bundled her closer and rubbed her arms to generate some heat. Darkness fell earlier because of the overcast conditions. She scanned the skies for a gap in the clouds, but they were solid.

Finally, the little girl woke. "C-come on S-Sarah, l-let's go," she said, rested and excited to reach the grand house.

"Don't tire yourself out. We still have a long way to go."

She nodded, and her small hand tightened its grip on Sarah's. "W-we g-go to the b-big house now," she said, jumping and skipping around.

At least at this time of day, the traffic was pretty much non-existent so they could make better time. The lane to the scenic viewpoint didn't seem to exist, or if so, trees and gorse obscured it. With the thick cloud cover, Sarah didn't have moonlight to guide her. Then the sound of water lapping over stones reached her ears. They were near the burn behind Weetshill. The mansion, windows radiant with the light of paraffin lamps, stood in the distance.

A hiss followed by an eerie yowl echoed through the still night air. Two yellow circles glowed like small fireballs in a tree above them.

"Wh-what's that?"

"I'm not sure." She pulled Jenny close. Wildcats were rare in Sarah's time. Their yowling was the source of banshee legends."Come on; we must go." She gripped Jenny's hand, and they ran toward the stream.

When they were almost there, Sarah skidded on a dew-covered rock and fell, twisting her lower leg in the process. An attempt to stand and support herself shot a searing pain through her right ankle, and she dropped to the ground. Using her left to push herself off, she tried a second time. The joint screamed in agony and gave out when she put any weight on her injured extremity. "You have to go to the house. Robert lives there. He's my friend. You can trust him. Tell him where I am."

"J-Jenny wants to s-stay with S-Sarah."

"No sweetie. You have to find Robert. Away you go."

The little girl ran off toward Weetshill; afraid whatever yowled at them might harm Sarah before she could bring back help. At the bank of the burn, her foot skated on the wet grass and she slid into the water with a huge splash. Struggling to her feet, she immediately fell again. She clambered up the slope and ran to the big house.

At the front door, she was too short to pull the bell cord, even when she jumped, so she pounded on it. A tall, fat man with long, bushy sideburns stood before her.

"A-a-are y-you R-Robert?"

He looked at the bedraggled child's wet, dirty clothes. "Nae, child, I isnae Robert."

"T-tell him I'm here."

"Who should I say is calling for him?"

"J-Jenny."

"You wait right here. I'll fetch Mr. Robertson."

"N-not M-Mr. R-Robertson. R-Robert."

Tears ran down her cheeks as the door closed in her face. She had done what Sarah asked, but no one was helping her.

A few minutes later, the door opened, and a shorter, thinner man with dark curly hair and a kind face stood in the opening. Behind him was the man who answered her knocks and an older woman with grey hair. Her vision blurred, and her stomach lurched.

"Do you recognize this waif, Sir?" said the man who first came to the door.

"Poor wee hen, she's in a' awful state," the woman commented.

"No," said Robert. "But something has her flustered. What's wrong child?"

Jenny's eyes rolled back, and she collapsed on the ground.

After she came to, she had no idea how long her seizure had lasted. The man with the caring eyes held her in his arms and stroked her forehead.

"A-are y-you R-Robert?"

"Yes, and who are you?"

"J-Jenny. S-Sarah t-told m-me t-to c-come f-find you."

"Where did you see her?"

"O-over there," she said, pointing. "S-Sarah's hurt. N-needs help."

"Sarah sent you?"

"Y-yes. S-sore a-ankle. C-can't walk. Over th-there."

"These people won't harm you. They work for me. You go inside with them, and I'll go find Sarah and bring her back."

The little girl nodded.

"Look after her, Mrs. MacEwen."

The throbbing in Sarah's ankle worsened by the minute. Maybe she shouldn't have sent Jenny to the house by herself. What if she got lost or had a seizure? Or what if she couldn't explain where Sarah was? Alone in the dark, Hamish's warning about the wildcat ran through her mind. She didn't believe they would attack humans, but what if it came after her because of her weakened condition. Cold and in extreme discomfort, she drifted in and out of consciousness.

Robert raced off in the direction pointed out to him. "Sarah where are you?" Frigid water seeped into his shoes as he scampered across the burn. A wild cat's scream echoed through the night, and its glowing eyes stared down at him from above.

Distracted by the animal, he tripped and fell face first on the ground. He scrambled to his feet and tried to focus his eyes in the dim light. Had he stumbled over a rock or a tree root? Another sound but not that of the cat but a human's moan.

"Sarah." He knelt beside the crumpled heap at his feet, scooped her up, and held her tight. "You're free from danger now. No one will harm you."

"Where's Jenny?" she mumbled as she wrapped her arms around his neck.

"At Weetshill. Mrs. MacEwen is seeing to her. Let's get you there and looked after, too."

"I need to go to her."

"Don't talk. Save your strength. I can't believe I'm holding you. When I discovered you had escaped from that abominable place, I thought I would never see you again."

"You came for me? Really?"

"Of course I did."

25

"Miss Shand, look at the state o' you," the housekeeper said when Robert toted her into the house.

Now he had Sarah in his arms; he was loathed to let her go.

"Mr. Robertson, bring her to the kitchen. I's got the wee lassie there in front of the fire gettin' warmed up now."

He cradled Sarah in his arms as the housekeeper spread a blanket over a chair near the enormous fireplace.

"S-Sarah."

"Put her down, Sir. I'll look after her. No harm will come to her here."

He reluctantly obeyed.

"You cannae stay in here whilst she is undressin'. Asides, look at you. You's all wet an' mucky. Go take off those things afore you catch your death." She shook her finger at him as she had done when he played in the burn as a young boy and come home soaked.

Outside the door, Robert leaned back

The housekeeper placed a tub of steaming water on the floor in front of the fire. A basin of cold water sat on the oak table. "Come, Miss Shand. Let's get you, and this wean saw to."

Sarah hugged the youngster. "You were a good, brave girl finding Robert." She fumbled with a button on the little girl's dress, but couldn't undo it because her fingers were numb from the cold. "Can you help me?"

"Och, dearie me," she said and unbuttoned their clothing. "Can you manage now?"

"I-I think so." Sarah's cold, stiff digits still didn't work as they should, but she managed to pull Jenny's clothes off over her head. She pulled her blouse off and shimmied out of her skirt.

"W-we h-have to g-give th-these c-clothes b-back. Y-you s-said we w-would. St-stealing is b-bad."

"We will. Don't you worry." She turned to the woman. "You'll have Maggie launder these things? We need to send them back to the people they belong to."

"Come nearer the fire."

Sarah hobbled to the hearth and stood in her underthings, letting the heat from the crackling blaze take the chill away.

Exposed body parts washed, the warm water and the woman's gentle touch soothed Sarah's skin. "Get these other things off an' scrub that part o' you. I'll leave you whilst you do it. Once you's done, wrap up in that blanket. It will be hot now."

Mrs. MacEwen turned to help Jenny wash, but the little girl cowered from her.

"She's afraid. It takes her a while to get used to new people. I'll look after her." Sarah dipped her hands in the basin. At first, the water burned her cold fingers, but as the numbness left, so did the discomfort. She assisted the child, then swaddled her in the warmed blanket and settled her in the chair in front of the fireplace.

The little girl's requirements looked after; Sarah attended to her own. She untied the ribbon in the waistband of her drawers and eased them down until they fell to the floor. When she stepped out of them, she supported herself against the table unable to put weight on her right foot.

The soft cloth and heated sponge bath were comforting, unlike the scratchy towels and cold water at the asylum. She wrapped herself in the homemade quilt and sat down.

Jenny crawled into Sarah's lap. "C-can w-we s-stay here?"

"We're safe here. No one will harm you. And you won't go back to that disgusting place. I promise," she reassured the little girl with a hug who smiled and closed her eyes.

Mrs. MacEwen came back and peered at the bundle held in Sarah's arms. "Ah, wee lassie, she's fast asleep." She looked at her feet. "You still be in your stockins."

"I have a small problem. My socks are stuck to my feet."

The housekeeper squatted beside her and placed Sarah's right foot on her thigh, but she stiffened at the woman's touch. Within moments, the stockings were pushed down her legs as far as possible. "Your feet are all blistered. How long was you walkin' in this state?"

"Not long after we escaped."

"You walked at least twenty miles in your stockin' feet. Och, child, whatever have you done to yourself?" She clucked her tongue and pulled a bell cord near the door.

Soon, the butler entered.

"Sorry to wake you, Archibald, but it be Miss Shand. She needs Doctor Burnett."

"No," she cried. "He's the one who authorized the order for the asylum. The Superintendent showed me. I don't want that man near me. I don't ever want to go back to that place."

The woman left the kitchen and returned with Robert. "She thinks he is the one what signed her papers. Surely, he wouldnae do such a thing. The man looked after her so well when she first came to us."

Robert knelt beside Sarah. "I spoke with him. He says he knew nothing of your commitment and I consider him an honest man. Quite likely the document was a forgery."

"Yeah, right," she snapped.

"I believe him," he defended, then took the servant aside. "Send for the physician anyway," he said in a low tone.

Mrs. MacEwen looked at Sarah then at Robert. "Like it or not, she needs him. Her feet, you ken, they's in a terrible mess. Her stockin's are stuck to them, and I cannae budge them."

"I'll get word to Callum. Dinnae fash," Archibald said.

The woman returned to her side. "Here you be. Put your feet in here to soak." She lifted Sarah's feet and slowly submerged them in the tepid water.

Jenny groaned from the change in position but didn't waken.

26

Robert took another chair and sat in front of Sarah. "You don't know how happy I am to have you home here alive and well. I was afraid I would never see you again."

"You're soaked." Patches of wet covered his suit. "You're still wearing the same clothes you had on when you brought me in here."

"Don't you worry about me. You're the one who needs worrying over. You and this wee lassie here in your lap."

"We be in here," the housekeeper said as she held the door.

"Doctor Burnett. We're sorry to rouse you at this time of night," Robert said as he walked across the room to shake the physician's hand.

"So what seems to be the problem? Your coachman only said it was urgent."

"I told you I didn't want him anywhere near me. Keep him away from me," Sarah argued.

Ignoring her protests, Mrs. MacEwen said, "Miss Shand an' this wean here."

Robert scooped the little girl into his arms.

She didn't fuss when he picked her up. The small child usually feared strangers, but she warmed up to him.

He stood back and allowed the doctor to take his seat near Sarah.

"Hmm... let's see what you did."

Blanket clutched tighter around her; she shrank back into the chair. "Keep away from me. You signed the orders. I saw them with my own eyes."

"I assure you, young woman, I was not involved. I knew nothing of your disappearance until this morning when Robert and his ghillie arrived at my surgery. If my name is on anything, it was a forgery. I intend to find out who was behind the deception and see the culprit punished to the full extent of the law."

"Prove it to me then."

"Would someone indulge me with a sheet of paper and a pen, please?"

Provided with the things he asked for, the doctor signed his name. "Does this look like what you saw?"

"No. Not remotely close." The doctor's handwriting was darker and backhand, unlike the lightly scrawled signature on the admission form.

"There. I told you I had no involvement in the scheme. Now please, let me examine your leg."

"I'm sorry I doubted you. Jenny needs looking after, too. She fell and skinned her hands and knees."

Doctor Burnett looked at the little girl in Robert's arms and pulled Sarah's left stocking off. "I'll tend to her, too, don't you worry, but first I'll look after you." He lifted her left foot from the tub and examined the extremity from different angles, hmming several times. "Not so bad. We'll clean them up with a carbolic acid solution. Mrs. MacEwen, might I have a quart of lukewarm water, please?"

The housekeeper provided him with a porcelain bowl filled per his instructions.

The physician took a vial from his bag, dispensed its contents into the water, and mixed the suspension with his hand. Next, he raised Sarah's right one out of the tub and picked away the remains of her stocking.

"Ouch," she yelped before clenching her teeth when his touch shot a searing pain through her ankle.

"I'm sorry, Miss Shand. Nasty sprain, my girl." He felt around pushing here and there and moved her foot. "I don't think you've broken anything, but the swelling is going to have to come down some for me to get a better idea. But these blisters. My word, what in heaven's name were you doing?"

"I couldn't stay at the asylum a minute longer. We were almost home when I turned my ankle on a rock on the other side of the burn."

The doctor sponged Sarah's feet with a clean, wet bandage. "There. That looks better now. Mrs. MacEwen, you'll have to do this every few hours for the next two days to ensure infection doesn't set in."

She nodded in acknowledgement.

"What's all the strushan down here?" Margaret asked as she swept into the kitchen. "Oh Sarah, I'm so glad you're back. Robert's been in a state since you disappeared. I saw Letitia today," she continued. "She says you saved her life?"

"Yes. She drank poison, and when I found her, she was almost dead. She's all right, isn't she?"

"Yes, she's alive now thanks to you. I don't know how you knew what to do, but I am very grateful you did. I am so sorry I misjudged you when we first met. I thought you were here to make trouble. Please forgive me."

"You're forgiven. I would have thought the same thing if I were in your place."

Margaret bent down and hugged Sarah, then took the tyke from her brother and cuddled her before handing off the child. "Who is this wee lassie?"

"This is Jenny. She was in the asylum – wrongfully. I prevented her from getting a beating and found she's a sweet girl. If not for her knowledge of the grounds, I never could have escaped that awful place." Sarah cuddled the girl.

"Let's have a look at those wounds," he said.

"It's okay sweetie. He's going to help you," she said reassuringly.

Jenny whimpered the whole time he sponged the scrapes on her knees, but she didn't cry or have a seizure.

"Keep Miss Shand off her feet, and this one elevated," he said, pointing to her sprained ankle.

"But we cannae keep 'em here in the kitchen. She needs to be in her room."

Doctor Burnett lifted Jenny off Sarah's lap and handed her off to the Weetshill employee while Robert bundled Sarah in his arms. With the blanket still securely around her, they made their way to her bedroom.

Outside the door, the physician took the little girl back from the woman and stood aside to allow the others passage. With slight unease, she took in her surroundings when Robert carried her in. The room remained as it was when she first arrived.

"Set her in the chair by the fire, Mr. Robertson. I'll gets her changed. You can sit the wean here on the ottoman, Doctor."

"Very well."

The woman brought Sarah a clean nightgown and drawers, then shooed the men out so she could put them on. "Janet," she called out into the corridor, "Can you look an' see if you can finds some of Miss Margaret's things from when she was a bairn. We's got a wean needin' a nightshirt."

"Aye, Mrs. MacEwen."

The sound of Janet's voice reassured Sarah she was back at Weetshill. She put on the items brought for her and draped the quilt over her shoulders.

The young maid hurried in carrying an armful of clothing. "I hopes they fit. I dinnae ken how big the wee lassie is."

Nightgown held up; the housekeeper clucked her approval.

Jenny scampered to Sarah and clung to her.

"You're all right. Let's get you ready for bed," she said and took the nightie and asked the servant, "Would you help me?"

"Aye."

The sleeves extended well past Jenny's fingertips, and the hem pooled on the floor. The excess fabric hung limply from her outstretched arms.

Doctor Burnett came back briefly and took Sarah to her bed, propped pillows behind her back and a large, fluffy one under her injured extremity.

"I'll be back to check on you tomorrow Miss Shand. Have yourself a good night's sleep. You've been through quite the ordeal these last days," he said.

After he left, the housekeeper pulled the heavy draperies closed.

Jenny rummaged through the hand-me-downs Janet found. She held up a blue velvet dress in her nightgown-covered hands. "P-pretty."

Sarah nodded, and patted the bed beside her. "Up here, you. Maybe you can wear that one tomorrow."

Mrs. MacEwen's astonished voice followed a creak of the door hinges. "Mr. Robertson, you cannae be in a lady's bedchamber on your own. Most of all a spinster lady's room," she clamoured.

"About now I don't care about proprieties. Miss Shand has been gone for far too long. It's imperative I speak with her."

"But Sir, it be well past midnight. She needs her rest."

"I won't keep her long. Could we have some privacy, please?"

Sarah looked pleadingly at the woman. "It will be fine. Robert is a man of honour."

"A mannerly gentleman and a lady wouldnae be in a bedroom unchaperoned."

"R-Robert and S-Sarah n-not alone. J-J-Jenny is here." the child said.

Trying to keep a straight face, Robert continued, "I assure you nothing untoward will happen. I only want to talk to her."

"Verra well, Sir, but I'll be right outside this door, so you best leave it open."

27

Robert waited for the housekeeper to leave before dragging the wingback chair to the side of the bed. The open door made him even more nervous. He pushed it closed until it remained slightly ajar, hoping that would appease the housekeeper.

Seated next to the bed, he took Sarah's hand in both of his. He took a deep breath and murmured. "I was so worried about you when you disappeared. I didn't know what became of you if you were dead or alive if I would ever see you again. Then I discovered some people in the village knew where you were, but lied to me. Their deception infuriated me."

"It was that awful ghillie who works for the Christies. He dragged me away from Letitia. "How did you find out they'd taken me to the asylum?"

"Angus and Callum were in the tavern, and according to them, there was quite a fuss. They managed to coax it out of Tommy Sievewright."

The door creaked open, and the housekeeper poked her head around it. "I's been patient long enough, Sir. It be time you was leaving Miss Shand to her sleep."

"Five more minutes, please," Robert replied.

"Five minutes, but not one minute longer. And this door stays put."

Robert nodded and waited for the housekeeper to return to the corridor. Before he lost his courage, he took a deep breath and began. "Miss Shand, I find you attractive, delightful, exasperating, but most of all, my world is empty when you're not in it. I love you. I love you more than life itself. I've fallen in love with you."

Robert breathed a sigh of relief. There, he'd said it, but she was sound asleep. He would have to make the entire speech again tomorrow when she was awake. Robert stood slowly and returned the chair to its position. Before leaving, he stopped at the bedside and kissed her on the forehead. "Welcome home. Sleep well."

"I love you, too," she murmured.

When Sarah woke the next morning, she wondered if the whole asylum ordeal was a dream, especially when she realized she was in the bedroom at Weetshill. Then she saw Jenny sleeping beside her. A stab of pain shot through her ankle as she moved her leg. It hadn't been a dream. She hoped that meant Robert's declaration of his love had been real, too.

"Miss Shand, you isnae to be out of bed! Doctor Burnett wants to you have complete rest," the housekeeper cried as she entered the room.

"But Mrs. MacEwen, I can't stay in bed all the time. I'll go mad. Can I at least sit in the chair by the fire or at the table? I promise I'll behave."

It took some doing, but Sarah convinced the housekeeper to let her sit in the wingback chair in front of the fireplace. Dressed in a navy blue wool skirt and a long-sleeved white muslin blouse, she settled with her left foot resting on a fluffy feather pillow on an upholstered footstool. Sitting around staring at four walls with nothing to do would drive her mental, and she would end up back in the asylum. If only, Sarah had her radio with the CD player or even her computer.

Jenny put on the blue velvet dress provided the night before and climbed up into Sarah's lap.

"Good morning," Robert said as he knocked on the door and entered the room. "Did you sleep well?"

"I think so. Um, Robert," she faltered. "Did you say something to me as I fell asleep last night?"

"Yes, I did. I said I love you, and I meant every word," Robert said, leaning over and kissing her forehead.

Sarah's heart skipped a beat. "That makes me feel so much better. I was so afraid I dreamt it."

"I wanted to stop in and see you before I left. I have some important business to attend to in Aberdeen, so I'll take my leave now. You rest as Doctor Burnett said, and I'll see you later."

28

What was Robert's important business? Mysterious. She didn't have much time to dwell on it though because Janet came in with a tray of oatmeal, ham, eggs, and hot chocolate. Jenny didn't wait for an invitation but scrambled up to the table. The young maid supported Sarah from the wingback chair as she struggled to walk across the room. Her ankle ached more today than the day before.

The aromas coming from the food filled the room. What they passed off as such in the asylum didn't compare. The oatmeal was thick instead of runny, and everything was fresh, having been grown or raised at Weetshill.

"Thank you, Janet," she said as she fixed a serving for the little girl. "Slow down. You don't want to give yourself a tummy ache. We only had a few apples yesterday." Sarah put a piece of meat in her mouth and chewed slowly savouring the flavour. "I'm thrilled to be home and eating Morag's cooking." Right after she spoke, she realized she called Weetshill home.

"Doctor Burnett is here," Mrs. MacEwen announced as she led the man into the room.

"I'm sorry to interrupt your breakfast, but I have many calls to make today so wanted to make an early start."

"I don't mind."

With the help of the housekeeper, Sarah turned her chair to enable the physician to examine her feet and ankle.

Once he completed Sarah's examination, he moved on to look at the small girl. "You're both doing fine. Remember to clean their wounds regularly. I don't anticipate any problems."

"I'll looks after the two o' them."

"Doctor, could I speak to you in private about Jenny?"

"Miss Shand?" He arched his eyebrow as he spoke.

"Can you get some information about her for me?" She fidgeted with her napkin as she talked.

"This is most irregular. After all, you're not related to the child."

"Please, I need to know," she said, emphasizing her desire.

"What do you require?"

"Well, she can't be more than eight years old."

"Aye, I would agree given her size."

"She has a speech impediment and epilepsy."

"Go on," he said and rubbed his chin.

Sarah balled the napkin up in her hands. "She was dumped there after she had her first seizure, but where was she before? They wouldn't give me much information. How old is she? What's her last name? Anything you can do for me? I don't dare go back there, not that they would talk to me anyway."

The doctor nodded. "I have every intention of going to that infirmary to determine who falsified my name."

"Wait. I just thought of something. When Tommy Sievewright dragged me into the police house, I saw him pass a paper to Constable Skinner. Maybe one of them forged your signature? At least, signed your name."

"Thank you, Miss Shand. I shall discuss the matter with the two of them as well."

"I saw Jenny suffer seizures, once when we were out on the grounds when something scared her. The other time was when an enormous woman attacked her. I know she needs love and affection, which I can do, but I want to adopt her. Make it a permanent situation."

"An unmarried woman adopting a child? Unheard of, but I'll see what information I can ferret out for you. It could take me some time, so you'll have to be patient." Doctor Burnett removed his spectacles and set them down.

"I'm sure with the right medication, and in a loving home she could live a normal life."

"You hold out great hope for this child. I trust it isn't misguided."

"No."

"I will also have to give her a thorough check-up. How do you think she'll react to that?"

The small girl shovelled in food like she hadn't eaten in her life. Would an examination trigger a seizure? Maybe if she stayed with the little girl, it wouldn't. "Give me a couple of days to prepare her, so she understands you're not like the people at the asylum. Oh, and something else. I think they're selling bodies there, too. I heard men and the superintendent talking about that when we escaped through the crypt."

"Most interesting. You're a very observant young lassie." Doctor Burnett put his glasses on as the cue he was about to leave. "You bring the wee girl to my surgery when you think she's ready," he said before closing the door behind him.

"How did your business go?" Sarah looked up from her book when Robert walked through the door.

Jenny amused herself quietly on the floor by Sarah's feet with a pair of dolls the laundress made for her out of some old socks.

"Can we speak alone?"

His tone worried her. She turned to the youngster. "Be good, and go find Mrs. MacEwen, and ask her nicely for a glass of milk. Morag might have some butteries or baps baked. If there are, I'm sure there's jam or something to have on them."

She scrambled to her feet, cuddled Sarah, and skipped out of the room.

"You have a way with children," he said once the library door closed.

She blushed. "I didn't know I did until I met her." The bond with the child was difficult to describe. She'd protected and nurtured her, and possibly improved her self-assurance. Sarah found it ironic she had been able to help the little girl in that way since Blair shattered her self-esteem when he broke up with her.

"How was your day? Archibald told me you came downstairs. Shouldn't you be resting?"

"I am. Curling up with a book is the most relaxing thing I can do."

"Did Doctor Burnett stop by this morning?"

"Yes. He checked the two of us over and was pleased with our progress." Sarah shifted her position on the sofa and cast her eyes downward. "I'm not sure how to say this," she faltered as she rubbed her fingernails over her cuticles on her thumbs.

"You're not unwell?"

"No, I'm fine. We both are ..."

"But."

"Well, she doesn't belong in the asylum. A speech impediment and epilepsy are no reason to stick her in that hell hole, but I'm frightened me bringing her here …"

"Yes?"

"Well, it isn't fair to you and everyone else. I want to take care of the wee thing, but I'll understand if you don't want the two of us here."

"What possessed you to come up with such an idea? If I weren't happy with having the girl in my home, I would have said something. I can see there is a special bond between you two, and I am grateful to her for helping you escape from there. Tell me, please."

Sarah told him how she came across the little girl and how she wanted to protect her. "I asked Doctor Burnett to look into Jenny's background when he was here this morning. When she's happy and feels safe, her seizures are pretty much nonexistent. They only occur when she's stressed," she said, standing and limping to the window. "That little girl needs as much affection and support as she can get. Someone dumped her there soon after her first seizure."

"You're a compassionate person, Sarah Shand, but don't you think you're taking on a bit too much?"

Tears pricked at the backs of her eyes. "I love that small girl. She's never had anyone care for her before. They're probably chuffed I got her out of there since she was only a nuisance to them."

"You feel strongly for wee Jenny. This illness she has, I'm afraid I don't know enough to understand its implications. When she came to tell me you were injured, she had a seizure, and it was frightening to watch. Not knowing what else to do, I bundled her into my arms and held her until the fit ended."

"You did exactly the right thing. I want to adopt Jenny. Be a real mother to her."

"You can't. Not on your own."

"Doctor Burnett said the same thing."

"I think I know a way I might be able to help you."

"'Tis time to gets ready for dinner, Sir, Miss Shand," the housekeeper interrupted as she knocked on the door and pushed it open.

"Thanks, Mrs. MacEwen."

"Shall we?" He reached for Sarah's arm.

"Miss Jenny is up in your room. Sent her that way an' tol' her you'd be there straight away."

"Thank you."

Sarah found it a struggle to climb the stairs, so she sat down to go up them backwards on her bum. Powerless to stand by and watch, Robert picked her up. "If you need to go up and down, say the word. I will be more than willing to assist you," he said as he carried her to the first floor.

"How's my pretty girl," she asked when she opened her door.

"J-Jenny happy! J-Jenny l-likes it here."

Sarah held Jenny's hand as they walked into the room. One of the servants set a place for the little girl next to hers.

"Are you and the wee lassie feeling better today?" Margaret asked.

"It's brilliant to be out of that place and back here. Last night you mentioned you saw Letitia. I feel terrible she tried to kill herself because of Robert and me."

"She has bigger problems than just the two of you. I asked her to stay with George and me in Edinburgh, but she refuses to leave her father."

"Getting away from that tyrant would be the best thing for her," said Sarah. "Almost like he's got some hold over her."

She knew her comment rattled Robert's sister by the fake smile on the woman's face and her forced laugh. She wished the woman would have elaborated on Letitia's more significant problems but didn't want to pry.

"You're a pretty little thing," Margaret said when the small child scrambled into the chair beside Sarah.

The little girl beamed.

"Did Robert mention I plan to adopt her?"

"A single lassie adopting? I never heard of the like. But then you are headstrong and can be quite charming, so I have no doubt you will succeed. I just pray if it all falls apart, you won't be too badly hurt."

"I tried to tell her so. Such things are unheard of." Robert turned to Sarah. "I don't want you to raise your hopes. It will be easier in the long run if things don't work out as you wish."

Sarah sighed. Adoption wouldn't be easy, but she wasn't about to give up on the idea.

After they ate, Sarah stood and said, "Come along there, and we'll get you cleaned up and ready for bed."

She leapt out of her chair, scurried to Sarah's side and hugged her.

"Mrs. MacEwen prepared the room next to mine especially for you. What do you think of that?"

"I-I l-like it."

Sarah settled Jenny into her permanent bedroom. While she waited for the little girl to nod off, she pondered the epilepsy diagnosis. Since the night they came back to Weetshill, she was seizure-free. Had her condition been an excuse for a single mum to dump her child? Once asleep, she kissed her on the forehead and went to her room.

Shadows cast by the dying fire and the dimly lit paraffin lamps created a spooky air. An icy draft chilled Sarah to the bone, so she climbed into bed and yanked the covers over her head. She was confident a woman's low musical voice said 'you're doing a beautiful thing for the wee lassie.' Sitting up, she said, "Who's there?" but the room was empty.

Sarah's mind raced. Who had spoken to her? She didn't dare tell anyone for fear of being taken back to the asylum. The ghostly voice reminded her of the visions she had of Margaret and Robert as children. All the strange things that occurred might be related to her time travel.

The first night she spent in this room, she had hoped she would wake up the next morning back in her parents' house. She sat up again, her heart pounding. What if she returned to 2010? That was what she wanted only a few short weeks ago. Now the thought of being sent away from Robert and Jenny terrified her more than going back to the mental hospital near Ladysbridge Station.

29

After breakfast the following morning, the physician arrived to check on his patients. He was changing the bandages on Jenny's knees when Robert walked in.

"There is every possibility Jenny would never have another seizure now she's away from that environment, but I wouldn't hold out hope," Doctor Burnett said.

"Medication. Epanutin."

"What is that? I never heard of it."

Sarah was more knowledgeable than the medical practitioner when it came to the wee girl's condition. How did she know so much? Robert stood back and listened.

"What would you give her then? Would there be anything else causing her seizures? It appears she only has them when she's upset."

"That's an astute observation. Now, if medication is warranted which I presume it is, then I would start with a course of bromide of potassium. And if that didn't stop the fitting, then there are other bromides we can try on their own or in combination."

"So her condition is treatable," Robert said.

"Yes, although difficult in some cases."

"Please forgive me, Doctor, but I am ignorant when it comes to this disease. You have taken a huge weight off my mind."

"I'm glad to hear that. Miss Shand and the wee lassie are coming along well. I don't think any further visits will be required."

"Have you been able to find anything out about Jenny's

background?" Sarah asked.

"I've not been to the asylum yet, but I will let you know as soon as I do," he said and closed up his medical case.

"Thank you for coming, Doctor." Robert shook the man's hand in gratitude and walked him to the front door.

30

The next morning dawned cold and damp, so Sarah bundled Jenny in heavy outerwear so they could go outside. Thanks to Archibald, she had the use of old Mr. Robertson's cane.

Today was the first time she had explored the grounds surrounding the grand mansion. Once the fog combined with chimney smoke burned off, the day would be gorgeous. Chilled, she rubbed her arms and wrapped herself in the cloak.

"Wh-where are w-we g-going?"

"Dunno. Where would you like to go?" She wanted to take her over to the stone circle, but after her experience with Tommy Sievewright, she was terrified to go near the Christies' estate. The only option at least for now was staying at Weetshill.

The walking stick made the roaming far easier. The two crept to the stables. A man walked the pony in the paddock, and Jenny ran ahead, squealing.

"Slow down, so you don't fall and do yourself a mischief," she called after her, but it was too late.

The youngster tumbled face first on the ground. Before Sarah could get to her, Hamish scaled the fence and righted her. "The wee lassie be a' right," he said and handed her off.

"Thank you, but I'll be the judge of that." She sat her on a slice of log and did a cursory inspection. Aside from dirt, Jenny was no worse for wear.

"C-can I p-pet the p-pony?"

Sarah didn't answer but slipped between the two middle rails and into the enclosure. She waved her arm in invitation.

Once they were both in, she hoisted the small child and walked over to the groom. "May I?"

Hamish stepped back and allowed them passage. Sarah lifted Jenny on the animal's back and put her hands in its mane. "Hang on tight, and we'll walk around." She clicked her tongue, and the pony trailed after her.

"You ken what you're doin' when it comes to horses. An' you bonnie one are a fine horsewoman."

The sound of his voice made her cringe, remembering her first encounter with him. She stopped and looked up at the rider. "Twice more around and then that's it."

With the last revolution completed, Sarah expected a fuss since she seemed to be having such a good time, but there wasn't.

"B-bye horsey," she called as she took Sarah's hand and left the stables.

"Bring her back anytime," Hamish said and winked as they walked past him.

On their way back to the house, she worried about the groom and his lewd wink. If Jenny didn't love the pony so much, she wouldn't go near the stables again.

After lunch, Sarah took Jenny into the library where she scanned the bookcases for children's books but didn't find any. It was odd since children grew up here. There were so many rooms in the mansion; most of which she had yet to see. "I know what we can do. We'll go exploring. Race you to the stairs." Not that she could run, but she gave the little girl a head start then hobbled after her. They reached the bottom step simultaneously.

At the first floor, Sarah explored the opposite wing to the one where her room was located. She had never seen the interior of Robert's and was curious. Slowly, she turned the knob on what she thought was his door and poked her head inside. The pieces were darker and bulkier than those in her room but otherwise comparable. The draperies were dark green, and the colour matched the quilt's square pattern on his bed. Books, stacked meticulously on a small table next to the chair facing the fireplace provided reading material. She pulled the door closed, and they meandered down the corridor.

"Th-this o-one?"

"No sweetie."

"Wh-why not?"

"Robert's grandfather died in there."

They worked their way down the passage, opening doors one by one on both sides. Every room had similar furniture and a massive inglenook. These must have been where the men from the hunting party stayed when they visited.

The door at the end of the hall was locked. Sarah squatted down and peered through the keyhole. The room was full of children's things. Footsteps sounded from behind, making her jump.

"What are the pair of you up to?"

She wheeled around. "J-just exploring the mansion. I'm sorry."

"It's all right." Robert reached for the top of the casing and retrieved a key. Sarah pulled the child aside. "Let's see what we have in here." He unlocked the door, turned the knob, and retreated a few steps.

She stood in awe of the sight in front of her. It was like a Victorian toy store matching the one in the movie *A Christmas Carol*. Nestled amongst the playthings, were a bed, wardrobe, and washstand.

Sarah let go of Jenny's hand, and the little girl ran towards the dust-covered toys.

"This room belonged to my older brother, John. My parents insisted the door was kept locked. They mourned his death until the day they died."

"I'm so sorry," she said and held him close. "Your grandfather mentioned him when he took me on our portrait tour soon after I arrived."

"Please, take anything you think Jenny might like, or better yet, let her choose the things she wants to take back to her room. I'll arrange for this door to remain unlocked, so you both can come and go as often as you like. The wee girl deserves higher quality toys than dolls fashioned from socks." Robert slumped into a chair.

Sarah moved to his side and cradled his head against her. "I'm sorry. Even though you probably don't remember him, you must miss him."

"Not until now being here with his things. I often wondered what he would have been like, and if we would have been close."

A small table with books, a slate board with a stick of chalk sat in the corner. Sarah walked over for a better look. One tome was *Grimm's Fairy Tales*, the other a collection of children's stories by Hans Christian Andersen.

Seeing her interest, Robert nodded. "By all means. Anything here at Weetshill is at your disposal."

Holding the bounty from their quest into the forbidden zone, they left the room and closed the door behind them.

After breakfast the following morning, Sarah and Jenny went for a walk. The cold, damp mornings made her injury ache more than usual, but she was determined not to stay cooped up indoors nor ingest any more laudanum, despite there still being a decent supply on hand. They kept to the footpath to Leith Hall but only went as far as the bridge over the railway line, leading to the cemetery. By then Sarah's ankle screamed in agony. She leaned against the stone parapet to rest. Once the throbbing subsided, she and the little girl continued.

As they approached the old man's gravesite, Robert's sister crouched in front of the headstone. "Margaret, I didn't expect to find you here."

"I-I felt the need to pay my respects. It's been so long since I left Weetshill," she said, standing up.

Recalling the discussion with the members of the hunting party over dinner, Sarah wondered if she should say anything. Not waiting for the woman to volunteer information, she asked. "At the funeral, I heard you had said something about it being finally safe to come home?"

"Yes, I did."

"Why?"

"You don't want to hear about my life."

"I've been told I'm a good listener."

Margaret looked at Sarah and started to walk away from the graveside to a nearby seat.

"Your marriage was arranged, too?"

"Yes. My parents saw to it long before Father's death."

"H-how did your dad die if you don't mind telling me?"

Margaret's eyes filled with moisture. "I was in the library with him. I had recently discovered I was to marry a horrible, mean, old man. I didn't like him, nor did Robert. On the occasions he came to Weetshill, we ran away and hid. He didn't like children. When I found out, I pleaded with both Mother and Father to not make me go through with it, and they said I was just silly. The marriage wouldn't take place for some time, and they said by then I would be old enough to realize they had chosen right for me."

Handkerchief extracted from her drawstring bag, she dabbed her eyes and continued. "I was just a wee girl, and I argued with Father, insisting he put a stop to the arranged marriage but he wouldn't hear of it. He got very angry with me and threw his pen down, stood, and ordered me to leave the room. The next thing I knew, he lay dead across his desk in a puddle of ink. Granda sent for the doctor, but it was too late."

"I'm so sorry," Sarah said as she put her arm around Margaret's shoulders. "So is this why your mother was so into arranged marriages?"

"Mostly Father. He never knew his mum. She died from complications in childbirth. Mother adhered to his wishes implicitly."

"So you got railroaded into a marriage you didn't want."

"Which is why I ran away and never came back. The old man I was to marry was still alive at the time of Mother's death, so I didn't dare return. I always prayed he would die before my parents, but he outlived both of them. He only perished earlier this year. I debated if I should come home for Granda's funeral."

"Come on. We'll go back to Weetshill." Sarah helped Robert's sister to her feet. "Time we were going," she called. "Where is Jenny?"

The little girl leapt out from behind a headstone and yelled, 'boo' making the women jump.

Suddenly, Margaret turned a sickly shade. "I'm feeling a mite poorly," she said. "Better now than this morning, though."

"Maybe you're pregnant."

The woman's face went pale, and she sat back down on the bench.

"You are, aren't you?" Not giving her a chance to answer, Sarah asked, "When are you due?"

"Early next year best as I can tell."

"Congratulations! You must be thrilled."

In her usual whirlwind of activity, Jenny ran to Margaret and put her hand on her stomach. "B-baby in th-there?"

She smiled. "Yes. There is a baby in there." She turned back to Sarah. "I didn't go home after the funeral because something doesn't feel quite right with this pregnancy. I've not told George I'm with child yet. I don't want anyone finding out either, in case something goes wrong."

"Your secret will be safe with us. Won't it? We'll let Margaret tell her news when she's ready, all right?"

Jenny nodded, smiling.

Hours later, in the middle of a novel, Sarah dozed off with the book face-down on her chest. Woken by the creaking door, she sat up. Robert stood at the window with his back to her.

"Why didn't you wake me when you came in?"

"You looked peaceful. I didn't want to disturb you."

Jenny scrambled up from the floor where she had the box of toy soldiers spread out. She ran to him and wrapped her arms around his waist. "J-Jenny likes R-Robert. L-likes th-this house."

"I'm glad to hear that. I like you too. Now can you be a good girl and run off and play someplace else, so I can speak to Sarah?"

"Off you go," she said.

After Jenny skipped out of the room, Robert spoke. "She thinks the world of you."

"And me, her, too. She's a great kid. Just had a lousy start in life. I want to make sure she gets a better middle and end."

"She isn't the reason I wanted to talk with you in private," he faltered as he sat on the sofa beside Sarah. "No, this is between you and me."

"I'm not sure I like the sound of this. You're scaring me."

"Don't be. The other day, I went into Aberdeen," he paused and swallowed. "Since your arrival, I feel alive. I smile and laugh. I'd never felt this happy. Then you disappeared, and my world crashed down around me. I didn't think I would ever see you again, and that's when I realized I fell in love with you, and I want us to spend the rest of our lives together." He got down on one knee, pulled out a box and opened it. "Miss Shand," he said and took her hands in his free one. "Would you do me the honour of becoming my wife and stay here with me till death do us part?"

Sarah gasped. The ring was stunning. Sparkling diamonds surrounded a glittering red centre gemstone. Speechless, she held out her hand. "Y-yes." She finally found her voice. Once Robert put it on her shaking finger, she embraced him, holding her hand out to admire the gorgeous piece of jewellery he'd installed there. "I love you, Robert Robertson."

"And I love you, too, Sarah Shand."

31

About half-nine the following morning, the minister arrived at Weetshill. "Good morning," he said after the butler showed him into the library. "What can I do for you young folks today?"

"We want to be married, Reverend."

"What about your arranged marriage to Letitia Christie, Robert?"

"That business is taken care of so I am free from that encumbrance." He pulled the signed copy of the release document out of the desk drawer and handed the paper to the clergyman.

"Hmm, well everything seems to be in order, albeit somewhat irregular. So when would you like the ceremony to take place and where?"

"Here in the chapel. It should be used for a happy event. The last time was for Mr. Robertson's funeral."

"Well, let me see," Reverend Mitchell took out his diary and opened it. "The banns need to be read on three consecutive Sundays. I could begin this coming Sabbath, twenty-sixth September with the reading of the first with the second and final readings taking place on third and tenth October. I could marry you immediately afterwards. However, you will both need documents to prove your identity, as well as you are clear to become husband and wife. The vicar must read them at your parish in Edinburgh, which he can do on the same three Sabbaths as when I proclaim them."

Sarah's heart sank. She didn't have any paperwork to prove she was, in fact, Sarah Shand and nothing to say she was free to marry. Worst of all, no one in the city she claimed to be from had ever heard of her.

"Documents? I don't have any."

"A trip to the Registry Office will solve that. They hold all the vital records," the minister said.

That was fine in theory, but she didn't exist in 1886. They could search all they wanted, but it would be time wasted.

"Don't worry, we'll obtain the documentation you need," Robert said, patting her hand.

"B-but what about getting the banns read in Edinburgh? My parents were far from religious, and I didn't go to church there. Was I even baptized? How can we manage that?"

"Your birth would have been registered which is a requirement of civil registration. Once you find that record, it won't be difficult to find the rest. Since you hadn't belonged to a kirk there, the readings don't have to be performed in that parish. Still, we'll require the documents," Reverend Mitchell said.

Sarah stood and paced about the room chewing on her thumbnail. "So, if we wanted our wedding around the end of the month, when is the latest I could bring you my certificates?"

"Preferably before the third reading, but so long as I have them before the day of the service." The minister thumbed through his book. "The only day I have available is Saturday, 30th October; otherwise we're looking at November. Would that be acceptable?"

"Yes, that's fine," Sarah replied, her mind on the lack of documents.

"Young people, you're in my book for that date and time. I will read the banns commencing this coming Sunday. "If there isn't anything else for today, I'll take my leave of you now. Wonderful to see you again, Miss Shand."

"Thank you, Reverend."

After the man left, Robert turned to her. "You're worried about what the vicar said, aren't you? Don't worry. We'll go to the Registry Office right away and find those credentials for you."

There was nothing to find. This particular Sarah Shand would not exist until January 1991. And when she could not provide proof of her identity, the wedding would be off.

That night, when everyone took their seats in the dining room, Sarah positioned her hand on the white tablecloth, so her engagement ring was evident.

Jenny spotted the glittering piece of jewellery immediately. "P-pretty," she said as she touched the centre stone.

"Do you like it? Robert gave it to me last night. We've also set a date for our wedding."

"Stunning. Even though Letitia is my friend, I'm happy for you both."

"Are you feeling better today?" Did that let their secret out? She hoped not since she was only asking after the woman who had been poorly the previous day.

"Yes, thank you. So kind of you to ask."

Sarah became quiet.

"You look worried," Margaret said.

"Robert and I can't get married until I have proof of my identity."

"What's the problem?"

"I don't have any," she cried.

"Maybe Kenneth McIntosh could help you?"

"You are a wise woman, Sister. I'm ashamed I didn't think of that. I'll contact him in the morning. If he can't find the documents, nobody can."

Jenny took Sarah's hand. "S-Sarah loves R-Robert?"

"Very much. I want to marry him and have all three of us be a family more than anything in the world."

Later, Sarah joined Robert in the library. "Your solicitor will never find any documents to prove I exist or stating I'm not already married." A tear ran down her cheek.

"Why not?" He brushed the moisture away with his thumb.

"After you hear this, you'll probably want to take me back to the loony bin yourself, but every word is true. I swear. I'm not from this time. I can't explain how, but I think it has something to do with the stone circle and the ley line that runs nearby. After I left it, I stepped in front of a ... well, I was in a bad accident that should have killed me, but I woke up here. Over the years, I saw what I thought were the ghosts of a boy and a girl playing up there. When Mr. Robertson took me on a tour of the house and showed me the portraits, I discovered that the children I saw were you and Margaret."

"How could that be?"

"Please just listen before you say anything else. I was born in 1991. When I left my time, it was the year 2010. That's how I know so much about Jenny's alleged epilepsy and its treatment, and how I knew what to do for Letitia when she tried to kill herself. My family's home is on the property you and Angus took me to, but in 2010."

Robert frowned.

"You do believe me, don't you?"

"I never told anyone this for fear people would think I was crazy," he said, "but I experienced strange encounters, too. Seeing things that don't belong. I saw a young girl at the stone circle when I was a wee lad and my sister, and I played in those fields. I have no idea who she was or where she came from, but I only saw fleeting images, so I dismissed it as an overactive imagination."

"Did she have short hair and lots of freckles?"

"Yes."

"That was me. How could this happen? Is it possible the strands of time had fragmented somehow, and we were able to see into each other's lives?"

"I don't know," he murmured.

"The first time I saw you and Margaret, I was with my gran."

"Yes, an older woman with a kindly face and grey hair. I remember seeing you two together. I tried to show both of you to my sister, but she saw nothing. How is all this possible? I don't understand."

"Neither do I."

"Whatever the cause, I am delighted because you came into my life," he said, taking her hand in his.

"I'm just embarrassed you saw me when I was young and awkward looking."

"You were beautiful then, too." Robert pressed his lips to her knuckles. His expression became serious. "You said when I found you on the doorstep Weetshill was a ruin. What did you mean?"

Sarah's mouth gaped open. "I-I was so confused; I probably said a pile of things that didn't make sense." She wavered before continuing. "What are we going to do about the documents? The banns are read for the first time tomorrow."

"Don't worry. I still plan on speaking with Kenneth to see if he can help."

"Thank you. I'll come with you then?"

"No. You shouldn't. It is considered bad luck for the bride to be in attendance."

Bad luck or not, Sarah and her charge would attend the next day.

"I don't think it's a good idea."

"But I don't have anything to hide. I did nothing wrong. I saved Letitia's life," she protested.

32

Sunday morning they rode to the service in silence. Robert pondered Sarah's revelation of the night before. She had been hiding something, and he had feared the worst. She had a husband who would turn up and take her away from him. Her real secret, outrageous as it was, relieved him. He still couldn't fathom her explanation of her statement about Weetshill being a ruin but didn't press her about that. They had more important issues to deal with, like the problem of her birth certificate.

At the church, Mr. Christie and his ghillie stood outside the door. The man glowered at them as they advanced. Robert surmised Sarah was the recipient of his foul expression. Horatio nodded and whispered something to Tommy as they walked by.

Spooked by their actions, she asked, "Wonder what they're up to?"

"I'm sure I don't know."

The elderly MacDonald woman stared at them from across the aisle as they took their seats. Suddenly, she stood and bolted from the building.

Reverend Mitchell was in fine form that morning. The sermon seemed to go on forever. A nudge in the ribs from Margaret prevented Robert from dozing off on more than one occasion. Soft snores were audible within the small sanctuary.

He looked to his left at his betrothed. The muted light softened Sarah's features, and she looked beautiful. To his right, his sister bowed her head and fiddled with the strings on her bag, presumably to stay awake.

At long last, the sole reason for their attendance this morning arrived. "According to the forms of the Established Church of Scotland, I read third banns of Alastair McDonald and Margaret Colquhoun." The minister repeated the introduction. "And first of Robert Andrew Robertson and Sarah Shand."

Thomas Sievewright leapt to his feet. "They cannae be mairrit! Miss Christie's blood is all o'er her hands. If it wasnae for the corrie-fisted wench, Miss Letitia wouldnae tried to kill herself. You must ken that. She and the mister cannae wed."

Robert stood and faced Sarah's accuser. "How dare you? I saw Horatio whispering to you when we came into the church. Did he tell you to object?"

They couldn't silence the ghillie. "Can this Miss Shand prove she is who she says?"

"You made your point, Mr. Sievewright. Please sit down so we can conclude our morning's worship," the clergyman snapped.

Once Reverend Mitchell restored order to the kirk, he finished the service with the Bible passage he selected for the closing.

At the conclusion, Mr. Christie scowled at them again. "I knew you were behind my wee girl's heartbreak, and now I've got proof. You two have made a fool of her, and I'll not stand for it."

"He had a strange look on his face when we first came in. At first, I thought he was staring at me," Sarah said to Robert and his sister.

"He was looking at the little one." Margaret glared at the man.

"Hmm. Wonder why? I mean Jenny's been at Ladysbridge her entire life and only just arrived at Weetshill. What would be up his butt to make him look at her in that way?"

Callum brought the open-topped carriage to the end of the walkway. The coachman helped the women board. Jenny scrambled up and hugged Sarah while Robert waited for the vicar.

The minister finally emerged and walked to the brougham. "I'm sorry about all that unpleasantness with Mr. Sievewright."

"Why can't the people of Kendonald bear to see me happy? Why did he have to say it was because of me Letitia tried to top herself?"

"Ignore his objection."

"You make it sound easy. I feel bad enough about it. Her father didn't need to tell the entire community like this. It would mortify and embarrass her, and I wouldn't blame her one bit. These people around us are the ones who had me locked away in the nut house. His outburst is the last thing I need."

"Have you had any luck yet obtaining the documentation we

discussed, Miss Shand?"

"N-no."

"There are still two more readings to go, so I trust you'll have your documents by the third. You go off home now and don't let this unpleasantness bother you. I have some parishioners who can't get out that I must visit."

"Thank you, Reverend." Robert shook the minister's hand and boarded the carriage.

In the afternoon, Sarah took Jenny to the steading. In the past, the pony was in the enclosure, but today there was no sign of the animal or the groom. She took the little girl's hand, and they wandered the perimeter the building. Callum's room where he kept his tools was empty, too. Strange. Where was everyone?

"Wh-where's the p-pony?"

"Dunno, sweetie." Sarah was worried because she had never seen the stable buildings so deserted.

They walked back to the main barn door. It was slightly ajar. "You wait here. I'll see if the horse is in its stall. Maybe Hamish hasn't had a chance to bring her out yet."

The hinges creaked when she pulled. Today was her first time inside the stables. She stepped across the threshold. It took some time for her eyes to adjust to the dim light.

Bang! Sarah wheeled around. The door slammed against the frame.

Before she could react, she was flat on her stomach with a knee in the small of her back. Unable to see her attacker, when she tried to scream, the person's weight made it impossible. He grabbed her hands and held them behind her back. She twisted on the floor, trying to escape his vice-like hold, but he only tightened his grip.

Her assailant flipped her on her back and drove his knee down between her legs, pinning her arms above her head with his hands.

"Jenny," she cried out.

"Shut your mouth, or I'll shut it for you," a ragged voice whispered.

Sarah screamed and received a backhander across the face. She took advantage of her arm being free and raked her fingernails down the man's face.

"You shouldnae done that," he growled and ripped her bodice.

The voice identified the man. "Hamish, what the hell are you playing at?"

He mashed his mouth on hers and pinned her wrists against the plank floor.

The door swung open, and Jenny stood there, eyes wide with fear. "D-don't hurt S-Sarah."

He lifted his head and loosened his grip on Sarah's arms.

"Run. I need help. Get Robert."

She remained frozen in place. Sarah prayed she didn't have a seizure. "Quickly, please."

The small girl turned and ran as fast as her legs could carry her. Breathless when she reached the mansion, she gasped, "R-Robert. S-Sarah n-needs y-you."

He and Margaret arrived at the front door at the same time. "Why are you so vexed?" Margaret asked. "Calm down. Take a deep breath and start again. We can't help you if you don't tell us."

Robert knelt beside her. "What is it?"

"S-Sarah," she managed between rapid breaths. "P-pony, m-man."

"Has there been an accident at the stables?"

She nodded.

Robert started for the barn.

"J-J-Jenny c-c-come, t-t-too." She tagged along behind him, but he was already strides ahead of her.

Robert flew into the stable as Hamish drew his fist back and punched Sarah in the face. "What the blazes is going on in here?" he demanded as he lunged for the man. "Callum, Angus," he yelled. "I need help."

The ghillie raced to his employer's aid. Once assured his man restrained the groom, Robert rushed to Sarah's side. He gathered her into his arms and moved her away from her attacker.

She huddled with her face buried and sobbed.

"What's the fuss? I heard the commotion and came as fast as I could, Sir," the coachman said, catching his breath.

"Don't let him out of your sight, Angus. Hold your shotgun to him if you must. You, Callum, fetch the constable and Doctor Burnett back here. Skinner had better bring that Black Maria of his so this no-good, evil bastard is secured all the way to the police house. Do you have some sturdy leather straps?"

"Aye, Sir."

"Then I want this man lashed to that beam before you leave. He's got much to answer for." He turned his attention back to Sarah and knelt beside her. When he tried to lift her head, she resisted. "It's me, Robert."

Without raising her head, she threw her arms around his neck and squeezed him.

"H-H-Hamish b-bad?" Jenny asked.

"Very bad." He gently put his arm around her. "You, on the other hand, were magnificent."

Once assured Hamish was secured and unable to escape his ties, he carried Sarah to the house. Jenny clung to him the entire journey.

"Whatever happened?" the butler exclaimed when he opened the front door.

"Please Archibald, not now. Callum is bringing the police and Doctor Burnett here as we speak so when he arrives, show him directly to Miss Shand's room."

"I shall carry out your wishes, Sir."

Robert took Sarah to her room and settled her gently on the bed. She immediately rolled over, turning away from him. What else had Hamish done to her that would make her not want to face him? If the brute had raped her, he swore he would kill him.

Jenny put her hand in his. He looked down into her fear-filled eyes. "She'll be all right. I'm sure. Don't you worry your pretty little head. Why don't you climb up there with her? I think Sarah would love a cuddle with you." Robert lifted the child onto the mattress where she nestled against her.

He paced while he waited for the physician to arrive, recalling how Hamish looked at her the first day and felt guilty because he never saw this coming.

Sarah groaned, and within seconds Robert was at her side. "You're out of danger. He'll not get near you again."

"Excuse me, Sir, but Doctor Burnett is here," Archibald announced.

"Good of you to come so quickly," he said as he shook the physician's hand.

"Let's see what the problem is then, Miss Shand?"

Sarah rolled over. The brute had split both her upper and lower lips. As a result, her mouth swelled. Scrapes covered her left cheek, and her right eye was swollen and bruised.

The doctor went to work and cleaned her wounds. She winced a few times but did not complain. He finished attending to Sarah's injuries and motioned to a location near the window where he and the Laird spoke in hushed tones before returning to her bedside.

"There is one question I must ask. Did Hamish MacMillan do anything else to you?"

"Not for the lack of trying. That man tore my clothes and said I led him on. I figure he would have raped me if Robert hadn't gotten there when he did."

"That's all I needed. I didn't mean to upset you," Doctor Burnett apologized. He turned to Robert and said, "Her cuts and bruises will take some time to heal, but she's a strong lassie. I believe she'll come through this just fine."

Sarah pulled the little girl close to her. Had the two most important people in her life not come to her aid, Hamish might have violated her or worse, beaten her to death.

After the doctor gathered his things and left, Robert said, "Police Constable Skinner will be coming to talk to you at some point."

The cop was the last person on earth she wanted anywhere near her. He'd taken her to the asylum on nothing more than the whim of Tommy Sievewright.

Robert leaned over and kissed her cheek. "You rest now." He started to leave the room.

Sarah reached for him, clutched his arm, and pulled him toward her. When he sat on the edge of the bed, she embraced him. The emotional upheaval bottled up inside now spewed from her, and her body convulsed with sobs as she clung to him.

"Sir, Miss Shand?" Callum knocked and stuck his head around the door. "Can I come in?"

"Please."

"I's sorry I wasnae there to keep Hamish from beatin' you. He sent me off lookin' for a loose horse. He left the gate wide open himself so the animal could wander off. I dinnae ken he would do anythin' like that to you."

Sarah groaned. "You couldn't know what he was planning."

"I do hope you's up an' around soon. Good night, to you both."

A few hours later, Robert brought Police Constable Skinner into Sarah's room. "She's sleeping. I'll wake her, shall I?"

"No, you're all right, Mr. Robertson. We'll let her rest for a while longer. You and I can talk. Say over at the table?" Once seated, the policeman began his inquiries. "Where were you when the incident took place?"

"Here in the mansion. Wee Jenny, she was with Miss Shand and came to get me."

"Do you have any reason to think why your groom would attack the young woman?"

"None."

"There is no delicate way to put this, but do you think perhaps she led him on?"

"Never. And I resent you thinking that," Robert said through clenched teeth.

"It's unpleasant, but I do have to ask." The man paused. "I just need to read this back to make sure everything is correct."

Sarah stirred and moaned, and immediately Robert went to her side. "Police Constable Skinner is here."

"I don't want to see him. After what he did to me? Tell him to bugger off." She waved her arm.

"I'm sorry about your injuries," he said, "and I'm even sorrier for my part in taking you off to the sanatorium. I only acted on the information given to me."

Sarah rolled back to face him. "You've known Doctor Burnett for a lot longer than me, but you didn't recognize the signature on the paper Tommy Sievewright handed you was a forgery?"

"No. The man was in such a state I didn't take the time to look it over. I should have checked more closely." He reached for her hand.

"Don't touch me," Sarah bristled.

"I won't then. Will you tell me what happened to you today? I have Mr. Robertson's account of things from the time he arrived on the scene. I need yours, too."

"And then you'll go talk to Hamish, and the old boy's club rules will prevail, and he'll be out so he can come after me again."

"I assure you, Miss Shand, that is not my intent. I can see you suffered a horrible beating."

Sarah plucked up the courage and related the events. She had to stop and regain her composure many times. Robert was at her side each time she broke down to comfort her. It took forever, but finally, the inquiries ended. Not deterred by the pain she was in; she was glad she had bruises because they were proof of the attack. At least, if Hamish was released, he would no longer have a job at Weetshill and would have to move on. Far away from Aberdeenshire was her choice.

"I'm sorry about this, but the more details this time around, the less I'll have to be back and put you through it again."

"Shall I walk you out?" Robert asked.

"No, you're all right, Mr. Robertson. I'll see myself out."

33

Sarah spent much of the following week in her room. Even though Hamish was still locked up, she had nightmares every night he would escape from his cell and come after her again.

When the day the second reading of the marriage banns arrived, she had mixed feelings. Should she go or stay home?

"After the last time, I think you two should remain here," Robert said. "I don't want to see you grieved like that again."

"My brother is right. Neither you nor Jenny needs all that grief. We'll tell you when we get home how everything went."

They took the decision away from her. Sarah wasn't upset but relieved. She waved them off and said, "I'm glad you didn't go with Robert and Margaret, sweetie. After the way Horatio Christie looked at you last Sunday, I don't want you anywhere near the miserable old git or his ghillie."

The country house was quiet with everyone gone. Sarah curled up with a Jane Austen novel on the sofa but couldn't settle her mind to read, too worried about the banns.

She took Jenny upstairs and read to her from *Grimm's Fairy Tales*, but even the little girl didn't relax.

"C-can we g-go outside? P-please?" Reluctantly, Sarah got their cloaks, and they went out. The aroma of wet, rotting autumn leaves and decaying windfall apples permeated the air with pleasant, earthy smells.

The strains of a woman singing in what might have been German floated towards them. Sarah was not able to determine where the music originated. Maybe one of the servants was in the kitchen garden, or Maggie was hanging out laundry. No one else was there. Listening closer, the voice sounded similar to the full, rich tone of the spectral voice in her room that night.

"M-music p-pretty."

Until the little girl said she heard the singing, too, she thought she had imagined it. "Let's go back in. I'm getting cold. Besides, it's getting close to the time Robert and Margaret will be coming home from church."

"D-do we g-gots to?"

"Afraid so, sweetie." Sarah took Jenny's hand, and they started back.

Inside, she went into the ballroom, and leafed through the sheet music on the piano. Nothing there resembled the song from earlier.

Soon after, the carriage wheels crunched on the gravel driveway. "You go upstairs and I'll be along shortly to read you a story." Once Jenny started for the first floor, Sarah hurried to the front door.

"The reading of the banns went well," Robert said, "and there was no sign of Horatio Christie or Thomas Sievewright."

"That's wonderful news. Now if we could solve my documentation problem."

"I'm confident Kenneth will think of something."

"But, we only have a week left." Sarah mourned. "Anyway, I promised Jenny I would read to her. I best go." As she walked down the corridor, a voice was singing the same melody she heard outside, but instead of a rich contralto, this one was high and clear. Before her earlier experience, no one in the mansion ever hummed. Sarah quietly opened Jenny's door.

The little girl sat in the rocking chair. This beautiful music came from her, and more unusual, her speech impediment vanished when she sang. A tear trickled down Sarah's face, and she wiped it away before entering the room.

Jenny stopped and looked up.

"Don't stop. That was beautiful. Where did you learn to sing like that?"

"D-don't know."

She doubted they had music of any kind in the asylum. The small child likely never heard singing in her life before the church service the previous Sunday. Still, didn't children sing loudly and off-key when they first learned?

She started the melody again. Awed by the child's talent, Sarah stumbled into a chair and listened.

"Would you like me to teach you a song? I'm nowhere as good as you, but I know a fun one you might like."

"Y-yes p-please."

She thought of a tune that would be easy to learn. "We'll do *Mairi's Wedding*, but instead of Mairi, we'll sing Sarah. It starts like this 'Step we gaily on we go,'" she belted out. "Your turn now."

Jenny repeated the words. Line by line, Sarah sang, and she followed her lead until they reached the last one. "And now the finale 'All for Sarah's wedding,' Think you can do the whole thing by yourself now?"

At the song's conclusion, she applauded. "You can sing it for Robert and Margaret later," she said enthusiastically and cuddled the small girl.

After lunch, everyone adjourned to the library. Robert's sister went back to her needlepoint. He chose a book off the shelf and sat in one of the armchairs by the sofa.

Sarah bent down to Jenny's level. "Are you ready?"

"Y-yes."

"Jenny has a surprise for you."

Both Margaret and Robert turned their attention to the little girl.

Flawlessly, she performed the four lines of the tune taught to her. At the last line, Sarah was sure she'd put extra emphasis on her name. They applauded her performance.

"It's the first time I heard that song," Margaret said.

"S-S-Sarah t-teach me."

"That's amazing. Did you notice, Sister, when Jenny sings, she doesn't stutter?"

"Why, yes I did. How does she do that?"

"Beats me. I'm as gobsmacked as you are," said Sarah.

"Do you know any other songs?" Robert inquired.

The little girl then sang the piece they listened to when they were outdoors.

"Where did you learn this?" Margaret asked.

"The l-lady was s-singing."

"What lady?"

"A woman was singing that while you were at church. I thought it might be Maggie when she was hanging clothes out."

"What kind of voice was it?" he asked.

"Similar to Letitia's only lower."

"No, wouldn't be Maggie. She can't carry a tune. The crows and jackdaws squawk better than she does," he said in a strange voice. His face turned white, and the siblings stared at each other.

Margaret and Robert looked like they had heard a ghost.

"What's wrong?"

"That song, that's *Auf dem Wasser zu singen*, by Schubert. It was one of Mother's favourites. I've not heard it since she died," he said.

34

Late Monday morning, a special messenger arrived with a letter from Kenneth McIntosh. Robert tore open the envelope and scanned the document. With trepidation, Sarah peered over his shoulder.

"Well, the man did it. He found papers for you."

"Th-that's brilliant." How had he managed to find something considering she wouldn't be born for over a hundred years? "How?"

"I wrote to him and told him the month and day of your birthday and your age. He did the rest," Robert replied. "Thank you, laddie," he said to the messenger. You have delivered excellent news. Tell Mr. McIntosh we'll be at his office on Wednesday."

After the young man left with a generous tip, Sarah asked, "What's wrong with tomorrow?"

"Kenneth is busy most of the day and unable to fit us in. That is the soonest he can see us."

"I wanted to go as soon as possible." Her voice choked with disappointment.

"I would rather go and get it over, too, but we have to abide by Kenneth's schedule." Robert kissed her lightly on the cheek.

Wednesday morning finally arrived. Still anxious about her documents, Sarah looked forward to hearing what he found for them. "Can we go shopping while we're there? I want to pick up some things for Jenny and maybe look for a wedding gown if that's all right."

"Of course. We'll have plenty of time after our meeting."

In the beginning, Margaret begged out of a day in the city, but after much persuasion from her brother and Sarah agreed.

"You suggested I try Kenneth. You should be there, too."

Janet accompanied the women on Mrs. MacEwen's orders since proper ladies didn't travel without their maid as a chaperone.

When the entourage arrived at the station, Robert bought their tickets. The locomotive chugged into the platform, belching black smoke out the stack and steam out the sides as he distributed their travel documents.

Excited, Jenny jumped up and down. For Sarah, it was just a day in Aberdeen, although there was much more at stake on this trip.

The conductor blew his whistle signalling their departure time. The engine hissed and lurched into motion. Janet looked around the carriage. "I hasnae rode in first class before," she said, rubbing her hands over the plush upholstery.

"I did once on the Strathspey Steam Railway from Boat of Garten to Aviemore on a family outing," said Sarah.

"Do you know what you want for a wedding gown?" asked Margaret. She fidgeted with her drawstring bag and it clunked loudly against the side of the opulent coach.

What did she carry in there to make such a racket? "Not really, but I'll know it when I see it." She smoothed her skirt as she spoke.

"Should I be here if you're discussing Sarah's clothes?" asked Robert leaning across the aisle toward the women and Jenny.

"You're fine, Brother. It's not like you're seeing her in it on or before your wedding day. And flowers?"

"Red and white roses with baby's breath in a cascade bouquet."

"Ye cannae have that. Red and white is bad. Means blood and bandages," exclaimed Janet.

"Really? More superstitious nonsense?" Sarah looked out the window on the opposite side of the carriage.

"Do you have trains in what you refer to as 'your' time?" Robert whispered.

"Yes, but their schedule keeping is nowhere near what it is now. ScotRail isn't known for their punctuality, but there are other rail companies worse than them. There are also cars and airplanes."

"What are they?"

"Well, cars are like this in a way but much smaller. Usually only room for four or five people. Planes may carry hundreds of passengers, but they fly."

"What? Like birds? Have you ridden in one?"

"Yes, it's lots of fun. I love taking off. The thrust of the engines pushes you into your seat. The only part I don't like is when the plane banks to turn, and you can look down and see the ground. Once up at the cruising altitude, I don't mind looking down. You're above the clouds."

"This future of yours sounds wonderful yet frightening."

About forty-five minutes later, the train pulled into the platform at the joint terminal in Aberdeen. The city didn't look or smell anything like the one from her time. Engrossed in the stonework on one of the buildings, Sarah backed into the street to get a better look. An unfamiliar sound became louder, and she turned in its direction. Janet yanked her out of the way in the nick of time to prevent her from being run over by a runaway horse-drawn carriage. Her brush with disaster brought the realization that everything was different to the fore.

Architecturally, most of the buildings were similar but had ornate window and door casings. The businesses occupying them were gunsmiths, milliners, drapers, merchants of wine and spirits, as well as fancy goods, accountants and silk mercers. The streets were cobblestones, not smooth tarmac. Petrol and diesel exhaust fumes no longer filled the air. The stench of human waste from chamber pots chucked out tenement windows mixed with the pong from horse urine and manure caught in her throat. The building housing the solicitor's premises was the Abbey Bank in Sarah's time.

Robert opened the oak door, letting the women enter. "Up the stairs and to your left," he said before following them.

Kenneth met them inside the spacious outer workspace. "Good to see you people. Come in my office. I searched for documents on Miss Shand, and was unable to find any marriage records."

"I knew there wouldn't be."

"So I turned to birth registrations for the years 1866 to1868 looking for a Sarah Shand."

"And?" Robert asked.

"I found a few, but I think this one is the best choice to use for your upcoming nuptials."

"This isn't what one would call above board, is it?" she said.

The solicitor blushed. "Hear me out. This particular woman was born in Musselburgh in January 1865. Her full name was Anna Sarah Shand, and she was the daughter of Charles and Barbara, maiden surname Abel."

"Would I have to change my first name?"

"Yes, but say you don't like your forename, and you go by your middle one. Many people do." He looked at Robert. "Your father did. Everyone knew him as Alex, but he was registered as John Alexander."

"But what if this woman or her parents come forward?"

"That's why I say this selection is perfect. Both this woman and her mother succumbed to consumption, and her father, a steeple-jack, died when he fell off the roof of a church he was working on."

Sarah sensed the man's excitement. "What about brothers and sisters?"

"There were no siblings," Kenneth said as he spread out the paperwork on the desk.

"But you could go to prison for this. So could we. Identity theft is illegal. Besides, Robert told everyone I was from Edinburgh."

"Aye, but folk do move. Don't you fret about these documents. You let me worry about that. You need to prove you are in a position to marry. I provided it. Plain and simple."

"Kenneth, I'm not so sure I like this," said Robert.

"What other choice do you have?"

"An irregular marriage. Perhaps one performed by a blacksmith."

"Abolished in 1854 by our good lady Queen with the inception of Civil Registration, and that same Civil Registration is allowing you to go through with your wedding plans. You see, my lad, you have no alternative but to take this opportunity I'm providing for you. Don't worry, if anything comes of it, I will take full responsibility."

Sarah clutched Robert's hands and held them tightly. "I think he's right. This is the only solution."

"I agree. I don't like the idea of being dishonest with a clergyman, but if it means we can wed, then I'm willing to do just that."

Running her hands over the registration certificates, she studied them until Robert took them and put them in his coat's inside breast pocket. "You ladies go attend to your other business here in Aberdeen. I'll stay with Kenneth, and we'll meet for the train at say, three-thirty for four?"

Business concluded at the solicitor's office, the women and Jenny left to shop. Sarah walked on air now she had the legal proof she needed to marry Robert. She wished he had come along with them, but if he was anything like the men from her time, he detested shopping with women.

As they made their way closer to the Castlegate, Sarah stopped and turned quite pale.

"Whate'er is the matter, Miss?" asked Janet.

She couldn't answer not without revealing her previous life. Where was the Salvation Army Citadel and the high-rise behind it? A conspicuously empty place in the Aberdeen skyline occupied the area its turrets and the roof lines would someday fill. Horses and buggies drove around the Mercat Cross – an area she knew was pedestrianized.

Margaret's heels clicked loudly on the pavement. "I told you Kenneth could help," she said when she caught up with Sarah.

"Thanks for suggesting him, but how did you know he could?"

"He assisted me when I escaped my arranged marriage."

"How?"

"When I first ran away, I came to Aberdeen. I didn't have anywhere to go and was living on the street. Kenneth found me and put me on a train to Edinburgh with the name of a solicitor friend who required a nanny for his children. He gave me a substantial sum of money to tide me over until I was on my feet. Mother, Granda, or that awful man they arranged me with in marriage never knew where I had gone. I needed false documentation, too, so George and I could wed."

Margaret's revelation shocked Sarah. "So you know my situation better than you've let on." She linked arms with the woman, and they worked their way along Union Street.

The sign in the window of Milne, Low & Co. advertised the latest fashions from Paris. "Let's go in. Even though a Paris original is well out of my price range, it would be fun to look at them."

Inside the shop, a well-dressed man approached. "Ladies, what can I do for you today?"

"I'm looking for some children's dresses. And wedding gowns."

He raised his hand and snapped his fingers, and a woman approached.

The female clerk guided the women and the little girl to a location in the back of the ground floor where girls' ensembles hung on racks. "Our bridal apparel is up there," she said indicating the staircase leading to the upper level.

Sarah and Jenny perused the clothing downstairs. "What about this one?"

She wrinkled her nose at the long-sleeved, green dress with white pinafore then pointed to a short-sleeved, burgundy one with snowy coloured lace trim. "J-Jenny likes this one."

"That is pretty. Is there a place to try it on?"

The shop worker showed them to an area at the back where Sarah helped her change into the chosen clothing. Once clothed, they went back to where Janet and Margaret waited.

"You look beautiful, just like a Princess," said Robert's sister.

"My thoughts exactly. It would be perfect for my wedding." After Jenny was back in her regular clothes, Sarah took the apparel and selected some hair ribbons. She laid them on the display case then went up to the room where the shop housed their selection of bridal wear.

She meandered around and examined each one. As she worked her way through the gowns, she spotted the dress, the most beautiful gown she had ever seen. Ivory satin, with off the shoulder sleeves which converged into the bodice coming to a point at the front and fit like a corset.

It was the one she dreamt of wearing when she walked down the aisle on her father's arm in her dream wedding. She searched for a price tag and found one, affixed with a straight pin. Six hundred pounds for the garment alone. The veil was extra. Sarah looked at it and back at the costume. "I've seen enough," she said. "I'd like to leave now." She paid for the items selected earlier. Once packaged, Janet picked the bundle off the counter, and they departed.

Outside the shop, Margaret patted Sarah's arm. "Are you all right? We've only been in one store."

"Yes, I'm fine. I want to go home."

The Trinity Centre mall which occupied the corner of Union and College Streets was noticeably missing from the landscape, too, as were many of the modern buildings from her time. The St. Nicholas Cemetery with its columned entry remained unchanged.

Janet touched Sarah's arm. "Ye look a bit pale, Miss. Is this tae much for ye? It hae only been a short time since yer ..."

"I'm fine. I'm just confused. I've shopped in many of these buildings, but they're not how I remember them. The shop where we looked at wedding dresses I know as the Orange store."

35

They arrived well before the next train. Sarah chose a seat near the platform from where they would leave.

"Miss, whatever has you so vexed?" Janet asked.

According to the time on the station clock, there was still over an hour to wait. She dropped on the wooden slats and stared off. "I'll be okay. I just need to talk to Robert."

Jenny climbed up beside her. "S-Sarah s-sad?"

"A little but not because of you."

The little girl hugged her then clambered up and peered over the back of their seat. "R-Robert," she squealed, pointing.

Sarah turned. "You're early."

"I could say the same. I didn't expect you to conclude your shopping this quickly."

"The wedding, I can't," she said bowing her head.

"What do you mean you can't?" Robert said as he sat next to her.

"All this money. I can't spend it on our marriage, not after you had to pay off Horatio Christie. I don't want you to waste that much dosh on things I don't need. I can't do that to you."

"I wanted to give you something lavish."

She swallowed. "I want to marry you more than anything. But ...,"

"Go on. I'm listening."

Fidgeting with the drawstring on her bag, Sarah persevered. "I thought I wanted the fairytale ceremony. The dress, the shoes, the flowers, the bridesmaids. As long as I'm with you none of that matters."

"What are you getting at, Sarah?"

"I don't want all the frills. A simple affair, just you, me, and two witnesses."

"If that's what you want, by all means." He brought her hands to his face and brushed his lips against them.

"There's more. I want the money you would have spent on this to go to something worthwhile."

"Such as?"

"The asylum. The place could use it. I know they need bedding and clothing, a garden and animals so they can become self-sufficient and not have to rely on the meagre handouts from the council."

"That's charitable of you." He squeezed her hand.

She sighed. Lost in her thoughts, she jumped when the piercing shriek shattered the relative quiet, and steam belched from the engine, filling the platform.

"All aboard!" the conductor called and blew his whistle.

They boarded, and Sarah turned around. The Robertson siblings remained near the bench, apparently in deep conversation. When he joined them in the carriage, she stayed behind. "Where's Margaret going?"

"Well, she decided to visit some friends here in Aberdeen."

"Oh." Something about his explanation sounded a bit fishy. If the plan was to see people in the city, Robert's sister would have said something before they left Weetshill.

"Do you think George and the children will come to our wedding?"

"I can't say. With Granda's ill feelings toward my sister after Father's death, I never met the man. I only know what Margaret tells me."

Sarah waved to the woman on the platform from her seat.

They rode the rest of the way home on the train in silence. Back at Weetshill, she ensured the little girl had a bite to eat and got her off to bed before joining Robert for supper.

Margaret waved until the last carriage vanished around the bend. She scurried back to Milne, Low & Co. unsure the hour they ended their daily trading. The shop remained open.

Winded from rushing from the railway station, she paused with her hand on the door knob to catch her breath before entering the premises.

The bell jingled, announcing her presence when she crossed the threshold. At the foot of the stairs, the same man who greeted their party earlier approached. She nodded, clutched her skirts and ascended. The treads creaked beneath her feet. Gowns for all occasions filled the room on the upper level. Where was the one Sarah fell in love with?

Many of the fancy costumes were displayed on mannequins. Margaret weaved her way throughout the maze until she found it. Footsteps grew louder as someone drew near. "I'd like to buy this," she said, "along with a veil and long gloves."

"You were in earlier with two other women and a wee girl?"

"Yes. I'm purchasing this wedding ensemble for my brother's betrothed. I saw the way she admired it."

The clerk brought over a selection of veils in the same shade of ivory and one at a time, held them up next to the dress. The intricacy of the lace work along the edges made the decision more difficult. In the end, Margaret chose one bordered with Trinity knots. "Gloves?"

"This way." The woman led the way to a display counter. She opened a drawer and lifted it onto the glass surface.

Margaret selected a pair and turned them over in her hand. The colour matched but they were plain. She picked up another. These ones had the same Celtic knot on the back of the hand as trimmed the veil.

The store employee took the gloves from Margaret and slipped the left one on. "The seam in the ring finger is open so the bridegroom can place your wedding ring on without you having to take it off. You slip your finger through the opening."

"I never would have thought of that. It's quite ingenious. I'll also need gloves for the flower girl in the same colour as well as myself. Wrist length will do."

Purchases packaged and paid for, Margaret left for Jackson's Shoe and Bootmakers on Upperkirkgate. The gas lamps cast an orange glow on the street below. Because of the late hour, she cut through the St. Nicholas Churchyard. The shortcut turned out to be a blessing in disguise, as it brought her out opposite the shop.

Again, a bell chimed when she entered the premises. The smell of tanned animal hides filled the small room. A short time later, a stout man in a stained leather apron, appeared from behind a grimy curtain at the rear.

"G'day. Can I get anything for you?" He smiled broadly revealing his dark yellow, rotting teeth.

"I need shoes to go with a wedding dress."

"Aye. An' what size would you be needin'?"

"I'm not sure. Whatever size this is." Margaret pulled the pilfered footwear from her handbag.

Mr. Jackson took the boot from her and disappeared into the back. He returned a short time later.

"I've chosen this style, but in this colour." She pointed out a different shoe in the desired shade. No way was she about to take anything out of the enormous bundle Sarah's wedding outfit was in – not in this place. It would be filthy in no time. Tins of shoe black and other polishes were stacked haphazardly on a sideboard behind the main display; its surface covered in splotches of colour.

"Nae tae worry. I's happy to make 'em for you. Custom-made and dyed shoes will be nine-pound, six and ten."

"That's a bit dear for a pair of shoes, don't you think?"

"Nae when you's getting the best in all o' Aberdeen."

The shop might leave much to be desired, but the man had a reputation as being the foremost cobbler in the city. "Can you send the bill to Weetshill by Duninsch?"

"Aye, but I am needin' some money up front."

"Is two pounds enough?"

"Aye."

"The wedding is on 30th October. Will that be a problem?"

"Nae. Two weeks. They'll be done in two weeks."

Margaret opened her handbag and extracted the deposit from her purse. "Can I take this home with me or do you still need it?" She pointed to the shoe she brought with her so he could get the sizing correct.

"I has the size. Doesnae need it any longer."

"Can you tell me how to get to St. Andrew Street from here? I'm looking for Mrs. Marr at number six."

"Very easy tae get there. When you leaves here, go right until George Street. Turn right there and straight on until St. Andrew Street. Takes a right there and she's nae very far down."

"Thank you very much for your help."

Margaret followed the shoemaker's directions and found the wax flower maker's house without any difficulty. After her last stop, it was refreshing to step into a neat and orderly shop that didn't reek of animal hides.

"The Robertsons of Weetshill by Duninsch are hosting a wedding celebration. We'll need flowers for the chapel, the great hall and ballroom as well as buttonholes for the men and bouquets for the women."

"Would ye like orange blossoms?"

"I'm not sure I know what they look like."

Mrs. Marr bent down and picked a wax bud and full bloom from the cupboard.

"These really are quite pretty. Is it necessary to get the flowers in wax? Can I get real ones?"

"These are real. They dip 'em in melted beeswax afore they ship 'em here tae Scotland. They would ne'er make the journey if they dinnae. I do the local flowers masel.'"

Margaret inspected the sample orange blossom more closely. "It smells like a real flower, too. They will do quite nicely. Can they be mixed with something more seasonal and native to Scotland?"

"Nae worries. And what aboot the bride's flowers? What do ye want for yersel'?"

"Oh, they're not for me. For my future sister-in-law. She mentioned roses. Deep red and white ones with lots of greenery and a bit of heather. I would like to incorporate tartan into the wedding. I think tartan ribbons on the flowers would be quite pretty."

"What aboot the pinnin' o' the tartan in the weddin' ceremony?"

"How romantic. Sarah would be thrilled."

Margaret spotted a wicker basket which resembled a small inverted saddle. Dyed, off-white, it matched perfectly with Sarah's dress and accessories. "I'll take that basket, too, and as many sprays of heather as you can provide. Wee Jenny can hand them out to the guests."

The order continued with a bouquet for herself, corsages for the female servants, fancier buttonholes for the groom and best man, and plain ones for the male servants.

The clock on the wall chimed once.

"Oh dear," said Margaret. "Is that the correct time?"

"Aye. Half six. You's lucky you got here when you did because I was closin' up."

"I must dash, or I'll miss the last train to Weetshill. If there's anything you need from the Robertsons, please let us know."

"When do you need your order?"

"29th October," she replied hurrying out the door to the train station.

By the time Margaret arrived on the platform, she was out of breath and her arms were weak.

As she settled into her seat, she wondered if she overstepped her bounds by shopping for everything. Would Sarah be pleased or outraged? Time would tell, but she had followed her brother's instructions implicitly.

About eleven o'clock that night, Sarah woke to the sounds of voices in the great hall. She opened the library door to Robert's sister speaking to the housekeeper who held an enormous package in her arms.

"Did you have a nice time with your friends?"

"What?" she replied. "Oh yes, very. Is Robert in there?"

"No. He went upstairs."

Margaret left Sarah in the entryway and swished her way to the staircase.

"Do you think George will bring the children to our wedding?"

"Probably not. The kiddies are in school, and he has to look after the shop. It isn't easy for a merchant to pick up and go. Also, my husband is as stubborn as Granda was. He says if the family didn't think he was honourable enough before, then he doesn't want to see them now."

36

Over the next while, Sarah kept close to Weetshill mansion. She and Jenny read, sang, and went for walks, always avoiding the stables. The little girl hadn't asked to see the pony. The strain of being a person down was hard on both Callum and Angus, but each had stepped up and shared Hamish's duties between them.

When they came back after one of their strolls, the doctor's carriage and the policeman's horse-drawn paddy wagon were parked in the driveway.

"What's going on?" she asked when she walked into the great hall.

"News of the utmost importance," Robert said as he greeted her. "Perhaps it would be better if Jenny is elsewhere for a wee bit."

"Why?" She persuaded the small child to go to the kitchen for a snack before following him to the library.

"I think you'll want to sit down," he said as he ushered her through the door.

Sarah flopped into the wingback by the window. In addition to the physician and the cop, Jean MacDonald sat in the chair at the far end of the sofa, looking worried. "What's she doing here?"

"I think you'll want to hear what the woman has to say," Police Constable Skinner answered.

"You asked me to find out about wee Jenny's condition," Doctor Burnett began. "Well, I made some discreet enquiries at the sanatorium and some not-so-discreet ones about my name being on your admission order. When I checked on the little one's background, I found she had been there since her birth. Her first seizure didn't happen until a few years later, most likely after suffering a head injury."

"Why would someone dump an infant in a place like that?" Sarah asked.

"Were me 'at took her there," Mrs. MacDonald said.

The police constable spoke. "Perhaps you should tell Miss Shand and the Robertsons what you told us at your cottage when we came to speak with you."

"Well, Mr. Christie paid me real good to attend the birth."

"Whose?"

"That wee lassie bidin' here. Be about seven-eight year ago now, Horatio sent for me. He were terrible bothered when I gots to Gleanstane house."

"Go on," Robert pressed.

"I ken it ain't polite but do you think I could has a dram?" she asked.

He passed the woman a glass of whisky.

The old woman slurped down the liquor. "Miss Letitia, she were havin' a bairn."

Sarah's jaw dropped, and she grabbed Robert's hand.

"I birthed the wean an' were told to take her away to an orphanage. Horatio said he'd pay me more to keep the secret. Well, there ain't one o' them in these parts, so I took her to the parish poorhouse. He went mad 'at I left her so close to home, as folk would find out. Tol' me if I wanted to gets my money I had to take the lassie far away. He threatened to slaughter the bairn if I dinnae. He said he was goin' there the next day, an' if she were there, he'd take her off and drown her in the Water o' Bogie."

"What are you saying?" Robert interrupted.

"I couldnae leave her there with Horatio Christie threatenin' to kill 'er, so I took her off to Ladysbridge asylum. Wasnae sure if they would accept a little un, but I hads to do somethin'. Took some doin', but they took her in. I said there was somethin' not right wi' her. They asked me for her birth certificate. Well, as the poor thing had jus' been born, I dinnae have one. When they asked the name, I said it were Jenny – after me own ma, and the da had run off, and the mother died birthin' the wee thing."

"How can you be sure the little girl here is the baby you took away?" Sarah stared at the MacDonald woman.

"I kent the minute I clapped eyes on her that day in the kirk. She be the image of her grandmother when she were small. I kent it for sure when I seen the heart shaped mother's mark ahind her left ear."

The first time Sarah saw that birthmark was when she brushed Jenny's hair at the asylum.

"Who was the father?"

"I dinnae ken."

"Well, um, Mr. Robertson you were arranged to marry Miss Christie," the constable said.

"I never had relations such as those with Miss Letitia. I would never bed a lassie before the wedding night. Sarah, you can't possibly believe this is true."

"I don't. Not for one minute."

"N-no. It was one of the Gleanstane servants," Margaret broke in, wringing her handkerchief in her hands. "Horatio found out and drove him away."

The stutter when speaking in her brother's defense and her actions made Sarah suspicious. She hoped the woman would divulge the truth later.

Robert asked, "But what does all this have to do with Hamish attacking Miss Shand?"

"He confessed. Horatio had paid him to get rid of her and the little girl by whatever means necessary."

"Exactly what do you mean by that?"

"Kill her. Now that was the most extreme, but Horatio was willing to fund that, too. And to do the same to the wee girl, if needs must."

"That bastard," Sarah hissed.

"The paper given to the police, well I managed to get the Superintendent to hand it over," the physician said. "Constable Skinner and I have had a good look the forged name.

"Whose then?" she asked. "Tommy Sievewright's?"

"Not him. He can't read or write," the policeman replied.

"Perhaps Miss Letitia?" Doctor Burnett suggested.

"Let me see that." Margaret took the sheet of paper and studied the signature. "That's nothing like Letitia's handwriting."

"I have an idea who it might be," said Robert. He took out the copies of the original marriage contract and the discharge document and distributed them to the doctor and policeman.

They spread the papers across the desk and examined them. Although the letters were different, the pressure and writing style were the same. "Look," Robert said, pointing to Horatio's signature, 'Horatio J. Christie.' "The J is identical to Doctor Burnett's first name on the commitment order."

Sarah stared at the men in disbelief.

"So it is. I do not doubt he has forged my name."

"So you've arrested the creep?" she asked.

"Well, no."

"Whatever do you mean?" Robert asked.

"Surely he isn't going to buy his way out of this?"

"Mr. Robertson, Miss Shand, there's more. When I went to arrest the man, he and his daughter had fled. Couldn't find any trace of Tommy either. Only Carlyle was there, and he knew nothing. Once found, I'll see Horatio Christie prosecuted to the full extent of the law."

"If you catch him," she said.

The information was too much to take in. In essence, the Laird of Gleanstane had taken a contract out on her and Jenny, and Hamish was his hit man. The situation was straight out of the movies.

Robert, still reeling from the revelations, escorted the men and Mrs. MacDonald to the front door.

"Wait. When is Jenny's birthday? Do you remember?" asked Sarah

"Aye. Were the evening of thirtieth April. The Beltane festivals were jus' gettin' started."

"What year?"

"Let me think. 1878, no 1879. I's sure now. The Tay Bridge fell into the river at the end o' the same twelvemonth."

Guests gone, Sarah turned to Margaret. Her face was a sickly greenish-grey. "You know something, don't you?"

"Let's go out to the chapel. No one will disturb us there."

Privacy ensured, Sarah asked, "Are you lying to protect Robert?"

"No. It's nothing to do with my brother."

"I would still love him even if he did sleep with her. Doesn't matter now. It happened in the past – long before I ever met him."

A tear trickled down Margaret's face. "No, he wouldn't have done that. This information is much worse."

"You're scaring me now. Tell me," Sarah urged.

"The day I called on Letitia after her suicide attempt, she said something that made me sick. I couldn't believe it, but I swore I would never tell a soul, and I have to abide by that."

"Oh no you don't; if you have information to prove Robert isn't the father, then you have to speak up."

"Well, Horatio had always kept Letitia away from other people. After Mrs. Christie's death, he took her out of school and had tutors brought in. I always thought it was strange since both my brother and I went on to The Gordon Schools." Margaret paused then continued. "Well, she told me he was preparing her for marriage. She didn't realize that wasn't a normal father-daughter relationship. She believed everything the man told her."

Sarah almost threw up. "You mean ... he and she ..."

"I'm afraid so. Letitia was always meek and easily led."

"So now what do we do?

"You must promise never to breathe a word of this to anyone," Margaret insisted. "I promised her; I would take the secret to my death to protect her, but maybe I'm not doing her any favours."

"I'm gobsmacked. I never liked Horatio Christie from the first time I clapped eyes on him. Now I could swing for him."

"Promise me; you'll not tell a soul what I told you in here today. Swear on that Bible, please?"

"We should tell the police."

"What could they do? Besides, we must think of her. She doesn't need to know about this. If anyone asks you about who Jenny's father was, you tell him he was a servant, and Letitia's father drove him away when he found out."

"All right."

37

"Should we visit Reverend Mitchell this morning after our meal?" Robert asked.

"Why?" Sarah asked as she fixed a breakfast plate for herself. She was still stunned over the drop in from the doctor, the policeman and Jean MacDonald, but more so with the secret, Margaret shared with her in the chapel.

"Your papers. We probably should have gone as soon as we got them."

"I feel bad about stealing a woman's identity."

"I know you do, but we decided that day in Kenneth's office there was no alternative. I feel guilty lying to a man of God, but as that is our only choice, we have no option."

"But what if he knows this woman who I'm pretending to be, and knows she's dead?"

"I don't think there's much chance of that. You're worrying too much."

"I'll have to see if Margaret will watch Jenny while we're away." She worried about leaving her behind after everything that had come out about the little girl.

"Already arranged. My sister said she would be thrilled," he said a sheepish expression on his face.

Outside the wind whipped the pouring rain in horizontal sheets. Callum gave Sarah and Robert a hand into the carriage. Within moments, they were off.

"Can you give me those certificates again, please? I want to make sure I have all the responses. I don't want to get tripped up, so I forget the correct answer. Or better yet, you quiz me, so I'm ready."

"You're fretting over nothing. You know the answers perfectly. Just take your time, and everything will be fine."

The rain pelted the carriage's soft top all the way to the manse making it impossible to carry on a conversation. It was a relief when Callum stopped in front of the minister's house.

"Good morning. You have your paperwork?" asked the vicar as he ushered them into his modest home.

"Yes," said Sarah.

Robert pulled his and Sarah's official documents out of his pocket and handed them to the minister.

Unfolding them, the clergyman gave them a cursory glance and beckoned the two to sit. "Robert, I've known you since you were born, and I remember baptizing you myself, so I have no doubt about the authenticity of your documents. However, seeing how I'm not acquainted with Miss Shand so well, I must ask you," he swallowed, nodded at her, and continued, "some questions. So, I see your first name isn't Sarah. What is your forename and why don't you use it?"

"Anna. I preferred Sarah so have used my middle name for as long as I can remember."

Reverend Mitchell acknowledged the response and scanned the citation further. "Does your father give his blessing for your marriage?"

"I wish he could. He died."

"Your mother then? Does she approve and will she be coming to the wedding?"

"No, sadly, she's dead, too. Tuberculosis."

"Pardon me?"

Remembering people didn't call it that back then, she corrected herself. "I meant consumption."

"I'm sorry to hear that. Any brothers or sisters?" he asked.

"No. I was an only child. My dad died when I was a little girl," she replied bowing her head. Despite knowing her words were untrue, saying them made her feel bad.

"Very well," he drawled. "How old are you?"

"Turned nineteen in January."

With the expression on the man's face, it was apparent he suspected something wasn't quite right. She became more nervous than she already was. Perspiration dripped from her underarms.

"Suppose you tell me how you made one another's acquaintance and how long ago?"

"It was....," they started to speak at the same time, looked at each other and giggled.

"Go ahead, Sarah. You tell the story."

"Well, a few days before the Glorious Twelfth." She moistened her lips with her tongue then continued, "I had been at the stone circle at Gleanstane. I don't remember what happened, but I was severely injured. Robert found me unconscious on his doorstep and took me in. Over time we fell in love."

Reverend Mitchell folded his hands and steepled his index fingers. "Marriage is not a step to be taken lightly. Too many young people do these days. Divorce rates are on the climb. Over one hundred this past year. Scandalous! People often fall out of affection due to life's difficulties. Do you think yours can stand the test of time?"

"Yes," they said in unison.

"I love Robert with all my heart and soul. Never felt this way about any man before him."

"What of you? Are your feelings for Miss Shand comparable?"

"I feel I have known Sarah all my life. We share many interests and adore each other as much as humanly possible. I reckon our marriage to be much the same as my Gran and Granda's. They were besotted and swore to love one another forever. Granda never once thought of taking another wife during my lifetime. I feel the same way about Sarah, and I know she shares my feelings."

"I look at you two, and I see a couple who are very much devoted to each other. Your commitment to one another is admirable. I will be more than pleased to conduct your ceremony on the date we've set."

Sarah breathed a sigh of relief. "Thank you, Reverend Mitchell."

"My sentiments exactly," Robert said and shook the man's hand. "You've taken a load off our minds."

The minister walked them to the front door. Sarah's answers were too perfect. But Robert fidgeted and could not maintain eye contact. Beads of sweat formed on his forehead. The clergyman prided himself on being able to tell when someone was lying. With the Robertson lad, it wasn't difficult. He shuffled back to his desk and examined her documents again.

The birth registration he stared at told him she was born in 1865. That made her twenty-one. She said she turned nineteen in January. His face flushed. They duped him.

While he pondered the situation, he went into his kitchen and made a pot of tea. Returning to his office, he examined the paperwork again. The only time he had been sure they were truthful was when they talked about how much they loved one another. He joined dozens of couples in matrimony every year, yet he had never seen two people so much in love.

Reverend Mitchell slumped into his chair debating on what he should do. "Dear Lord, guide me in this matter. The couple adores each other, and I believe their union is the right thing. Still, the documents aren't hers. If I join them in marriage, then I'm guilty of lying in your house. Please help me." He cast his eyes downward at his open Bible and a phrase leapt off the page at him 'hatred stirs up strife, but love covers all offences.' Those words certainly fit Sarah and Robert's situation. They were willing to risk legal prosecution and lie in a house of God so they could become man and wife. The strength of their feelings covered the deception. Much as it behooved him to do so, he would marry them and accept the false documents as factual.

On their return to Weetshill, Sarah sought out the housekeeper. She found her in her small room at her desk. "I need a favour from you."

"Aye, Miss Shand. What can I help you wi'?"

"Do you have Margaret's address in Edinburgh?"

"Why would you need that? She be here. You can jus' talk to her."

"Her husband is the one I want."

The woman took off her glasses and beckoned Sarah to sit. "What do want with him?" she asked as she rummaged through the compartments in her desktop.

"I want to surprise Margaret. Bring George and her children here for our wedding."

"Fair nice o' you." Mrs. MacEwen pulled out a tattered piece of paper. "Here you be. Dinnae expect much."

"Thank you. When I'm finished, where do I put it?"

"Archibald has a bag in his pantry. He'll show you."

After obtaining the information, Sarah crept into the library and sat down at the desk, hoping to have the letter written and into the mailbag before anyone interrupted her.

After careful deliberation, she was finally happy with the way she expressed herself.

Dear Mr. Esslemont,

You don't know me, but my name is Sarah Shand. I will be marrying your brother-in-law on 30th October and would love for you and your children to come to Weetshill to celebrate this occasion with us. Margaret misses all of you something terrible, and it would be wonderful if you could surprise her. She is going to be one of my witnesses. It would be brilliant if my fiancé and I could meet you, too.

I look forward to hearing from you. I hope you'll say yes.

Sarah Shand

The response was unknown, but she reached out.

38

The wedding day had finally arrived. Since the final reading of the banns, servants scurried from room to room, dusting, tidying and polishing. Sarah, in awe of their work, asked to help many times, but they refused her offers.

The housekeeper turned up with a tray at Sarah's bedroom door as she was leaving. "I brung you your mornin' meal, Miss Shand."

"Thanks, Mrs. MacEwen, but I'm perfectly happy to go downstairs."

"Nae on your weddin' day. Asides, Mr. Robertson, is in the breakfast room, and you cannae see him until the time."

That was the one superstition with which Sarah was familiar, although she didn't believe in such things.

"Janet says you's chosen the frock you wants to wear?"

"Yes. I asked her to get it ready for me some time ago."

"Dinnae fash. It will be a'right," she replied and looked away.

The housekeeper's mannerisms bothered Sarah. Something was wrong.

The suggestion of a walk thrilled Sarah. With being kept out of Robert's way, there wasn't much for her to do, and she welcomed the change of scenery and fresh air. Under a clear and cloudless sky, the day was perfect for late October, and marrying the man of her dreams made it more special.

"I suppose Mother and Father would roll in their graves knowing neither one of their children abided their wishes and went through with their prescribed marriages."

"They would be thrilled to know you were happy in the lives you had chosen for yourselves; I'm certain of that." Sarah cringed as she imagined the type of man her dad would have selected for her.

"My parents didn't know of any other way since theirs was a pre-arranged marriage."

"What are you saying, Margaret? I mean, your grandfather suggested Robert get out of his arrangement."

"We were told it was Granda's idea. He said it had to be, because of the way he was left to cope on his own with a bairn. He negotiated for Father to marry Mother when Father was a wee laddie. Mum's family were the Leslies of Leslie Castle."

"So was money the only motive behind all the arranged marriages?"

"They wanted to ensure ample provision for their children and their grandchildren, too."

"Did your parents love each other?"

"I think they did."

When they came back from their walk, it was almost two o'clock.

"Where are you going?" Margaret asked when Sarah made the turn towards her room at the landing of the staircase.

"My room. Why?"

"Not today. Come with me."

Intrigued, she followed.

"In here," she said as she stopped at the last door on the right.

After opening the door, Sarah slowly crept in. Looking around, she could tell it had been cleaned and made up. The furnishings were like those in her room, except for the enormous four-poster with a canopy and burgundy, velvet curtains tied at each corner.

"The wedding room," Margaret said. "Granda and Gran spent their first night of marriage here. Father and Mother theirs, and now you and Robert."

Sarah nodded in acknowledgement although her surroundings left her in wonderment. She walked around the bed running her fingers over the plush fabrics. A white-wrapped parcel with a note attached sat in the centre of the mattress. She picked it up and read, *To my beautiful bride. All my love, Robert*. With trembling hands, she tore off the ribbon and decorative paper. The gold lettering showed *Zamek and Edelshain, Jewellers, Aberdeen*. A delicate strand of pearls surrounded a dark blue velvety neck form.

Through tear-filled eyes, she gingerly took the necklace out of the box and held it up. "They're beautiful," she whispered.

"Follow me." Margaret opened another door and stood aside for her.

When Sarah walked through into the adjoining room, she gasped. On a dressmaker's mannequin in the corner was the gown she had fallen in love with in the shop in Aberdeen. "It-it's gorgeous! Where did it come from?"

"The day we went to the city, I saw how much you liked it. My brother and I talked before you came home on the train, and I stayed behind and went back and bought it."

"I-I-I don't know what to say."

"You don't have to say anything. Now you relax in that hot bath Janet prepared for you, and then we'll help you get dressed once you're finished."

"Thank you," Sarah said hugging Margaret.

The library door squeaked, and Robert looked up. Kenneth McIntosh stood in the opening with a broad smile on his face. "Well there, today is the day. You're not getting nervous now are you?"

"Not at all, but I still don't like this deception." He glanced at the mantle clock, and reached for his pocket watch out of habit but stopped. By now, Margaret should have revealed the first of the surprises. Sarah might have said she didn't want the fairytale wedding, but no matter how many times she said no, she still did. He had ensured she would have it. He told Kenneth he wasn't nervous. Terrified was a better description of his emotions. "Would you join me in a dram?"

"I thought you would never ask."

Janet styled Sarah's thick, wet hair. She pulled the sides back and fastened them in place and curled the rest of her hair in ringlets. The tongs sizzled as the water boiled off the hot metal.

The young maid helped Sarah into her wedding finery and clasped the string of pearls around her neck.

Sarah pinned the brooch from Robert's grandfather to the bodice.

"You have something old and something new. Now for borrowed and blue," Margaret said.

"So, what do I need?"

"Here, Miss, my lace handkerchief. Isnae much but was my mama's." She handed Sarah the delicate heirloom.

"It's beautiful, Janet. I couldn't ask for more."

Robert's sibling gave Sarah a bedraggled teal garter. This was the one traditional thing I had at my wedding. It belonged to George's sister and maybe her mother before her. At first, I was angry with you over the discharge of Robert and Letitia's marriage contract, but you are good for my brother. He laughs and smiles. He's happy, and that's what's important. Today especially."

"Thank you. You girls have looked after me so well."

A knock reverberated through the door. "Who's there?" Sarah called.

"Mrs. MacEwen."

Janet rushed to the door and let her in.

"You gots e'erythin' you need?"

"I think so."

"Somethin' old?"

"Yes, the brooch from Robert's grandfather."

"And new?"

"These pearls – a gift from Robert."

"Aren't they bonnie," she said, leaning forward for a better look. "Borrowed?"

"The handkerchief."

"And blue?"

"The garter from Margaret."

"So sounds like you is about set."

"What's missing? I can tell by the tone of your voice."

"This." The housekeeper pressed a coin into her hand.

"I don't understand."

"An' a silver sixpence for your shoe. It be part o' my savin's. I would be most pleased if you would take it."

"Of course I will," Sarah said as she embraced the woman.

Robert, dressed in his best navy blue suit, awaited Sarah's appearance outside the chapel. When she rounded the corner, her beauty overwhelmed him. A lump formed in his throat. Although he found her attractive since her arrival, it was never so much as it was at that moment.

Sarah drew next to him, and Robert held his arm out for her. The flowery aroma of the toilet water she used wafted in the air, and he drank in the fragrance. He wanted to take her in his arms right then and there and hold her close to him and never let go. A few more hours and they could make love without any pangs of guilt. By then they would be man and wife.

Jenny walked ahead, and Sarah prayed the wee girl didn't have a seizure. If ever a situation warranted, this was it. The little girl fulfilled her role perfectly, passing sprays of heather to the guests and smiling like she enjoyed herself.

Although focused on the minister near the altar, Sarah couldn't help but notice the room was full. She recognized the other men from the hunting party and Doctor Burnett. Best of all, there was no sign of Jean MacDonald or the miserable ghillie who worked for the Christies.

Reverend Mitchell began. "Dearly beloved, we are gathered here in the presence of our Lord to unite this couple. If there is anyone here who knows why they cannot be legally married, let them speak now or forever hold their peace."

The door creaked open. Sarah worried someone was going to object. Then a little voice called out, "Mama."

A tall, slim man in a charcoal tweed suit, with two children beside him stood at the back of the chapel. The boy had a head of curly brown hair, freckles, and a big smile minus one front tooth. The little girl wore a blue sailor dress, and dark blond ringlets bounced around her face.

Margaret crouched down and held her arms out. The children ran to her and squeezed her. "John Bryce, Mary Elizabeth, my precious bairns. I'm so happy to see you. I missed you terribly."

She stood and embraced the man who had arrived at the front of the room. "George. What are you doing here?"

He nodded in Sarah's direction, making her blush. "This young lassie sent me such a gracious invitation I couldn't refuse. Said you were missing the kiddies and me, and would I come up today for the wedding and surprise you."

"You did that." Tears streamed down Margaret's cheeks. She turned to Sarah, beaming then introduced the man to her brother and soon to be sister-in-law.

"My pleasure to meet both of you. Now before we hold proceedings up any longer, I suggest we take a seat and let you folks carry on."

Reverend Mitchell led the assembled guests in the recitation of the 23rd Psalm. Another brief pause and he began. "Robert Andrew Robertson, will you have Anna Sarah Shand to be your lawful wife? Will you love, honour and keep her in sickness and in health and forsaking all others keep only unto her so long as you both shall live?"

"I will."

The minister turned to Sarah," Anna Sarah Shand, will you have Robert Andrew Robertson to be your lawful husband? Will you love, honour and obey, and keep him in sickness and in health and forsaking all others keep only unto him as long as you both shall live?"

"I-I will."

The ceremony went on. Kenneth reached into his waistcoat pocket, pulled out the plain gold wedding band and handed it to the minister who blessed it. "Robert Andrew, take this token of your fidelity and place it on the third finger of the bride's left hand."

While he took it off the Bible, Sarah passed her bouquet to Margaret. He eased her extremity out of the open seam in her glove and gently placed the gold band.

The clergyman spoke again. "Repeat after me, with this ring..."

"..., I thee wed."

"Let us pray." After the Lord's Prayer, Reverend Mitchell looked out over the guests and back at the bride and groom. "Before God, you two have made your vows to one another."

She smiled.

"Now, you both take wine from the quaich. As the couple shares this drink, they set down the way they will share their lives." He passed the silver cup to her.

Sarah held it nervously in her hands, took a sip and gave it back to the clergyman who in turn gave it to Robert.

"And now, the pinning of the tartan. In so doing, the family welcomes Anna Sarah to the clan."

Kenneth handed Robert a small rosette of the Ancient Robertson Hunting plaid of green, light blue, and purple with narrow red and white stripes. Robert turned to Sarah and carefully pinned it to her bodice.

"By the powers vested in me, I now pronounce you man and wife. You may kiss your bride."

Robert placed his hands on her waist and kissed her full on the lips. Her fears about time travel and returning to 2010 disappeared from her mind. She wound her arms around his neck and caressed the back of his head with her left hand.

"A-hem." Reverend Mitchell cleared his throat. They broke their embrace and stood to face him. Margaret gave Sarah's bouquet back to her.

"May I present Mr. and Mrs. Robertson?" They turned to face the invitees. "The bride and groom have asked me to remind you of the feast followed by a ceilidh in the ballroom. There will be people outside to escort you there."

Kenneth and Margaret remained in the chapel with the newlyweds to witness their signatures in the marriage register after the guests left.

"While Sarah signed the registration book, Robert leaned forward and whispered, "I have another surprise for you."

"Another one? This gown, the flowers, the pearls. They must have cost a fortune. I told you I didn't want a fuss."

"It would not be befitting of a Laird not to have his wife look her best on such an auspicious occasion. I've persuaded, Geordie McDougall, the proprietor of the photography studio in Duninsch to join us. Apparently, wedding pictures are the thing these days. Now, he doesn't like to bring his equipment out. Says it's not good for it. He prefers to take his photographs at his place of business. However; I managed to convince him."

The chapel door opened, and the man entered. He was about Robert's height but much stockier. After he introduced himself, he set up his large box camera, heavy black hood, and flash unit. The first images he captured were of Sarah and Robert signing the register. Afterwards, he took a picture of the entire wedding party. The blinding burst of light from the flash created spots in front of Sarah's eyes for quite some time, and she imagined the others suffered from the same problem.

"That's me off then."

"Can we take a few more? I would like some in front of the grand staircase. It is beautiful there," said Sarah.

"Is that all right with you, Mr. Robertson?"

"Yes."

Angus prepared his bagpipes and played the recessional leading Sarah, Robert and the others out of the chapel. Some of the guests lingered in the great hall but most had made their way into the ballroom.

The wedding party gathered in front of the grand staircase. The photographer quickly grabbed some of the floral arrangements from other locations in the hall and placed them on either side of the stairs. Again, he took a picture of Robert and Sarah alone followed by one of the newlyweds and Jenny, and lastly with the entire wedding party.

"Robert, can Mr. McDougall take one of me alone? I'd like the one with my veil and train out in front of me and Jenny's and Margaret's bouquets on it."

"If you like. Do you know what she means?"

"I think so."

Margaret arranged Sarah's gown and veil to her liking, then placed hers and Jenny's flowers on the floor on it around the edges. Sarah stood at a bit of an angle and turned her head directly at the photographer; her bouquet held in front of her. Geordie took a few more photographs.

Sarah was disappointed but at the same time relieved with all the picture taking, colour photography didn't exist. At least with the current 1886 technology, the wedding party wouldn't have a terrible case of red-eye.

Placing her hand on Margaret's arm, she whispered, "I don't know if I should be pleased or mad, but thank you so much for everything you've done. Today wouldn't be the same without you and Robert conspiring to get the job done."

"It was my pleasure. Just promise me you'll be a good wife to my brother."

"I will."

The photographer packed up his cameras for the journey back to his studio.

"You've come this far at a bad time of day. Stay and dine with us. There will be plenty to eat," said Robert.

Geordie accepted the invitation and joined the other guests in the ballroom.

The tables groaned under the weight of the food on them. Roast geese, haunches of venison, bowls of potatoes, turnips, and other seasonal vegetables, along with bread, butter, and assorted cheeses and wine filled the space not required for the diners' place settings.

Sarah, Robert, Jenny, Margaret, Kenneth McIntosh, and the minister took their seats at the head table. Archibald ensured the placement of three more for Margaret's family. Reverend Mitchell gave the blessing, and the meal commenced.

The little girl peered around the adults and smiled at Mary Elizabeth. Sarah noticed the exchange, and was pleased George and the children made the journey. Jenny needed people close to her age to play with, and hopefully, the two would someday be friends. The peek-a-boo game at the table suggested they would.

Partway through, Robert stood. He clinked his knife against his glass to get everyone's attention. The room quieted. "As a gift to my beautiful bride, I provided the asylum by Ladysbridge Station a financial endowment for the administration to spend on items they desperately need. In addition, I contributed livestock so they can become self-sufficient and those patients who are well enough will tend to the beasts. Also, come spring, I will hire and pay for a permanent gardener to help plant the fruits and vegetables and teach the shut-ins how to grow them."

"Thank you. This gesture means much to me."

"Oh, there is another detail. The small lassie on my wife's left, Jenny. She will receive the Robertson surname and we'll raise her as our flesh and blood child."

"Oh, Robert." She jumped to her feet and hugged him. "You've made me so happy." Tears of joy fell from her eyes and down her cheeks. The child would want for nothing. In time, she would inherit the Christie fortune and would also be entitled to a sizeable portion of the Weetshill assets, too. Knowing the little girl's future was well secured added to Sarah's happiness.

In the meantime, the ceilidh band were warming up. The leader announced the first dance would be the Gay Gordons.

The music started, and Sarah immediately turned the wrong way. They laughed.

"You always do that. Must be because you're left-handed."

Sarah smiled at him and replied, "I fell head over heels for you the first time we danced this together, just like my great-grandparents did."

"That's when I knew I had fallen in love with you, too," he said as he led her through the steps. "We will be dancing for years to come." During the night they did the Eightsome Reel, Strip the Willow, and the Dashing White Sergeant among others. Sometime later, they discreetly left the ceilidh for the room specially prepared for their wedding night.

Sarah moved behind the screen to undress. Item by item, she slowly disrobed and tossed her clothes over the frame. "Are you ready to see me, starting here?" she asked and stuck her full naked leg out around the edge. "I've got more than just this if you think you can handle it."

"Jimmy, come here," Moira called from the front door. "I was about to close the door, but something's odd over at Weetshill."

Her husband joined her a few minutes later.

"Look, lights and music are coming from there," she said nodding in the direction of the ruins.

"I don't see or hear anything," he answered as he put his hands on her shoulders. "It's likely from the pub and bouncing off the hills. You only think that's where it's originating from."

"But look. There are lights over there."

"And you heard they're to restore the old ruin, so you're seeing things. You're missing Sarah. I am, too. She always talked about the strange things she saw up there. Don't stand out here too long. You'll catch your death and be no good to the lass when she decides to come home with her tail between her legs." He turned and walked back inside.

Mrs. Shand remained in the open doorway a while longer staring off at the derelict mansion beyond the distillery. She glanced off in the other direction briefly toward the stone circle that was barely visible from where she stood. The transparent images of a young man in a dark suit and a woman in a long white dress hovered there. She blinked. Was that her missing daughter? When she looked again, the man and woman were gone.

39

The following morning when Sarah woke, the pre-dawn light filtered through the opening in the drapes. Her husband's soft, rhythmic snoring came from behind her, and she felt his body next to hers. She wriggled down under the covers closer to him, content and filled with the promise of her life at Weetshill with Robert.

Soon after, he rolled her on her back and made love to her for the second time, and it was just as beautiful as the first. His tender touch made Sarah glad she had not given in to Blair's demands and had remained a virgin for her wedding night.

It was almost noon before they satisfied their hunger for one another.

"Well Mrs. Robertson, I suppose we must be making a start to the day."

"Mmm. I like the sound of that," she murmured.

He got out of bed and walked to the washstand. "Why don't you go get yourself ready, and I'll see you in the breakfast room."

"Somehow, I don't think they've held it for us. It's lunchtime." She giggled.

Robert and Sarah arrived within seconds of each other. As she suspected, the staff didn't hold their meal for them.

"Good mornin' to you both," the housekeeper said. "I thought I heard voices. E'eryone else is waitin' in the dinin' room. It be lunchtime," she said and smiled.

Kenneth stood when Sarah and Robert entered the room, and Jenny ran over and embraced them. "First thing Monday, I'll draw up the documents to give this wee lassie a worthy last name," he said.

"Thank you," Robert said. "In a way, she has a surname now. She shouldn't forget her family ties. Her name could be Jenny Christie Robertson."

"I think perhaps a better middle name for her would be Philomena," said Sarah. "She doesn't need to remember him. So sad Letitia has such a beautiful daughter, and she'll never get to know her. Everyone says Mrs. Christie was a wonderful, warm person."

"Yes, you are correct. As much of a skinflint Horatio is, she was charitable. Always making sure the poorhouse had what they needed, despite her having to do so secretly lest she angered him."

In the end, the child would choose her new name. Sarah turned to her. "Would you like to be known as Jenny Philomena Robertson?"

"Y-yes."

"It does have a nice ring to it, and I agree with Miss Sh..., oh I mean my lovely wife. She should never forget her mother and grandmother."

The butler preceded the other servants into the room with lunch, one of Morag's famous broths, most likely made from the leftover meat from the wedding feast. She hoped the woman hadn't been up all night making it. Accompanying the soup, was homemade bread and butter, cheese and pickled beets canned the previous autumn.

"Robert, I want to take you and Jenny to the stone circle," Sarah said. "Make it a family outing."

"Wh-what's a st-stone circle?"

"You eat up, and when you're finished, I'll show you."

Eager to find out what this thing was, she ate the rest of her lunch so fast she ended up with the hiccups. Margaret's children were restless, too, so she excused them from the table. John Bryce whined about having to play with girls, but when one of the adults suggested a match of Jackstraws, he soon stopped. "I'm the best player at my school. I'll beat you," he bragged.

"I-I d-don't know how to p-play."

"It isn't hard. I'll help you," replied Mary Elizabeth.

The children spread out on the floor playing their game.

George and Robert talked like they were old friends.

"So what sort of a shop do you own?"

"Books and stationery."

"I'd love to visit you there sometime. I love books. Dickens is one of my favourite writers."

"Mine, too."

After the adults finished their meals, the newlyweds excused themselves from the room and took Jenny with them.

On their way to the stone circle, Sarah said, "Today is Halloween. Do kiddies go trick or treating here, Robert?"

"I'm not sure I know that term. Could you explain?"

"Children cut faces in turnips or more recently pumpkins, put on costumes and wear masks or makeup, and go from house to house for treats."

"Hmm. Guising. It sounds interesting. Would you like to carve a turnip and dress up tonight?" asked Robert.

Jenny smiled and nodded.

"There will be a bonfire in the village this evening. We could go if you like."

"Let's. Maybe Margaret and her family would join us? How about you, sweetie?"

"Y-yes, p-please!"

When they reached the crest of the hill, Sarah sat on one of the stones, and the little girl clambered into her lap. "This is a stone circle. There's not much left now, not with the digs that have taken place."

"Why d-did they p-put the st-stones this way?"

"Well, they could have been arranged like this to use as a calendar or a clock," she said, recalling a discussion from her childhood. "Robert and I first saw each other here."

He moved behind them and put his hand on Sarah's shoulder.

Today was eerily similar to the times she came here with her grandmother and listened to her stories of the olden days. Except for this time her husband and adopted daughter were with her. Weetshill looked resplendent in the afternoon sun.

"L-look. Th-there's a house down there." Jenny pointed toward Kendonald.

Sarah turned and blinked in disbelief. The longer she stared the clearer the image became. It started fuzzy and transparent but over time came in to focus.

"Are you all right?" asked Robert.

"I-I'm not sure. M-my house. There," she said. "Can't be." She looked away and back again. The farmhouse was where it had always been in her time. "Do you see it, too?"

"The stone cottage in the valley," he replied.

"Yes. You both see it," Sarah repeated, moving Jenny aside and standing slowly. She took their hands and walked hypnotically down the slope toward her home.

When they stopped in the gravel driveway facing the house, Sarah reached out and touched the leaded glass front door. It was real. Shocked by the reality, she jumped back.

Robert encircled her waist with his arm and drew her close to him.

The deadbolt latch scraped, and then clicked into the unlocked position. The hinges creaked as the door opened. Sarah's mother stood in the doorway holding a broom. Her eyes were red and tired, and a worried expression covered her face.

Mrs. Shand was about to sweep off the small step when she looked up. "Sarah, I can't believe it's you!"

"You can see me?" She asked nervously.

The woman dropped the sweeper and pulled her into a hug. "Of course I can, you silly girl. Where have you been? We've all been worried to death about you?" She stopped talking and embraced her wayward daughter again.

Overjoyed to be held in her mum's arms, she returned the warm cuddle. Terrified Robert and Jenny disappeared, when she checked, they remained at her side.

"Your dad is going to be thrilled to see you. Let me ring him," she said turning to grab the cordless handset from the table inside the door. Before she turned around completely, she froze and stared. "Are you dressed for Halloween? And who is this?"

Sarah wanted to tell her mother everything, but it seemed so farfetched even she didn't believe it. Jenny tugged her skirt, and she discovered the little girl hiding behind her. "Don't be afraid, sweetie. This lady is my mother."

She peeked out and smiled.

"I love you. You do know that."

"Of course I do, you silly girl. I've always known. Even when we row." Mrs. Shand made the call and soon afterwards, her father appeared at the front door.

"Where the hell have you been, young lady? We have been fraught with worry." He'd taken his boots off at the back like always and stood there in his bright, white socks.

Footfalls on the stairs preceded her sister's arrival at the door.

"You're back," exclaimed Rachel.

For a second she was the little sister Sarah defended from bullies at school.

"What are you doing in that get-up? You going to a Halloween party or something?"

The Victorian era clothing had become the norm. Gone were the days of denims, hoodies, and trainers. She choked down a sob and said, "I love you, Rachel."

Her sibling blinked. "And me you, Sarah."

"How did your date with whatshisname go?"

"He was a total jerk. I don't ever want to see him again."

"Don't worry. The right guy will come along someday. Trust me; I found mine."

"What have you been playing at young lady?" Mr. Shand asked balling his hands into fists. "Running off that night the way you did. Go to your room and don't come out until I tell you."

Her father's voice reduced Sarah to tears. "I-I'm sorry, Dad. Not thinking straight."

"Who are these people with you?"

"Th-this is my husband, Robert. Our wedding was yesterday at Weetshill mansion, and this is Jenny, the wee orphan we're adopting."

"What in the name of Sam Hill? Married? And taking in a child when you're just a kid yourself. That Blair is the cause. I knew he was no good for you. Now you've gone and taken up with the first guy the comes along since breaking up with him. Your mother wouldn't let me, but I would still like to give him the thrashing he deserves."

"Not related to Blair, Dad. I forgave him and you should, too. I love Robert, and I'm staying with him."

"You must come in, please," Mrs. Shand insisted.

Sarah didn't budge; petrified if she crossed over the threshold, she would go back to 2010. Suddenly, it occurred to her that perhaps it was her wish to be elsewhere that opened the rift in time. She turned towards Weetshill, and the grand house still appeared new. Did she step into the house and possibly go back to her own time, or did she stay outside?

Robert leaned toward her. "If you want to go back to your time, we will come with you."

She looked at him then at Jenny. "Would you do that for me?"

The little girl nodded and squeezed Sarah's hand.

With the advances in technology and the bullying that prevailed in the twenty-first century, Sarah couldn't take a small child with disabilities into the future. It would be difficult for Robert, too. She couldn't do that do either of them.

"I'll raise Jenny on my own with Margaret's help should you decide to go without us."

Eyes blurred from crying; she couldn't expect them to live in her time, but she couldn't leave without them.

"No. My mind is made up. I'm staying with you two." Sarah kissed him. "I'm so sorry, mum. I can't do it. I belong with wee Jenny and Robert, the man I love and married yesterday."

"What do you mean, you can't come home? You'll always be welcome here. Don't ever forget that," her mum cried.

"I'll take excellent care of her Mr. and Mrs. Shand. You have my word as a gentleman." He reached out and shook their hands and bowed slightly.

"Please, don't go."

She hugged her parents and sibling goodbye, turned and walked off. One final look back; her mother broke down in her father's strong arms; Rachel with hers wrapped around them both. Sarah focused on the stone circle.

Her sister said, "Where did they go? They just faded away."

Halfway there, Sarah looked back again. The farmhouse and her family had vanished into the mist.

Also by Melanie Robertson-King

A Shadow in the Past out of print)
(4RV Publishing)

Sarah Shand time travel romance series
A Shadow in the Past (second edition)
Shadows From Her Past

The Consequences Collection
Tim's Magic Christmas
The Secret of Hillcrest House
YESTERDAY TODAY ALWAYS
Cole's Notes (Revised version)

It Happened Series
It Happened on Dufferin Terrace

(King Park Press)

Cole's Notes (A Short Story)
EFD1: Starship Goodwords – a cross genre anthology
(CARRICK PUBLISHING, 2012)

Future Titles in the *It Happened* Series
featuring the Layne and Scott families

It Happened at Percé Rock

It Happened in Gastown

It Happened in Niagara Falls

Thanks for reading *A Shadow in the Past*. If you loved the book and can spare a moment, I would really appreciate a review as this helps new readers find my books.

MELANIE ROBERTSON-KING

https://melanierobertson-king.com

Melanie Robertson-King has always been a fan of the written word. Growing up as an only child, her face was almost always buried in a book from the time she could read. Her father was one of the thousands of Home Children sent to Canada through the auspices of The Orphan Homes of Scotland, and she has been fortunate to be able to visit her father's homeland many times and even met the Princess Royal (Princess Anne) at the orphanage where he was raised.

www.ingramcontent.com/pod-product-compliance
Lightning Source LLC
Chambersburg PA
CBHW050506260626
47157CB00004B/1213